DARE TO BE MIGHTY

(A Collection of F&SF Stories)

TODD J. MCCAFFREY

A Foxxe Frey Book

DARE TO BE MIGHTY

Dare To Be Mighty is a collection of fiction stories. Names, places, and incidents are either products of the author's imagination or are used fictitiously.

> *Dasher* Copyright © 1984 by Todd J. McCaffrey
> *Never Use A Rocker* Copyright © 1992 by Todd J. McCaffrey
> *EMS Brevity* Copyright © 2004 by Todd J. McCaffrey
> *The Terrorist In My Kitchen* Copyright © 2011 by Todd J. McCaffrey
> *Coward* Copyright © 2010 by Todd J. McCaffrey
> *Kiss* Copyright © 1992 by Todd J. McCaffrey
> *At The Bottom Of The White* Copyright © 2019 by Todd J. McCaffrey
> *Rhubarb And Beets* Copyright © 2014 by Todd J. McCaffrey
> *Golden* Copyright © 2013 by Todd J. McCaffrey
> *Red* Copyright © 2016 by Todd J. McCaffrey
> *The Dragonkiller's Daughter* Copyright ©2017 by Todd J. McCaffrey
> *Small Bird's Plea* Copyright © 2019 by Todd J. McCaffrey
> *Red Roses* Copyright © 2014 by Todd J. McCaffrey

Books by Todd McCaffrey

Science fiction

Ellay

The Jupiter Game

The Steam Walker

The Canaris Rift Series

Collectionst

The One Tree of Luna (And Other Stories)

Dragonriders of Pern® Series

Dragon's Kin

Dragon's Fire

Dragon Harper

Dragonsblood

Dragonheart

Dragongirl

Dragon's Time

Sky Dragons

Non-fiction

Dragonholder: The Life And Times (so far) of Anne McCaffrey

Dragonwriter: A tribute to Anne McCaffrey and Pern

Books by The Winner Twins and Todd McCaffrey

Nonfiction:
The Write Path: World Building

Books by McCaffrey-Winner
Twin Soul Series:
Winter Wyvern
Cloud Conqueror
Frozen Sky
Wyvern's Fate
Wyvern's Wrath
Ophidian's Oath
Snow Serpent
Iron Air
Ophidian's Honor

To see the full list, scan the QR Code below!

Dedication

For Bill Fawcett

Contents

SCIENCE FICTION	9
Dasher	11
Never Use A Rocker	31
EMS Brevity	45
The Terrorist in My Kitchen	73
Coward	81
At The Bottom Of The White	91
Kiss	125
FANTASY	141
Rhubarb And Beets	143
Golden	151
Red	161
The Dragon Killer's Daughter	181
Small Bird's Plea	195
Red Roses	219
Acknowledgements	229
About the Author	230

SCIENCE FICTION

HERE ARE SIX SCIENCE FICTION STORIES STARTING WITH MY FIRST, DASHER. *THE TERRORIST IN MY KITCHEN* is arguably my most terrifying and challenging story.

Dasher

Dasher was the first story I ever wrote.

THE OFFICE WAS WELL APPOINTED BUT OBVIOUSLY NAVY. BEHIND THE huge mahogany desk was a plush chair whose back was just a little too straight; the bookcase had several carefully selected classics, including "Spock's World", arrayed on the top shelf but the lower shelves all contained books of naval tactics and regulations; the pictures on the wall were all elegantly framed but all of great naval encounters. The walls were covered in dark-grained wood, bespeaking more money than mere naval pay. Incongruously the desk sported a replica of the long lost space shuttle *Challenger* nose up, ready for its last flight and a detailed model of the first probe to leave the solar system, *Voyager*.

In the plush chair sat a gaunt, wiry naval Captain. The Naval Captain was attired in dress uniform, declaring to every knowledgeable onlooker that here was an officer who spent more time in the staff room than the bridge. In front of him, in front of a much less well-appointed chair, in fact a standard issue chair, stood a Navy Lieutenant at attention.

Captain Poindexter allowed himself one more intimidating minute of staring at the Lieutenant, one eyebrow arched, before he growled: "At ease." As the Lieutenant unbent, he added: "Be seated."

Trudeaux was not standard Navy issue. For one, she was a woman. That was not terrible in itself but she was also a test pilot, an engineer, a physicist and just about everything the Navy frowned upon. And, Poindexter's eyes narrowed, she was so plump as to be almost overweight. All these, however, were to be expected of the Navy's experimenters. The rumors about her singing in the rare times that she was not talking to either her computers or their ghosts he dismissed as unimportant.

However, her Officer's Evaluation Reports followed a disturbing pattern as she moved from post to post: always they started off warm and glowing until, as time passed, her superiors slipped from praise to insult and innuendo. Such OERs could be read two ways: either Trudeaux's ineptitude was hard to discern immediately or she was so brilliant that her commanders sought to discredit her. Poindexter had seen both. What *was* unusual, however, was Trudeaux's continued requests for combat duty or command, preferably both. More alarming was her superiors' refusals on the grounds that she was "too valuable in her present position" to let her go.

Even *more* unusual was the fact that she was nearly one billion kilometers from her post. That fact prompted the court martial papers now lying in plain view on Poindexter's desk and this preliminary investigation.

"They tell me that the *Dasher's* right engine is mere shrapnel somewhere back in Jovian orbit and that the left engine has fused." Poindexter began, civilly. He saw her relax somewhat and chided himself, barking: "You've set back the Navy's Matter/Anti-Matter propulsion project a good ten years! Explain!"

Margaret Trudeaux winced, clearly upset and uncertain.

"*Dasher* was ambushed." Maggie began.

"Ambushed!" Poindexter roared. "Ambushed! *Dasher* has the best stealth electronics of the Navy!" He spluttered: "Ambushed!"

"Ambushed." Margaret maintained icily. Good! Poindexter thought to himself, pleased that his antagonizing tactics had not worked. He raised an eyebrow to indicate that she should continue, reminding himself that he was supposed to be the hard captain, intent only on the facts.

"They took out the right engine, combustion chamber and feed lines, in the first bolts. They also hulled the ship. In the next, they got the communications gear and the Reaction Control System."

"And just where were you when they attacked?"

"I was indisposed." Trudeaux replied.

In response, Poindexter slammed his finger on Naval issue voice recorder. "I want every detail."

Margaret Trudeaux nodded slightly, closed her eyes and remembered.

Dasher was the Navy's test ship for MAM, Matter/Anti-Matter, propulsion systems. It was a modified courier, unarmed, relying on its incredible speed and unsurpassed stealth electronics to protect it. It had been the test ship for the Polarized Radiation MAM engines until two pilots had died from gamma radiation poisoning and now it was the Navy's Chaotic Flow Chamber MAM test bed. CFC had proved a winner: computer controlled injections of a secondary propellant (hydrogen) had not only given the *Dasher* a specific impulse of $0.05c$ but had produced a control room that was absolutely free of any radiation other than space normal levels. And it was so safe, "Even a woman can drive it!", as Dr. Brenschluss had crowed. Margaret had refrained from giving the Professor a chance to examine his heart firsthand in order to be selected as the female to prove his boast. The old Prussian did it to needle her, resentful of the breadth of her engineering skills.

Dasher had already made three flights from retrograde Sinope to Amalthea, the satellite most blindingly near to Jupiter, and the test results had been perfect: the test pilots almost boring in their praise of the reliability of the engines and the handling of the modified courier. The most intriguing episode of the three flights had been one pilot's recounting of flying straight through an enemy fleet without causing the slightest blip on their radar; *Dasher's* stealth electronics and hull coating were the best the Navy could boast.

So Margaret Trudeaux, test pilot, chief engineer, leading and only architect of MAM combustion chambers, was selected for the fourth and final flight of the *Dasher* before it was replaced by a larger ship equipped with a production version of the CFC MAM drive - the drive that would give humankind, particularly UN humankind, the stars.

In mis-response to Margaret's outrage at being chosen to fly *Dasher* only when it was proven safe - those were *her* engines, dammit! - the chief test pilot, "Red" Nelson, a relic from pre-historic times, had consoled: "Don't worry, it'll be a milk run." A milk run! She had hoped she would not be bored silly and prayed that Red was merely displaying his usual cultivated calm.

#

In fact, Margaret Trudeaux was in the galley trying to figure out how quickly to eat her ice cream when the enemy ships attacked. A sudden savage lurch of the ship was immediately followed by tearing noises and the hiss of vacuum. She clapped her hand over her mouth with no time to swear as she leaped up, and lurched to the control room. The air in the control room was fogged with water vapor to condensed by the sudden pressure drop.

She strapped herself into her chair and saw a sea of red lights glaring balefully on the control panels. First, hull integrity was gone. Ship's internal oxygen lines were functional. Margaret turned her seat, grabbed a facemask and slipped it on, pulling the straps over her head and tightening them. She set the regulator and was soon breathing pure oxygen. As a precaution, she located and started charging the portable oxygen system. With the regulator set at a mild overpressure she could work until the ship's own pressure dropped below two per cent of standard. After that she would have to don a hardsuit.

"Let's see what we've got here!" She said to the ship's computer in her best "pilot's calm". Another blast shook the ship. Margaret checked her radar: two destroyers were hot on her tail. A quick look forward showed only Jupiter. Another scan of the panels showed no new major damage. Outside, the stars were visibly moving in response to the roll of the crippled ship. The brighter star, Margaret guessed, was Amalthea, not that it would do her any good. The Navy kept no ships on that tiny dustball.

"They've got you pegged!" She said to the computer, expecting it to plan evasive actions. Somehow they must have found out about the *Dasher* and the Navy's experiments and simply waited until a reliable engine had been developed. Now they wanted to steal it.

"No way, José!" Margaret swore, shaking a chubby fist at the distant enemy. How did they find me? She wondered.

Margaret glanced over to the stealth electronics panel. It was still functional. She sucked her teeth in consternation. "Ohmigod, they've got a counter to our stealth gear!"

This information was probably worth as much to the Navy as a working

MAM engine was to the enemy. The computer still had not responded. Margaret checked its panel and found that the main unit had been destroyed in the second attack. She frowned, fingers poised above the destruct switch for the stealth electronics - if she was wrong, she was destroying her only chance - and pressed. The panel glowed brighter and then went dark.

Committed, Margaret switched her attention to the engines. The panel showed that the starboard main engine was scrap, Maggie's fingers moved quickly to stop the hemorrhaging of valuable fuel, a loss which had made *Dasher's* course an erratic heloid and probably had saved her from being further assaulted or boarded by the enemy.

The left engine was functional at reduced power but *Dasher* relied on the twin thrust of the left and right engines. Using only one engine would put the *Dasher* into fast right turn. Attitude Control thrusters could counter some of this, Maggie gave a gargled groan when she noted that the Attitude Control System was so much junk. Either the enemy had been incredibly lucky or it had known just where to hit *Dasher* to immobilize her.

Margaret decided that it was not luck. But it hadn't gone all their way: *Dasher's* roll about its long axis meant that she could thrust the left engine by itself and wobble in a path that was mostly forward. She would have to be careful with her motions though: the laws of energy conservation were such that a roll about the long axis would try to convert itself into a yaw about the center of gravity, just like a top falling over to its side. One of the early Explorer satellites had done just that.

"Don't bother checking the comm gear." Margaret told the defunct computer, then shrugged when she realized her mistake. With a dismissive wave she responded to herself: "Doesn't matter, they probably took out the main antenna and, besides, you don't have enough power with just one engine to punch a distress call back to *Sinope*."

She reviewed her options: the enemy wanted *Dasher* intact, Margaret herself would be an added bonus; she had only one engine to use but it was fully functional; *Dasher* had no armaments, relying on speed and its now-destroyed stealth gear. She was not far from Jupiter.

Jupiter! "Period, period, period -- what's this goddammed rotation period!" Maggie chanted to herself. She locked her eyes on a bright star that could have been Amalthea and counted *Dasher's* roll rate at three revolutions a minute, more or less. Margaret plotted a thrust that would vector her towards Jupiter.

"How much can that chamber take?" She asked herself, hoping that as the designer she might know and knowing, as the designer, that she had never bothered to calculate it - *Dasher* was never expected to make even one gee thrusts. "Never mind that, Trudeaux! Just get moving!" She ordered.

Maggie fired the engine manually, the computer being hopeless. She set the matter and anti-matter flow rates to produce first one half gee, then one gee and finally, in a mixture of devil-take-all abandon and sheer desperation, five gees. She cut the engines quickly and tried to determine how fast the ship was turning. When she thought it was just about aligned for Jupiter, she thrust again, countering the turning moment.

Then, aligned to head towards the huge planet, she started a corkscrew towards the leviathan of the skies.

"What's your speed? You've got to go faster Trudeaux, you've got to *run* away from the enemy!" Maggie barked aloud, forcing herself to play hard captain. She was disappointed to admit that she could think of no easy way to calculate *Dasher's* speed.

Dasher had been on a trajectory designed to swing around Amalthea and back towards Sinope but, as Sinope moved other-clockwise around Jupiter than Amalthea, Margaret and *Dasher* would have to execute a very fuel costly direction reversal which few chemically fueled ships could do - one of the reasons that the Navy felt orbits between Amalthea and Sinope were safe. In order to facilitate the maneuver, *Dasher's* trajectory was arranged such that the ship would be travelling at the lowest possible velocity when the reversal in direction was made.

At Perijovian, the lowest point of her orbit, she would have had the same speed as Amalthea - slightly over thirty kilometers a second. To get into a low Jupiter orbit she would need a speed of just over forty-two kilometers per second, a difference of twelve kilometers per second. And she wanted to get to Jupiter fast.

"Two gees?" Maggie asked to herself, taking the time to review the panels in front of her. "Let's see: t equals delta vee over a; at two gees, nineteen point six-two meters per second squared, delta vee is twelve thousand, t is about - uh," She glanced nervously about for a working calculator or *something* that could do simple math and swore when she found nothing. "Call it twenty meters per squared second, that's six hundred seconds - ten minutes at two gees!" She mulled the figures over.

"Maybe it'll shake 'em, it'll sure give 'em a rough ride!" Her captain voice agreed, adding: "Won't be too easy on you, either!"

Maggie crouched onto the command chair for extra security, set the flow controls and fired. The enemy were taken by surprise. It was a long thirty seconds before they fired off in pursuit of her.

Maggie spent the long minutes en route to Jupiter alternating between checking the enemy, pulsing the one engine, watching her fuel, and wracking her brains for a way out of her predicament. Just outside the atmosphere, she stopped her two gravity thrusting, waited a quarter of a corkscrew and made another thrust, a wrenching, bone-jarring six gees. She countered it ten seconds later with another agonizing six gees.

Now *Dasher* was in the pull of Jupiter's gravity and on a course deep into Jupiter's clouds.

"How much pressure can this hull take?" Maggie wondered scientifically, continuing captainly: "Can it take more than they can?"

Under more normal circumstances, Margaret would have addressed these questions to the ship's computers but there was no computer to talk to. Then she remembered that the ship was holed - the internal and external pressures would both be Jupiter's. Her ship could take more pressure than theirs. The question was, could she?

Switching from the chair's oxygen to her portable supply, Margaret made her way to the suit locker. With much grumbling she managed to pull her deepspace suit over her shipsuit. With it she could take more pressure but would lose dexterity. She returned to the control room and found to her disgust that she could not fit herself into the command chair and was bouncing out instead. Abashed, she remembered that she had to activate her magnetic soles.

Now the question is: how much can this suit take? She asked herself.

"One way to find out!" Maggie waited until she figured the good engine was almost above her, fired another four second burst, counted to six and repeated the operation, plunging *Dasher* deeper into Jove's thin air.

She glanced at the displays: *Dasher* was ten kilometers inside Jupiter's atmosphere. The enemy ships were following her with no difficulty: the atmosphere was mostly opaque at this depth. Navy manuals did not take into consideration mad dives into the Jovian atmosphere; it took Maggie quite a while to guess a depth she was willing to risk her life with.

"Even if you can go lower than them, Maggie, they'll just wait until you come up for air." She noted tactically.

"You've got to sucker 'em into letting you get away." She decided captainly. She thought about it as Jupiter's atmosphere thickened from tenuous to visible. She forced herself to glance at the hull temperature gage - it was already edging into the red. *Dasher* was not supposed to make atmospheric entries, no one had ever envisioned *Dasher* trying to smash its way through the Jovian atmosphere.

"You can outrun 'em if they don't knock out the other engine." She advised with her engineer's tone, noting that she had over twenty kilograms of precious anti-matter contained in the ship's magnetic bottles. Then she sighed: "Won't work, Maggie, they'll just radio ahead. You've *got* to loose them somehow."

Whatever happens, she continued silently, they can't get this ship. She smiled as that dark thought led her through a darker series to an image of *Dasher's* anti-matter evaporating through the magnetic containment in one vast explosion. Twenty kaygees of the stuff would probably shake up ol' Jove himself! She mused.

Pressure was rising rapidly in the spaceship. Vibrations through the floor plates and groans in the thin air warned Margaret that, even holed, *Dasher's* hull was feeling the increased pressure. Margaret was glad when *Dasher* passed below the ammonia ice clouds, the thinnest of Jupiter's clouds: it gave her the first little something to hide her ship under.

Later, at a pressure of slightly over six atmospheres, under the rusty orange of Jupiter's ammonium hydrosulfide clouds, Margaret made two rapid firings to keep *Dasher* from descending further. When *Dasher* groaned threateningly against the light thrust of the MAM engine, Margaret hastily reduced the thrust and increased its duration. She understood the tiny ship's predicament: movement in her hardsuit was laborious and several times she had had to stop herself hyperventilating from the fear that her suit was leaking or worse, buckling. Overriding the suit's controls, she increased the internal pressure to five atmospheres - adding nitrogen as she knew that oxygen at this pressure would literally cook her from the inside out. The increased internal pressure reduced the difference between outside pressure to one atmosphere. Margaret hoped that the suit would handle the one atmosphere difference; she was depending on it.

She checked radar. The two destroyers were over ten kilometers behind her and seventy-five kilometers above her - high up where the pressure was less than one atmosphere. *Dasher's* speed through the thick atmosphere was heating the ship up at an alarming rate. From the cockpit, Margaret could see the near-white glow from *Dasher's* nose. The temperature inside her suit was also rising. Maggie started sweating profusely and cursed the fact that the extra pressure of her suit made her sweat just stick to her skin.

"Drink your water, Trudeaux!" She growled to herself and suited actions to words, squirming in her helmet to drink from the water nipple. Dehydration in these circumstances would be fatal.

"Damn, now I'm hungry!" She complained. "Low blood sugar." Her scientific side noted.

"Well, the ice cream's melted for sure." She told herself flippantly. "Probably spoiled, too." She checked the pressure gage: it was dropping, telling her that *Dasher* had started its ascent from its roller coaster plunge through Jupiter's air. Gratefully, she vented some of the excess pressure in her suit.

"About time too. Now, you've got two choices: continue up and surrender and stay down here. Either way your goose is cooked." Her stomach growled at her poor choice of words.

As if in response to her stomach, the quart of ice cream she had left in the galley chose that moment to waft serenely over her head and bounce sickly against the forward viewport. With a sense of irony Maggie noted that outside was liquid, something she had been trying to accomplish when the enemy had first attacked her only - she glanced at the chronometer - twelve minutes before.

"Well now, Trudeaux, you've got two riddles to solve: how to get away from two enemy destroyers before you burn up and how to eat ice cream under six atmospheres!" She noticed that her words were somewhat slurred now and that made her worried that her suit might be leaking. A quick glance at her inboard monitor panel reassured her; she decided that her tongue was feeling the effects of the extra pressure.

"Or is it because you're starving?" She wondered.

Now what was it they had said at the Academy? "When you have several problems, sometimes the best solution is to combine them into one large problem and solve *it*."

So where did that leave her? Nowhere. The two problems were separate.

Well Maggie, she thought to herself, you always wanted a combat job! She snorted. "How could you have guessed that your only weapon would be ice cream!"

How do you get away from two enemy destroyers using only ice cream?

"That's simple," Margaret voiced, "throw it at them." She pursed her lips while she pondered the possibility. If she just kicked the ice cream out the door, it would continue on in the same orbit until she thrust *Dasher* away. The differences in velocity between the ice cream and the destroyers would be negligible. Aside from which, the destroyers would pick the ice cream up on radar long before it was a danger and vaporize it. But if the destroyers did not know it was ice cream and did not detect it until it was too close, say a kilometer, then the destroyers would have to make a massive orbit change to avoid the mysterious projectiles. And if the ice cream did actually hit -

Margaret frowned as she worked the numbers through in her head - and sighed: all it would do was make a loud noise.

"Now all you have to do is shoot the ice cream at them and make it invisible!" Maggie muttered aloud. Well, shooting it wasn't difficult: stuff the ice cream in the airlock, tight against the outer door, override the mechanism enough to force the airlock to open only to the diameter of the ice cream containers and - whoosh! - out it flies at a fair clip. Maggie worked the numbers out and found that her airlock thrust chamber would give her a respectable 700 meter per second velocity difference. She calculated the impact energy for eleven two kilogram objects and grinned. "Now to make 'em invisible!"

With part of her next problem solved, Maggie focused on the present and examined the control panels, noting that hull temperature was well within limits. Through the viewport she could see that she was passing through Jupiter's ammonia ice clouds. Soon she would be outside of Jupiter's atmosphere and a good target for the destroyers.

"Time's almost up, Trudeaux." She told herself. "Think! You've got to make them blink."

"Let's see: they're going to see the ice cream liquid or solid. The containers will hardly make a blip but they haven't got any mass and no one's going to jump away from something they can't see." Maggie shook her head. "The only chance is to make a hot radar blip when they aren't expecting it. They know you've got anti-matter aboard, a quick blip on their screens would probably scare 'em all the way out to Pluto."

Maggie sighed, looking out the viewport in an effort to distract her conscious from a problem best left to her subconscious. The last wisps of Jupiter's clouds were passing off to one side. Maggie thought about those ammonia ice crystals and how they must look as they fell, warmed on the outside, solid ice cores surrounded by liquid. "That's it! They'll light up like Christmas trees!"

Radar beams going through the liquid ice cream at distance would probably produce a very weak or non-existent return, just faint enough to convince the enemy that they were nothing to worry about. And radar beams going through solid ice cream would only produce a slightly greater return. But while neither liquid nor solid were much on radar, a liquid-solid boundary layer was a fantastic radar reflector. If she managed it just right the enemy would suddenly see incredibly powerful returns on radar and think she had unleashed some secret weapon. No telling what they would do. "Except they'll certainly blink!"

Now, how to deliver that heat when required? She glanced around the cabin and made her way to the rear. Because *Dasher* was an experimental ship, lots of spare equipment was left aboard for ease of use.

In the rear of the craft, strapped in or magnetically attached, were all sorts of measuring equipment. There were thermocouples, ohmmeters, magnetometers, vibration transducers, all sorts of useful equipment for dealing with the effects of an enclosed matter/anti-matter unit. But Maggie could see nothing that could be used to *generate* heat.

As her search grew more frantic the rear of the cabin became a dangerous constellation of flying discards as Maggie flung them away in disgust at their inability to meet her simple needs.

"Just one radio controlled heating unit!" She begged. "Even one would do the job!" No good. She had completed her inspection and re-inspection as cast-offs floated back in and out of her vision. A glare at the control panels assured her that she didn't have the time to make one.

"Face it Margaret Trudeaux, you're licked." She shook her head while saying it, as if her body was in revolt against her mind's conclusion. It was her first command! And she didn't have anything that could even *scare* the enemy!

An idle, detached part of her mind noted that soon the enemy would be in range again, they would finish the crippling of *Dasher* and board her, their magnetic boots clanging on the hull. They would cycle the airlock and they would find Maggie there -

"Singing!" Maggie exclaimed. She scanned the scattering debris of her earlier search with renewed energy. Margaret was looking for only one thing: a vibration transducer. It was nothing more than a microphone which was attached by suction or magnetism. The microphone would pick up the noise of unwanted vibration and transmit it back to the receiver. Margaret whooped for joy when she found the receiver - it was a transceiver. Often it was desirable to not only to record the vibrations of a test item but also to induce vibrations. The gear on board *Dasher* could do both: it could receive the vibrations picked up by the transducers or it could transmit vibrations through the transducers. And vibrations would produce heat! At resonance, the ice cream would heat up fastest and produce the required thin liquid layer. It did not have to be much, less than a tenth of a millimeter would do nicely.

Margaret picked up the box of transducers and the transceiver and brought it back to the galley. She left the box in the galley and brought the transceiver forward to the control room. Up in the control room, she secured the transceiver by its magnetic clamps and reviewed the positions of the enemy through her radar.

The two destroyers were now closing up on her, the range was about forty kilometers. Another twenty kilometers closer and the enemy would be within firing range. A couple of flashes on radar indicated that the destroyers were willing to try for a lucky shot even at this range. Margaret cursed them and hope that their weaponry blew up. For her plan to work the enemy would have to get a lot closer. She would have to let them within ten kilometers of *Dasher* before she could launch her gastronomic artillery.

Margaret kicked the circuit breakers, plunging *Dasher* into darkness and cutting all power from the batteries. The emergency lights snapped on, as did her helmet light and *Dasher* was illuminated in the baleful red of a dying ship. Margaret hoped that the enemy would decide that the strains of Jupiter had been too much for the small courier, that all power was lost. She wanted them to think that *Dasher* was dead and not bother to fire on it. The superconducting magnets could contain *Dasher's* anti-matter forever, if need be.

Decision made, Margaret went over to the airlock and used the emergency override to open the inner door. She checked the monitor and was glad to note that it showed no signs of leaks in the airlock. If the enemy's blasts had hulled the airlock, Margaret's plan would have been doomed.

She went back to the galley, opened the refrigerator door and pulled out the remaining eleven quarts of ice cream.

"The things I do for the Service!" Maggie groaned theatrically, placing the transducers on the tops of the ice cream. She turned on each transducer and checked it for functionality. Satisfied, she carried the ice cream over to the airlock.

She placed the quart containers one on top of the other just at the seam between outer airlock door and the airlock itself. That done she stood back in the airlock and inspected her work. Satisfied, she left the airlock, closed the inner door and pressurized. Then she spent time overriding the standard airlock cycle. Instead of evacuating the air in the airlock before opening to space, the airlock door would pop open under the pressure of one atmosphere just enough to allow the quarts of ice cream be forced out.

"Of course the airlock'll be useless after this, you know." Maggie noted with the hurt tones of an engineer about to damage an artifice.

Back inside the cabin she checked her suit's chronometer: four minutes to go. Of course, the enemy could have accelerated to overtake her - in which case all her plans were useless.

Relentless, Maggie tore off the cover to the propulsion control panel and started tinkering with the injector controls. There was no way that she could use the anti-matter in its hyper-strengthened, shielded containers for offensive purposes but she could rig a dead man's button which would force the MAM engines to full acceleration; even if the stresses did not splinter the courier all over creation, the resulting thrust would certainly kick *Dasher* well out of the Solar System.

She checked the CFC controls and tied them into the dead man's stick so that not only would *Dasher* accelerate at inhuman speeds but the thrust chamber would be irradiating gamma rays in all directions instead of photons directed only rearward - making *Dasher* too 'hot' for anyone to ever get near again. She was very pleased with the dead man's switch itself: she had rigged it to monitor her heartbeat, a second after her heart stopped beating the dead man's switch would trigger.

Satisfied but even more apprehensive from her precautions, Margaret watched the seconds tick away on her chronometer. To take her mind off the wait, Maggie worked out the thrusts she could use to get back to Earth; she was certain that *Sinope* had been infiltrated by spies and might even have been destroyed. Earth! With only twenty kilograms of propellant! No, she corrected herself, forty kilograms of propellant: twenty of matter and twenty of antimatter. *Dasher* was a light ship, massing only one thousand kilograms, one metric tonne. The destroyers behind her were ten times more massive. With forty kilograms of propellant, *Dasher* had a mass ratio of 1.040. Burning all that fuel between Jupiter and Earth would result in a measly 1.4% gee and take nearly fifty-two days.

"Rats!" Margaret snarled. If the thrust efficiency could be brought up, if she could up the specific impulse, then she could get back to Earth faster. She knew a few ideas she'd been wanting to try but Professor Brenschluss had *nicht'*d her. She leaned back into the Chaotic Flow Controls and dickered. Changing the beat frequency to just below the first resonant frequency of the thrust chamber should produce the same effect as twice the hydrogen damping, which would halve the hydrogen being kicked overboard merely to protect the chamber and increase the specific impulse accordingly.

"Of course if you're wrong, Maggie me dear, you're going to get cooked for sure." Her engineering side warned her scientific self as she checked her handiwork. Her detached side wondered why she was always making food jokes.

She glanced at her suit chronometer. "Cripes!"

Ten seconds. She raced back over to the center control panel, one hand poised over the radar circuit breaker, the other over the radar gain.

"Eight ... seven .. six .. five .. " She counted. "Lights, camera, action!"

She punched in the circuit breaker and the radar screen warmed up. The test lights blinked on the radar display and then the central tube starting glowing brighter.

"Come on, come on!" She implored. Finally the tube was fully on. She changed the gain, searching for the enemy ships. Twenty kilometers, fifteen kilometers -

"Bingo! You boys stay tight and you'll win the prize!" The two ships were close together and ten kilometers behind *Dasher*. She switched axes and took an azimuth reading. The angle between the top of *Dasher's* control room and the ships was about one hundred and thirty degrees - forty degrees from the airlock.

Margaret raced to the lock counting seconds to herself. "Three .. two .. one - oh shit!" She was still rushing to the airlock when the time passed! *Dasher's* airlock was not pointed at the enemy!

"Count Maggie, count!" She extolled, terrified that the enemy ships had noticed her radar. "You have to count down until the 'lock is lined up again!"

"Nineteen .. eighteen.. " A bright sear appeared in the ceiling to her right. The enemy was firing. A shiver of fear lanced up her spine.

"Sixteen .. fifteen .. c'mon! .. fourteen .." Another bolt tore into the hull to her left. Maggie jumped to the right. "Twelve .. eleven .."

The ship made a horrible groaning noise. "*Please* not the left engine!" She shrieked, right hand poised over the airlock override, left hand coming up to her emergency suit vent - if they boarded, she'd blow her suit open and when the air ran out … well, hypoxia was a great way to go.

"Eight! Seven!" Her voice rose in anticipation. "Six! Five .. four .." Another bolt glanced on the hull. "three .. two .. *now* you bastards!" She hit the lock override. Alarms flashed and klaxons sounded noiselessly in the vacuum. The airlock pressure blipped out to zero. Rushing to the control panel, Maggie started counting again.

"Twelve .. eleven .. ten - oh god, what's the frequency?" She stop, horrified. "What's the resonant frequency for the ice cream!?" Terror and visions of cold death beat at her, her breathing doubled and her sweat turned to ice as she imagined the next bolt searing through her suit and her body.

"Think Maggie, think!" She shouted uselessly in brash military.

"Time! Time!" She shouted scientifically. Her heart beat was racing and she was hyperventilating.

"NO! No, Maggie not now!" She told herself. "Breath slower! Control!"

She took a deep breath, held it and let it out again slowly in iron-tight control.

"Again!" She ordered herself. The second breath was more controlled. She willed her breathing back to normal.

"Okay, time." She said quietly, desperately. She flicked the broadcast switch on the transceiver, linked in the input to her suit mike's output.

With a bittersweet grin Maggie remarked: "It's not over until the fat lady sings", and started singing.

"Johnny could only sing one note and the note he sang was this: Aaaaaaaah!" Maggie checked the radar while singing: still two blips, closing fast. She peered a bit closer and thought she could just detect the smudges outlining the containers but it might also be space dust. She switched songs, going to Wagner's Valkyrie, tearing up and down the scales as fast as she could. There! The radar showed spots! They were getting brighter. She sang up the scales, zeroed in and held it.

Blips, seven, eight, eleven burst into brilliance on the radar screen. They were practically on top of the first destroyer.

"Now!" She told herself, singing the word. She punched the controls, fired the left engine, spun the ship, countered the spin and punched up a steady five gees.

Looking back at the radar she watched the tiny blips disappear, merging with the first destroyer. Nothing had happened. She took several deep breaths to retain her calm. The two ships were pursuing.

"Wait a minute!" She exclaimed, straining against the five gee thrust to get a better view.

"*Allllll* right Maggie!" She yelled. "Way to go!"

Her shrieks filled her helmet and resounded achingly but she kept them up nonetheless. The two blips merged, became one larger blip and separated again into many smaller blips.

"Jeeze! Have they got egg on their face!" She cackled. "What are they going to tell the base commander?"

Then she sobered up. "What am I going to tell the base commander?"

#

The office was cool but Margaret Trudeaux was hot as she finished retelling her story. Captain Poindexter had stopped his irritable finger drumming somewhere through her account and was now scribbling numbers on his notepad.

"So I shaped orbit for Earth and got here as quickly as I could." Maggie finished. "I rigged up a simple comm circuit on the way back and called in as soon as I was near base." She made a rueful face. "They had to cut away the airlock, it was so badly warped."

He looked up momentarily when he realized she was silent, then returned to his scribblings. Margaret started to feel more uncomfortable. She could not tell that Poindexter was using those moments to regain the calm detached manner of an investigating officer: her account was pure Naval history. Finally, Poindexter laid down his pen.

"You got here in a little under six days?" He asked. When she nodded, he continued: "That's a specific impulse of just over forty-two per cent of the speed of light."

"Well," Maggie began slowly, "I explained about the changes to the CFC, didn't I?" For the first time, Poindexter noticed how hoarse her voice was. He nodded sharply for her to continue.

"Well sir, I did figure out another way to get more thrust from the chamber." She hastened to add: "It would have been a long trip unless I could figure out a way to get better performance, so I tinkered a lot." She had hummed to herself quite a bit after her victory over the destroyers and had quickly decided that she wanted to hear other music than her own. The audio/video gear was still functional but the speakers had no air to vibrate.

"So I rigged the speakers to the hull and then I got the music from the vibrations through my suit." Margaret explained.

"What does *that* have to do with increased performance?"

"Everything! The vibrations traveled through the hull to the combustion chamber and influenced the chaotic flow. I experimented a lot, tried everything. Finally, I found that if I sang along with one particular song, I got a tremendous boost in performance."

When it became apparent that the lieutenant would have to be enticed, Poindexter raised an eyebrow encouragingly.

Maggie swallowed before saying: "Beethoven's *Ode to Joy*: the soprano line. I'm afraid that only a woman can sing it." She added hastily: "Though doubtless further experimentation would allow a mere recording to suffice."

"Doubtless," the captain agreed. He turned to the tape recorder and flipped it off. "Lieutenant, as you know this was a preliminary investigation for your court martial."

"Yes sir." Margaret's voice held neither hope nor regret.

"I have reached my conclusion." With elaborate motions, Poindexter collected the papers listing the charges against her, and tore them to bits.

Then, to Maggie's great surprise, intense elation and overwhelming joy, he solemnly rose from his chair, held his body rigidly erect and with steel precise movements brought up his right hand into a perfect salute and held it there for a long, long, long time.

Never Use A Rocker

This story was written at Clarion West Writer's Workshop in 1992. I have a soft spot for it in my heart.

She never listened, you see. Sure, she was sweet enough when she was a young thing but she didn't listen even then. We met when we was young and knew right off that we were meant to be. More than fifty years together. Fifty. It seems like only yesterday.

She never meant no harm by it, I guess she was just afraid that if she ever stopped talking I might leave her. As she got older she got worse. In the end, she might as well have been a river.

It wasn't that listening to her jabbering all the time was something awful, her voice was nice enough, I suppose, and I learned to ignore it most of the time but she'd never *listen!*

For all her talking though, my Hazel was no dimwit. She'd be thinking while she was talking and it was her thinking that left us with a tidy pile when came time for me to retire. Yep, she was a thinker.

Of course she's not the only one that didn't listen. Kids. I suppose that's what did in Mrs. Porter next door, her kids were talking about putting her in a home. She must've got a fright and lost her concentration or something. Of course if it weren't for that, Hazel and me would have never found out. It might've been better considering how quiet poor Hazel is now.

Anyways, we'd come out to the porch to set a bit and watch the sun rise - neither of us needed much sleep them days - and we saw Mrs. Porter's arm chair next door out in the yard, rocking away all by itself.

"Why Hubert, isn't that May Belle Porter's best chair?" Hazel asked. Of course she gave me no time to answer, just babbled on, "Whatever would she be doing leaving that chair out in the rain like that? It's going to warp for sure."

She went on some more like that but I'd already tuned her out, rising from my chair and crossing over to May Belle Porter's yard. I had to go around 'cause our picket fence was just too tall for me to step over these days.

The chair was a mess. It was all wet, of course, but the seat was covered in wet gray ashes that had soaked into the fabric - it'd been nice fabric - and were dripping onto the grass. There was a book on top of the ashes, its cover all wet. I pulled the chair back under the cover of the porch. Then I peered through the screen door. The front door was open and the screen door wasn't latched.

"May Belle?" I called. We weren't on the best of terms but we were still neighborly; she had our key and we had hers. "May Belle are you all right?"

No answer. I hesitated a mite outside her door but figured that she'd look in on us in the same straights so I went on in. I checked the kitchen, the bedroom, the bathroom, the basement and the living room. No May Belle. She didn't have a car. She might've gone off with that no-good son of hers, he'd been talking about putting her in a home, but I told you that already. Anyway, she wasn't there.

Hazel, of course, had lots to say about the whole thing when I came back. She went on and on about how I'd catch my death of cold, all wet like I was, how I should never have gone into May Belle's house and who did I think I was to lift a heavy armchair like that at my age? She sent me back inside to change, "And dry your hair!"

I changed like she said but I called the police while I dried my hair. I would have called May Belle's no-good son but I had no more time for him than Hazel. Besides, I didn't know his number. Tom, the Sheriff, was a youngster - about fifty - but he heard me out before he told me not to worry and that they'd check on it.

We talked about it for the rest of the day, leastways Hazel did and I grunted every now and then, but Tom never showed up. Towards dark, the clouds drew together again and we had a real good lightning show just like we'd had the night before. The thunder was great, even Hazel couldn't talk over it.

In the morning I went back over to May Belle's. The ashes had all blown away or soaked right into the fabric of her armchair - a real pity. The book was still there. I picked it up. It was a book on astronomy, "Burnham's Celestial

Handbook". May Belle Porter had never so much as looked at the stars in the thirty years we'd known her. I took the book back with me to Hazel.

"Why Hubert, why ever would May Belle Porter be thinking of to want to read a book at all," Hazel declared. "It's not as if there aren't enough soaps on and all the game shows are just dandy."

Hazel liked the soaps. I used to watch them - just to set with her, you know. Sometimes I'd sit with her and read the newspaper. Other times I'd sit and let the noise flow over me, just like the Hazel's babbling.

Tom came over towards dark. Hazel offered him some ice tea but any fool could tell it was too cold already for ice tea. I offered Tom a nice cold beer.

"No thanks," he said, "I'm on duty." Well, that perked me up.

"Did you find that no-good son of hers, Tommy?" Hazel demanded. She could never get used to the fact that he wasn't still in high school and mowing our lawn on weekends.

"We found him," Tom Grady replied. "She's not with him, though. He hasn't seen her for a while." Tom paused. "He's offering a reward."

"A reward!"

"How sweet," Hazel exclaimed. "I always said he was a nice boy." Tom gave her a look and I choked back a hoot; Hazel would do that, you see, switch sides in a flash.

"Well," Tom said, rising, "if you all see anything, let me know."

"We will," I promised. Hazel pestered him to stay for dinner but he said he really had to go.

They never did find her, either. After a week, we stopped talking about it except at sunset.

It was a Tuesday - or was it a Wednesday? — no, it was a Tuesday - it was the Tuesday two weeks after May Belle disappeared that the newspaper had an article on spontaneous combustion. They said that around the country over the years hundreds of people had vanished and left behind only ashes.

Hazel read the article first, I reading the sports pages, you see. She passed it over to me wordlessly. Well, as near as wordlessly as she got, "Read this, old man."

"Read what?"

"This." She marked the headline with her thumb. I read. Apparently hundreds, maybe thousands over the years, had vanished and left behind only a pile of ashes. Always they were in their chairs. Mostly they were indoors, not too far from a fire.

"So?" I said when I'd finished reading. "May Belle Porter's chair was out in the rain, it aint the same thing at all, not at all."

Hazel snorted. "Old man, what about the ashes? You can't go telling me that there weren't ashes all over May Belle's favorite armchair. And where does she sit when she sits in the armchair?" She never gave me a chance to draw breath, my Hazel, "In her living room, old man, in her living room. You'd think, after all these years, that you would've learned something."

"Sure I learned something, I learned never to listen to you, you old witch. If May Belle's armchair's always in the living room, then why was it outside? Tell me that!"

Hazel shut up. She always upset me when she shut up; she got me to worrying that she might not talk again. It was like when a river dried up and the land was parched. Scary.

"Hazel?" My voice was low and my hand reached towards her. She batted at it, "Old man, I ain't gone yet so don't git yer hopes up! I'm thinking, leave me be."

Well, she'd never before needed to be quiet when she was thinking. It was one for the records.

"Show me that book," Hazel ordered. I rose and got the book from the hall table where I'd left it. Hazel all but snatched it from my hands. She locked onto that book like it was the Good Book itself. After a while I sighed and went inside for some blankets. She smiled up at me when I wrapped one around her shoulders and threw another over her legs.

"You're a good man, Hubert," she said, "now leave me alone." Women! She was still up when I fell asleep.

Hazel was humming when I got up for breakfast. When she hums its always because she's figured out something new, like a cat when it gets the canary.

"Good morning!" she sang out from the stove. She was flipping flapjacks. Now Hazel's been shoving cold cereal at me every year for the last ten - "You ain't no baby, Hubert. You want something else, you make it." - so I was sure she'd figured out something real special.

"What'd you do, woman?" I asked her, not forgetting to get those flapjacks from her.

"Oh," she waved her hands airily, "nothing much."

Hazel ain't never done *nothing much* in her life. Long as I've known her, I know when she's playing games. And after so many years together, I'd figured out how best to play her games, so I finished my breakfast, put the dishes in the sink, gave her a peck on the cheek and went out to watch the sun rise.

She let me stew about five minutes before she came out, too. "I went to the stars last night, Hubert."

I closed my eyes wearily. She's slipped away from me and I'll never get her back, I thought. Oh, Lord, please not yet!

"To the stars." I repeated dully.

"Yes, Hubert, to the stars," She picked up that book of May Belle's, "Burnham's Celestial Handbook", off the railing and flipped it open. "I went to Alpha Centauri. I used my chair."

She pointed at her favorite setting chair, it was out on the lawn, toppled over. With a sigh, I pushed myself out of my chair and lugged hers back to the porch. It was singed a bit on the back and legs, like it'd been burnt.

"Hazel -"

She held up a hand to stop me. "It's true, Hubert. I figured out what May Belle did and I did it."

"What'd May Belle do?" I asked gently, trying to guide her into her chair but she shook off my hand.

"I can seat myself, thank you!" she did, though she sniffed mightily at the scorch marks and burnt wood. "Mustn't have got it quite right."

"Give me that book," she grabbed it out of my hands and flipped through the pages, muttering, "Centauri, Centauri, ah, here it is: page 549."

Poor girl, I thought, poor, poor girl!

Hazel slapped at me. "Stop that! Don't think I can't tell what you're thinking Hubert Rollins, I know that pitying look. I'll show you. You just wait until this evening when the stars are out. Hmph!"

She went inside and turned on her soaps. She wouldn't talk to me for the rest of the day and I knew what a sacrifice *that* was for her.

#

"Now, are you ready to *listen* to me, Hubert Rollins?" she called from the door as the last of the sun sunk below the horizon. We hadn't passed a word between us the whole day and I realized just how much I was used to her pretty voice.

Well, I'd had a lot of time to think about it. Seemed to me that if Hazel wanted to believe she'd gone to the stars, there wasn't any harm in it and I'd sure miss her.

I nodded from my chair. She could see my back clearly but it wasn't enough. "Reckon so, Hazel."

That was enough. She swung open the screen door, paused long enough for some mosquitoes to get inside and then sat herself in her chair. She put the book in her lap and ordered: "Turn on the light, you old fool, I can't see in the dark."

"You can't see too well in the day, either," I allowed but I turned on the light anyhow. Hazel ignored my comment and bent closer to the book.

"All you gotta to do is know where to look and how to feel," she told me.

"That easy, eh?"

"Hubert!" I reckon she must have caught my tone. "May Belle must've got it all wrong or something. She's got notes in margins. She said you needed a good birch wood chair to get to Alpha Centauri but mine's oak and you know it."

"Oak."

"Yessir, oak," She was mighty testy for a body who claimed to have gone to the stars in a straight-backed chair.

I played along. "Maybe if you used birch wood your chair wouldn't be all scorched."

She made a rude noise at me. "May Belle was wrong, I tell you. That's what happened to her."

"What?"

"Them ashes! She tried it with the wrong chair or she didn't do it right, I don't know, but whatever she did she toasted herself."

Well sir, I've lived with this woman for over fifty years, like I said before, and I've never heard her talk so crazy in all that time. Of course, I knew all the stars were suns like ours or bigger, and some of them were mighty odd but I couldn't see no old biddy figuring to go space traveling to the stars sitting in her armchair.

"So you just set in your chair and say, I want to go to Mars, is that it?" I asked, trying to sound normal. "It's a wonder all them NASA boys never did figure it out. We'll just phone up the President right now and tell him."

"Hubert, you old fool!" Hazel snapped at me, eyes flashing. "May Belle's notes say *nothing* about going to Mars. And the President's too young."

"Too young." You'll probably understand that all this was beyond me.

"Yup. Only old people can do it," Hazel told me. I just nodded. "Of course you, you old goat, you're probably too old."

"Why old people, Hazel? How'd May Belle figure all this out?"

"I dunno. I guess she was sitting out one night thinking just how much she'd love to be up with the stars and - oh, if I say more I'll be up there with her."

"She's at that Alpha whats-its you was talking about?"

"Alpha Centauri," she corrected absently, "and no, she's not. She didn't pay attention and turned herself to ashes."

"Lord's wrath," I suggested.

Hazel sighed. "I suppose the only way is to show you." She looked my chair over. "Alder. It would be. Alder's only good for long distances. You'll get the Andromeda Galaxy, probably. Of course your chair won't be good for nothing afterwards."

"I *like* this chair."

"Don't be a baby." She got up and stood behind me, her hand pointing to the sky above me. "Look there, no there! See? That blob? Here, look in the book." I looked. It looked like one of them tie-dye shirts them hippies used to wear with "You are here" written at the top. "Says here that it looks like the light of a candle shining through horn. It's two point two million light-years away."

"Light year?" I was going say more but she beat me to it.

"A light-year is how far light travels in a year. Don't let it bother you none. Just understand that it's a fair piece."

"How come no one but May Belle ever did this afore?"

"Who says they didn't? How'd you think May Belle found out and her not too bright, poor dear."

"I don't want to go."

"You'll go." It wasn't a question, it wasn't a prediction but it wasn't quite an order. Hazel was always like that.

She grew enthusiastic, arms waving in front of me. "Hubert, it's something special. You're gonna love it! It's just for old people. People with time to look up at the stars and sit in their chairs thinking. People with nothing else to do and nothing else to lose."

I looked up at the stars. They sure were pretty. We'd said it to each other often enough of an evening. Sure pretty. I sighed. "Okay, tell me how."

"Just look where you're going and pull it closer to you. Set tight and concentrate."

Well, I tried. I swear. I looked up where she'd pointed and I saw that thing in the book, only it was awfully small. I imagined rushing up to meet it, leaving the clouds behind, passing the Moon and whizzing out through the stars -

"No, old fool, not like that! Bring it to you."

"Hazel -" I began in a patient tone.

"Don't you 'Hazel' me," she snapped. "Do it."

Well I did. I focused on that small blur, that galaxy, poured all my attention on it and just when I felt that I had it, I pulled that it to me. And it *came*. And suddenly I was too close, I was right on top of it, I was going through the stars, planets whizzed by around my ears and -

"*Hubert!*" Hazel's shriek brought me back. She patted at my shoulders.

"Ouch! That stings."

"Burns's more like it," she kept up her patting. "You were on fire. Honestly, a man your age…"

I jumped up but with less spring than I usually had. My legs were like rubber, I was awful tired from that gallivanting, and scared too. Still a bit wobbly, I looked down at my chair as Hazel finished patting out the sparks on my shirt.

The legs were smoking and charred. I must have looked awfully wild-eyed because Hazel just up and laughed at me. I can't say I saw much to laugh at — my best chair was no better than kindling.

"How do I get back there?" I put a hand on my chair — it wobbled unevenly on its charred legs. I guess some of the feet had been burnt off.

"Well," Hazel said, pushing the chair out of my grasp, "first you get yourself a good night's sleep. And then you get yourself another chair."

I opened my mouth to protest but she cut me off, pointing up: a low fog had rolled in, obscuring the stars. "It's time to sleep. Tomorrow you can get both of us new chairs."

Come morning, I figured that before we went into town to buy new chairs I should take another look at May Belle's house, particularly *her* chairs. I wasn't up to no harm, just to have a good look and see what sort of chair she'd liked best. If you could only use a chair once, like Hazel said, then I figured if May Belle had done much in-ter-stell-ar sightseeing she must've used up a fair number.

Well, she only had about five other chairs in the whole place. In her kitchen I found the remains of two kitchen chairs: cheap steel tube chairs with vinyl seats. One of them had some red dirt on its legs. Up in her bedroom was a light walnut chair, its legs were badly charred and in the guest bedroom, which used to belong to her George, was a cane chair, which hadn't fared at all well to judge from the way it was mangled.

Downstairs in her living room was May Belle's old rocker. It was a beauty made in some sort of mahogany. I couldn't see any marks on it at all. That surprised me so much that I made a point of mentioning it to Hazel when I got back but she waved it off with a flip of her hand, "Pshaw! That rocker was her favorite. She'd never have used that."

Afore she could start up that engine and run on for hours, I said, "One of her kitchen chairs had some red earth on it."

My Hazel was never slow, no matter how much she liked to hear herself. Her eyes went wide. "Mars! She must've been to Mars!" She flipped through the book, found a spot and read avidly. When she looked up again it was to snap, "Don't just stand there, ol' man. Get me a pencil and paper. I'm going to make you a shopping list."

Me. I took the old pickup to town. Town ain't so big, never had been. But we got a furniture store and Goodwill. Between the two, I managed to get what she wanted. I also found me a dandy rocker. Made of rowan wood. I found it at the Goodwill. Now I'm not much partial to them myself, poor old Beauregard, my old setter, had lost his tail to one some years before he passed on and I never cottoned to them since, but I knew Hazel loved them dearly and pined for one. It was perfect and going for a song, too good to be true.

"I can't believe anyone would sell a rocker like this," I chuckled as the youngster helped me load it in the truck.

"I suppose." The youngster wasn't much for talk but he opened up a bit more, "It's funny, this one came from an estate sale."

"Really?" I was interested, you get to be my age and every passing seems to get you nearer to the head of the list, as it were.

"Yup. Fellow by the name of Jurgens, from up the road a ways," he explained. "We're the only Goodwill in two counties."

"That a fact," I said politely but I had another question, "That wouldn't be Amos Jurgens, would it?"

The youngster looked at me and really saw me for the first time. I guess he must've figured I wasn't all that far behind. "You know him?"

"Not to speak to," I replied. "I read about him in the papers."

The youngster shook his head, "Pretty weird, wasn't it? They said spontaneous combustion." He nodded at the chair we had just loaded. "That was his favorite chair. All they found was ashes."

"You don't say," I replied, shaking my head. It got me to figuring that there was something wrong with rockers.

I said as much to Hazel when I got back. Between the Goodwill and the furniture store, I'd picked up a baker's dozen of chairs. It took me and Hazel until sundown to get them off the truck.

"There ain't nothing wrong with rockers," Hazel said as soon as I'd finished speaking. "I read the notes in the book carefully. It says nothing about rockers."

"Hell, Hazel, May Belle wrote all them notes! What's she know about anything?"

"How dare you speak ill of the dead, Hubert Rollins," Hazel wagged a finger at me fiercely. "She figured out enough to write all these notes and she went to Mars, the Moon, and all them other places. If she said nothing about rockers, there's no problem."

"But what about Mr. Jurgens? And why didn't May Belle use her rocker if there was no problem with them?" I wanted to know.

"I told you that May Belle Porter loved that rocker of hers and wouldn't have done anything to hurt it. As for Mr. Jurgens, you can't say for sure if he was trying to get anywhere or just burnt himself up setting in his chair." It didn't bother her none that old man Jurgens had ashed himself in that rocker, she'd fallen in love with it the moment I'd pulled in the drive. Now it was setting on the porch and Hazel was pondering on using it or saving it for a setting chair. It was an odd moment, because with all her thinking she forgot to do any talking.

That old rocker worried me a fair bit but we didn't use it that night; we used the aluminum chairs. Yes, sir! I can tell you that the Earth sure is a pretty sight from the Moon. Hazel and me pulled the Moon down to our front porch and then under the house so just the porch and our chairs were all that remained. We got a good look at the Earth. We would have stayed there longer but it got awful cold and the air was getting kind of stale.

The chairs were good for nothing when we got back - parts of the legs must have froze to the Moon. It got me to wondering if there was a way to get somewhere without leaving part of a chair behind.

I should have known that Hazel was way ahead of me. "Hubert," she began in a slow voice that told me she'd been doing a lot of thinking, "what if May Belle *had* been using her rocker?"

"Huh?" I shook my head. "Look here, Hazel, I told you that it was still in her living room."

"She could see out the window."

"But there wasn't a mark on it!"

Hazel shook her head at me like I was some simple child. "That's because it's got rockers, Hubert. Rockers don't set down hard like chair legs."

"You're mad, woman!" I should have known better than to say that. Hazel just looked at me pityingly and tut-tutted me. "Anyways, it's late."

She sighed. "I suppose you're right." She got up off of her rickety chair and pushed it over to me. "Best put these two around back." She tottered over to that rocker. "I'll set here until you get back."

I stacked my chair face down on hers and made to drag them off, warning her, "Just make sure all you do is set."

Hazel made a face, "Go on, old man! We haven't got all night."

I went, dragging the chairs down the porch stairs and back around the house. The legs on Hazel's chair had been ate up a fair bit when we was sitting on the Moon so the stumps snagged in the grass and it was longer than I would have liked afore I came back around to the front.

"Okay, old woman, I'm back." I couldn't see much because the porch light was in my eyes. "C'mon, stir them stumps, it's time for bed."

She didn't answer. I knew just from that but I rushed up them stairs as fast as my old legs would carry me.

Ashes. That's all there was. "Oh, Hazel!" Then I got mad. "You wouldn't listen, would you? You just had to go and do it." Silly old cow. "You silly old -" but I could never say them words aloud.

I couldn't leave her like that either. I figured I had to do something. So I went inside and got a Dust Devil, put a new bag in it and cleaned her up good.

It got awful quiet after that. Too quiet. I took to reading that silly book of May Belle's. I was right about May Belle not being smart enough to figure all this out, I found a name written in pencil inside the front cover: May Belle had got her copy from an old man named Jurgens. Seems he was quite the egghead and worked on astrophysics and such before his health gave out.

I spent some time tracking him down, it appears he just up and vanished one night. Him and his favorite rocker. Once I heard that I re-read that book, particularly his notes. It seems that May Belle weren't all that smart at all, not at all, because on the last page old man Jurgens had scrawled a note.

"Took several types of wood with me last trip. All traveled well, except for rowan wood which turned to ash immediately. I resolved never to use rowan wood in any chair." May Belle's armchair was made of rowan wood.

May Belle's rocker wasn't, so I took it. And sure enough, Hazel was right – you *could* use a rocker. Hazel was probably also right that May Belle just hadn't wanted to risk her favorite chair.

At first I just went all around the place: Tau Ceti, Epsilon Eridani, Sigma Draconis, all them big names in space. But whenever I came back I would hear the silence. And that rowan rocker would tempt me sorely.

So I got to thinking. If I could see the stars, why not the planets? I'd gone to the Moon, hadn't I? If I could get on the planets, then maybe I could find someone, someone who could take Hazel's ashes and do something with them – bring her back.

And that's how I got to be here. You're the ninth type of people I've met. You wouldn't know how, would you?

She never did listen but *Lord!* I do miss her babbling voice.

EMS Brevity

EMS Brevity, what can I say? What happens when you have an engineer who's allergic to light and wants to drink blood? Or a first officer with pointed ears?

"Surgeon to the bridge! Surgeon to the bridge!" the voice shouted over the intercom. Dr. Jessica Cohen — Jess to the small circle of intimate acquaintances which, at the moment, only included herself — groaned and rose from the chair in her office to head up to the bridge once again.

She'd been on the *Brevity* long enough to recognize the voice as belonging to Mr. Rock. She wasn't sure if it was Mr. Rock with the pointy ears or Mr. Rock with the turtle on his head — the *Brevity*'s exec suffered from a most peculiar form of schizophrenia.

Mr. Rock — in either incarnation — was convinced that the *Brevity* was being shadowed by some unknown ship and had decided that the doctor was his natural ally in combating the alien menace.

In view of the other possibilities, Dr. Cohen had to concede that Mr. Rock (both of them) had probably made a good selection.

As Jess climbed into the lift tube and pushed off for the bridge she recalled the ancient Chinese curse — although it had all the hallmarks of good Yiddish, too — "May you get what you wish for."

As she floated up toward the bridge, aware that only such an ancient ship as the *Brevity* had a lift tube that was nothing more than a zero-gee tunnel running the length of the ship, Dr. Cohen regretted her decision on an early lunch. And, again, she regretted that she had got her wish.

#

Of course, at the time, it had seemed like a wish come true for Dr. Jessica Cohen, junior medical officer on the great cruiser *Commander*. From the first,

Captain Kellmann's near-anal attention to detail and insistence on repetitive drills had run completely counter to Dr. Cohen's more relaxed manner.

In no time, Jess found herself wracking up poor ratings on her efficiency reports and was constantly assigned extra duty or punishment detail. So what if she let her sick-bay attendants sleep on duty? Nothing was happening, was it? And if she joined them in the occasional game of poker, what was the harm in that? Of course, if she let them take some sack time it was only fair that they reciprocate and no one had actually died from it, had they?

The Captain was a stickler for the rulebook while Jess was not — clearly there were going to be problems. Only she hadn't anticipated the problems becoming so large, so quickly.

She supposed she should have guessed that Captain Kellmann would have expected her to be on her toes, perhaps even misplaced in a surgeon's role, when Jess's own parents were a combat admiral of renown and the fleet's best starship designer. But, honestly, with all the glory her parents had acquired, didn't it just seem natural that their only daughter would want to rest on their laurels?

It wasn't as if either of them were around long enough for her to acquire any of their good habits. When one wasn't trying to get herself blown up for the good of the service, the other was trying to go faster than anyone had gone before.

The few moments Jess had spent with her parents were tedious and strained for all of them, to be sure. Neither her esteemed combat admiral mother nor her stellar engineer father could for one moment grasp Jess' fascination with the workings of the human body — and mind.

She had exerted herself to the utmost in getting into medical school — despite her parents. And then she'd found herself constantly bing measured against *their* standards!

It wasn't enough that she could diagnose any ailment in record time nor that she could perform the most delicate brain surgery at the same level as any of the best in the field, no! She was expected to command starships in battle while redesigning their interstellar drives in her spare time, too.

So it was natural, to Jess' way of thinking, that she would expect after all her effort in med school and the patchy officer training demanded by the service of its surgeons, that Jess should take it easy for a while. Years, in fact. Perhaps her whole life.

Captain Kellmann, unfortunately, had other expectations. "Capable but uninspired," was the least of his critiques in her officer's evaluation report.

Jess, for her part, recognized a bad fit when she saw one and decided to take action. She put in a request for transfer to the next available ship.

Captain Kellmann tried to argue her out of it but she was adamant and, in the end, he relented, filing the request 'approved and pending' while waiting for another ship.

It was just Jess' luck that the first ship that needed a medical officer was the *Brevity*.

Brevity was short-handed and had an immediate need for a ship's surgeon. In fact, she had a priority need *and* the slot was for a ship's surgeon, not a junior surgeon. Jess couldn't believe her luck.

"She's a mother ship," Captain Kellmann told her when she reported to him for her orders. He frowned. "I don't understand how a mother ship would leave port without a surgeon on board."

"Mother ship?" Jess asked, confused. Kellmann glared at her until she added, "Sir."

"She's got some forty thousand fertilized embryos onboard en route to Theta Upsilon," the captain explained. "That should keep you on your toes," he added, eyes twinkling. He scanned the ship's records. "Crew of twenty, captain, exec, comm officer, engineer, and ship's surgeon — that'd be you — for officers."

He glanced down at the rest of the records.

"Uh-oh!" he said, scowling as he flicked through screens on his console. He sat up straight, gave Jess a searching look and said slowly, "Maybe you'd like to wait for another ship."

"No sir, first available," Jess said. She couldn't wait to get away from this martinet. Anything *he* didn't like about *Brevity* was probably good news to her.

The captain took a breath, preparing to dissuade her but caught the stubborn look on her face and decided against it.

"Very well, be at the docking tube, prepared to depart, in twenty minutes."

#

Twenty minutes later, Jess was back in the captain's cabin.

"Sir, Chief Rollins insisted that I wear *this*!" Cohen exclaimed, holding up a cross. "She said it was your orders."

Kellmann sighed. "It was," he said. He held up a hand to forestall her further protests. "I know that you're Jewish but —"

"This is an outrage, sir!" Jess protested. "I would have expected —"

"Lieutenant, it's for your own good," Captain Kellmann replied. "You *did* read the ship's records, didn't you?"

"I haven't had time, I've been busy packing," Jess retorted. Besides, she didn't want to read anything that might force her to change her mind.

Captain Kellmann bit back a quick retort and merely shook his head. "Very well, don't wear it. But you *will* wear a hard suit."

"Sir?"

"*Brevity*'s an old ship and I don't trust their docking tube," Kellmann lied. "I'll have the chief put search and rescue markers on your suit, too."

Jess acknowledged his reply with a curt nod, a sloppy salute and hastily left his cabin to return to the docking tube.

#

"What's this?" Jess exclaimed as she looked down on the bright orange reflective tape being laid across her chest.

"Search and rescue marking, ma'am," Chief Rollins said without looking at the lieutenant. "We'll have you all done in a moment and then you can depart."

There was something in the chief's tone that made it clear to Jess that Chief Rollins would be happy to see the last of her.

"It's a cross!" Jess protested.

"Yes, ma'am," the chief replied. "That's the best shape for radar reflections, makes you stand out. You'll be wanting that sort of protection from their engineer."

"Why? Is he so bad that he'll blow a simple docking procedure?"

"Well, it's best to be safe," the chief replied. "Okay, we're sealing your helmet now."

The chief put the helmet on Jess and twisted it shut. Instinctively, Jess checked the telltales and gave the chief a thumbs-up.

"All right, ma'am, lock's opening now," the chief's voice rang out over the suit radio. "If you'll just step in. *Brevity*'s just finished taking on cargo, so they're ready to depart."

As Jess entered the lock, the chief stepped in with her and clipped a wire to the front of her suit.

"What's that for?"

"Safety wire," the chief replied still avoiding her eyes. "From *Brevity*. In case anything goes wrong, you're attached to *her* now."

The thought of being attached to her new ship sent a thrill down Jess' spine. A new ship, and ship's surgeon!

The lock closed behind her and she started her way across the docking tube. With each step she took, she grew more elated that she was leaving *Commander* and more apprehensive that she was boarding *Brevity*.

What was it that bothered Captain Kellmann about *Brevity*'s captain? Could it be that she was wrong and that Kellmann was really trying to protect her? Or was he just annoyed that Jess would be getting the surgeon's slot?

Halfway across, the tube lurched. Jess spread her arms to balance herself.

"*Brevity! Brevity!* You've still got a passenger in transit!" *Commander*'s comm officer shouted on Jess' frequency.

Another lurch, sharper and harder this time and then Jess gaped as the docking tube suddenly split and she could see stars through the gap.

Jess couldn't remember how she got from the middle of the docking tube to the airlock of the *Brevity* but suddenly she was there, slamming the hatch controls with a speed that would have amazed her previous captain. Just as the hatch spun closed, Jess saw the shredded middle of the docking tube break free and drift off into space.

Her heart was still pounding as she activated the inner lock control and stepped aboard *Brevity*. She came to attention, ready to request permission to board when she realized that the corridor was unlit and empty.

"Hello?" she called after a moment. "Lieutenant Cohen requests permission to board."

No one answered her. Perhaps, she thought, there was some emergency that had called all the crew away — that would explain the bizarre destruction of the boarding tube. She looked around and found the environmental controls.

She turned up the lights to get a better view of her surroundings, deciding to keep her spacesuit on until she was sure of the hull's integrity.

"The lights!" A voice wailed in pain. "Turn off the lights."

"Sorry," Jess said, instantly turning the lighting back down to its previous dim level. "Lieutenant Cohen, requesting permission to board," she repeated in the direction of the voice — at least where she guessed it to be — spacesuits weren't equipped for stereo sound.

"Lieutenant MacDowell," the speaker answered, stretching out the last syllable of his name. "Ship's engineer."

Jess waited in vain for the engineer to add the standard "permission granted."

"Should I report to the captain?" she asked, as the silence stretched out interminably.

"The captain's sick," MacDowell replied after another long silence. "Step over by the door."

Jess suppressed her irritation at the brisk order and complied, stepping closer to the exit from the docking back.

A sudden loud hiss made her freeze in place. She was afraid that perhaps the ship's hull had been breached and it was leaking air. Could Captain Kellmann have known that *Brevity* was holed? Was that why he insisted on her wearing a spacesuit? Could this old ship be so leaky that she'd have to wear a suit for her entire *deployment*?

"The cross! Go! Leave me!" MacDowell wailed, and Jess had a fleeting impression of someone hurtling into the shadows of the boat bay.

"Cross?" Jess looked down at her suit. "Yeah, I don't what it those jokers were up to, demanding that I wear it —"

"Go!" MacDowell hissed again from his hiding place.

With one final backward glance towards the engineer, Jess left the docking bay wondering if perhaps the ship's engineer wasn't suffering from some strange photophobia.

Jess found the ship's lift tube, discovered, with a lurch in her stomach, that it was an old-style zero-gee tube, and made her way to the bridge — where the situation worsened.

"Lieutenant Cohen reporting," Jess said as she stepped out of the lift tube and onto the bridge. Her voice trailed off as she looked around the cramped bridge, noted its dim light and empty chairs.

"The captain's sick, lieutenant, and in his quarters," a tenor voice spoke from behind her. Jess whirled around and caught sight of an officer seated in the tactical chair.

"Rock, first officer," the man identified himself. Jess noticed that he seemed to have a slight palor to his skin and — what was wrong with his ears? Not wanting to make a bad impression, she tabled the question for her later perusal of the ship's medical files.

"Should I attend the captain, then?" Jess volunteered.

"I doubt that will be necessary, lieutenant," Commander Rock replied. "The captain's been sick before and nothing Dr. Metron prescribed ever helped."

"Well, maybe I…"

"If you'll excuse me, I have work to do," Rock said, turning back to his consoles and clearly dismissing her.

#

Jess spent her first week aboard *Brevity* putting away her gear, familiarizing herself with the most important surgical gear — all ancient — and tending the forty thousand embryos in her storage lockers.

Brevity was an old ship, nearly fifty years old. She was small and a first generation micro-jumper built just at the dawn of the star travel. While mankind still strived to develop genuine faster-than-light travel, micro-jumping, instantly displacing from one point in space to another, filled the requirement nicely.

As a first generation micro-jumper, originally *Brevity* could only jump a thousand kilometers each jump — but she could do that a thousand times a second for an apparent velocity of over three times the speed of light. New gear let her increase this to thirty times the speed of light which was nothing compared with *Commander*'s impressive 10,000 kilometer jumps made 10,000 times a second — for an apparent velocity of over three hundred and thirty-three times the speed of light. And her father's *Speedy* was getting jumps of over a million kilometers — but her father was trying to break the mechanics of making instantaneous jumps from one star to another.

Brevity's first several years had been spent exploring which meant that, at least early on, she was a lucky ship — too few of the explorers returned to the home world with news.

As more and more inhabitable planets were found and the technology of micro-jumping advanced, larger colony and trade ships were built.

Many of the original colony ships were built for one-way trips but it soon became more practical to build fleets adapted both to transporting colonists and trade goods.

The planet *Rainbow* had been the first colony world to turn net exporter — only a mere five years after the first colonists set foot on the planet.

Since then, over forty star systems had been colonized by the human race, eager to expand beyond its still-polluted home world.

One of the greatest needs of colony worlds, once they'd gotten beyond scrabbling for mere survival, was colonists. It quickly turned out that for the richer colony worlds, it was cheaper to import colonists *in utero* than any other way.

So *Brevity* found herself with a new lease on life, hauling embryos from the home world to desperate colony worlds.

As a command, *Brevity* did not demand much of her crew — basic maintenance, simple astrogation, that was all. That suited Jess just fine even though, as ship's surgeon, her job overseeing the embryos and their uterine replicators was probably the most demanding on the whole ship.

Jess quickly mastered the supervision of the replicators and found tending them to be a plodding, mechanical operation that she conducted in the first part of her watch with half her attention. Alerts and monitors would waken her if anything extraordinary occurred.

At the end of the first week, Jess felt sufficiently at home with her new duties that she found time to indulge in her curiosity about the crew.

The first thing she noticed, perusing their medical records, was that all the enlisted crew of the *Brevity* were woefully far behind in their regular medical exams. In fact, she realized with a frown creasing her forehead, none of the enlisted crew had a medical more current than ten years ago.

Jess flipped from their medicals to the records of Dr. Metron, wondering if perhaps the lack of medicals was a result of his lethargy.

Her frown deepened as she dug deeper and deeper into the medical database. After a while she slumped back in her chair — just what *had* Metron been doing?

Come to think of it, what had happened to the former surgeon, Jess wondered. She leaned forward again to her console, scrolled through the database, looking the answer — and couldn't find one.

"Well, this is just *too* weird!" Jess declared, pushing herself to her feet, and heading for the bridge, determined to tackle the captain on the issue.

#

The bridge was as dimly lit as she'd found it on her first day. She stood in the hatchway, letting her eyes adjust and scanned the room.

"Are you the surgeon?" A voice asked from her left, causing Jess to jump.

"Lieutenant Jessica Cohen," Jess said automatically, wondering if she was finally meeting the captain. Then it registered that the voice was a woman's. Not the captain, then. "And you are?"

Jess found herself looking down at a mousy-haired lieutenant wearing too much makeup, all badly applied.

"Lieutenant Monroe," the other said, her tone just short of frigid.

"You're the comm officer?" Jess asked, remembering the watch list, she turned toward the other and held out a hand. "I'm glad to meet you."

Lieutenant Monroe examined the hand but did not take it.

"Could you tell me something," Jess asked, trying a new tack. "When was the last time your saw Dr. Metron?"

A shadow flicked across Monroe's eyes. "I'm taking my meds," she said defensively.

Meds? Jess thought to herself. She made a note to go over the officers' medical records as soon as she got back down to the sickbay.

Jess waved a hand at the nervous comm officer, saying, "I didn't mean to imply... it's just that my records —"

A message popped up on Monroe's console. The lieutenant turned to it hopefully. As she read it, her expression changed and she turned back to Jess with a look of near-triumph.

"The cook's got your lunch ready in the sick bay," Monroe told her.

"Cook?"

"Yes, you'd better go," Monroe said, preventing herself at the last moment from making a shooing gesture with her hands. "You wouldn't want it to get cold."

"But why in sick bay?"

"That's where you work, right?" Monroe said. She continued before Jess could answer, "The cook's always being thoughtful." Monroe motioned again to the hatch. "You'd best go before it gets cold," she repeated.

Bemused and baffled, Jess turned to the hatch. Just before she swung into the zero-gee field, Monroe asked with a slightly embarrassed tone, "Doctor, could I come see you after lunch?"

Jess turned her head rapidly to catch at the comm officer's expression and immediately regretted the effect the quick movement had on her sense of balance in the zero gee field.

"Uh, sure," she managed to say before clamping her mouth shut and pushing off, hoping to reach her sick bay before she was sick herself.

#

Jess couldn't believe the lunch the cook had laid out for her on her desk. All her work, writing tablets and floating notes, had been carefully moved aside and a tray covered with a cloth placemat had been spread in their stead on which had been placed a plate with a warming cover, a glass and real flatware.

Jess frowned as she realized that instead of assaulting her stomach, still queasy from the zero-gee tube, the clean fresh smells wafting toward her were welcome and appealing.

Appreciatively she lifted the cover and saw that the cook had placed not a warm lunch but a light lunch of greens covered with a pungent dressing. A clear glass of water stood in front of the cutlery which was neatly arranged on top of a napkin. A printed note to the left of the napkin said, "With the cook's compliments."

"Thank you very much, cookie," Jess murmured, seating herself and diligently digging in to the salad. She murmured in delight with the first bite and soon found herself emptying the plate. This was much better than anything she'd had about *Commander*!

Replete, Jess rose, took the tray to the recycling receptacle — even on such an outdated ship as *Brevity* there was no such thing as trash — and sat back at her desk, pulling her work towards her.

She had barely settled in when her door chime sounded.

"Come in," she called. Lieutenant Monroe entered, looked nervously around the room, relaxing just slightly when she caught sight of Jessica.

Jess noted her apprehension but presented a smiling, cheerful face to the comm officer. She gestured to the chair opposite her. "Have a seat."

Monroe slumped into the chair.

"What can I do for you, lieutenant?" Jess asked, leaning forward intently.

Monroe's eyes slid away from hers and the lieutenant looked momentarily nonplussed. A long silence stretched between them.

"I'd like to have my implant removed," the lieutenant murmured finally.

"Really?" Jess was intrigued. "You want assignment dirtside?"

The lieutenant looked up at her, shocked. "Oh, no, not that!" she replied, shaking her head emphatically. "I like it here, it's just that…"

The fleet of ships which plied their trade through the stars were not organized into a formal fleet. In fact, few were owned by the same companies, much less the same planets, but they had all started with remarkably similar operating procedures and those procedures had grown more similar rather than less as the harsh lessons of space travel were learned the hard way. Early on it had been decided that pregnancy in space was to be avoided, so any woman who wished their contraceptive implant removed would normally be assigned off-ship.

"But without your implant, if you engage in any sexual activity, you run the risk of pregnancy," Jess reminded her patiently.

"I know that," Monroe said with a touch of acerbity in her tone. "I'll be careful."

"Hmm," Jess murmured, tapping on her touchpad to check ship's stores. "I see that we *are* stocked for such contingencies," Jess said, mildly surprised. In her experience ships didn't carry extraneous stores. She wondered why *Brevity* did, perhaps this was not the first time the lieutenant had made such a request. Jess tabled the notion for later investigation.

"Well, you are of age," Jess said with a smile, rising from her chair and beckoning the lieutenant to follow her. "I've cautioned you and you know you can always have another implant if you want."

Monroe nodded as she followed Jess into the sickbay proper. She sat in the chair Jess indicated while the surgeon hunted around for the right implement. She quickly found a sonic probe and ran it over Monroe's forearm. The probe beeped when it located the implant and Jess nodded to herself.

"It'll be a bit painful," Jess warned, as she searched the drawers for an extractor. She was surprised to see how neatly the drawers were laid out, Dr. Metron must have been very meticulous. Jess, for all her lackadaisical nature, approved.

"It's all right," Monroe said, looking away.

"Ah, the things we do for love," Jess said, looking at the lieutenant.

The Lieutenant's face snapped back to her, frowning. "How did you guess?"

"I didn't," Jess said honestly. "I just couldn't imagine any other reason you'd want your implant out."

The sharp frown lines eased a bit in the lieutenant's face. "It might not even work," she whined. "But maybe, just maybe, once a month he'll look my way."

"Who?" Jess asked in spite of herself. Who would be so bizarre as to worry whether a woman was menstruating? Someone with a bizarre religious aversion?

"Commander MacDowell," Monroe replied, flushing. "I thought that perhaps —"

"I see," Jess replied firmly. She held the extractor up over the site of the implant. "Well, I hope it works for you."

The incision was quick, painless, and the implant was quickly removed. Jess put a simple bandage over Monroe's arm and patted the comm officer on the shoulder.

"There, all done," she said. "It'll take about a month or so. If there's any problem, come let me know."

Monroe gave her a nervous smile and a nod and promptly left the sickbay.

#

Given Lieutenant Monroe's request, Jess thought it only natural that she start her review of the officers' medical records with the comm officer. She called up the officer's personnel records first.

Marla Monroe was the first in her family to enter space service. She was the youngest of a family of seven on *Rainbow* — the colony world was wealthy but large families had become a rarity since the colony world had grown rich. Jess wondered if Marla had felt out of place.

Lieutenant Monroe had been an uninspired but average student. How did she manage a commission, Jess wondered but the answer fairly popped out at her as she continued her scan of the records. Lieutenant Monroe's commission was bought, probably a gift from her father.

Monroe in short order found herself aboard *Brevity* and there she remained for nearly twelve years. Jess found herself surprised at that. Twelve years was a long time to be on one ship, let alone at one rank. Apparently Lieutenant Monroe had —

Jess' eyes had spotted something that interrupted her thoughts. She looked at it again, then indexed the records. Hmm, Lieutenant Monroe had a rather long listing for treatments for sexually transmitted disease.

"Goodness!" Jess said aloud, surprised. She would not have thought the mousy lieutenant to have wracked up such a great number of encounters, but judging by her medical records alone, Marla Monroe had managed a long line of conquests — or at least enough lovers to garner over two dozen separate treatments.

As Jess looked at the dates of Lt. Monroe's treatments, she noticed that the lieutenant's appetites — at least to judge by treatment for STDs — had slowed down significantly upon joining *Brevity*. Of course, Jess realized, that may simply be due to a lack of suitable partners, as evidenced by her most recent request.

Still… Jess looked at some of the most recent treatment dates and medicines used, performed a quick cross-reference and —

"Ah!" Jess' eyes danced. Perhaps the captain wasn't suffering from gout after all! It was fairly obvious, given two personnel both being treated at the same time for that particularly *rare* form of disease, that Captain Cahuyaga had found some special ways to communicate with his comm officer.

Jess wondered why Dr. Metron hadn't seen fit to report this — such abrogations of the chain of command were considered very grave offenses. The possibility of sexual harassment or sexual coercion aboard a ship as small as *Brevity* was a major concern.

And, even more worrying, Jess thought, was why Dr. Metron hadn't done something to relieve Lt. Monroe of what was pretty obviously a case of poor self-esteem.

Come to think of it, what *had* happened to Dr. Metron?

#

"Dr. Metron left," Commander Rock told Jess when she asked him later. His tone brooked no further discussion.

They were on the bridge and it was, as always, dimly lit. This time Jess' eyes were drawn to a strange mottling on the Commander's head and forehead.

I didn't realize he was bald, she thought to herself. It looked like some accident, perhaps involving acid or something, had left the Commander with a large part of his scalp bald and mottled — like he was wearing a turtle on his head.

"Hnh," the commander growled, peering down at his readouts. "It is as I thought."

"Pardon?"

"This does not concern you," Rock told her stiffly. He turned to her and she got a better look at his face. Why are his eyebrows so bushy? Jess asked herself.

"You should leave," he told her. "Only authorized personnel are allowed on the bridge."

"I am authorized," Jess replied staunchly. "As ship's surgeon, I have full run of the ship."

"Your duty station is the sickbay."

"Are we at duty stations?" Jess asked, looking around for the telltale alerts. "Is there some danger?"

"The captain has not ordered us to duty stations," Commander Rock replied. Rock's tone told of heated arguments grudgingly lost. "But *I* remain vigilant," Rock said, almost to himself.

"Commander," Jess began again, a bit more hesitantly. "About Dr. Metron…"

"He left, as I said," Rock replied shortly. "Now, if you'll excuse me, I'm sure you have duties in the sickbay." The word "lieutenant" was left unspoken but clearly implied in his tone. Jess had spent enough time in the service to recognize a dismissal when she got one.

#

Jess' search through Commander Rock's medical records made no mention of either premature baldness or indications of pointed ears or an explanation for a greenish tinge to his skin. The commander appeared from the records to be in robust health. However, Jess noted with some surprise, that Dr. Metron had prescribed a number of low-grade mood altering drugs for the commander. Some would increase aggression, while others would increase a sense of detachment. Yet nothing in his prior records indicated that the commander was suffering from a chemical imbalance.

Had Dr. Metron been drugging the crew, Jess wondered. She called up the records for Captain Cahuyaga. Carlos Cahuyaga was a veteran of space with over twenty-five years' worth of experience. Hmm, Jess wondered to herself, so why's he here?

The answer came quickly from her scan of the records. Apparently the captain had blotted his copybook rather profoundly when in command of the *Albatross*. The *Albatross* had been one of the fastest ships at the time and Cahuyaga had been entrusted with her on her maiden voyage. When he'd arrived late at his destination, with the engines hopelessly burnt out, no one believed his story that he'd picked up signs of aliens and had to put them off his trail.

In all the years since the micro-jump had been perfected and star travel had become a reality, no one had ever seen any sign of aliens. Of course, it was true that micro-jump ships were hopeless at tracking — because they moved in near-instantaneous jumps, light and all other forms of electromagnetic radiation had a difficult time keeping up with them and it was more than impossible to collate the microsecond data collected before each jump into a meaningful scan of anything but the nearest kilometer or so — light traveled too slowly for micro-jumpers.

So it was to be expected that no one believed Cahuyaga's story. How he managed to maintain his commission was beyond Jessica. Well, perhaps not, she mused, seeing as the captain was now in charge of *Brevity*, the nearest thing to a spaceworthy hulk in the known universe.

The captain's fall from grace perhaps explained his disinterest in preserving the chain of command, or indeed, in even accepting a courtesy call from the ship's surgeon.

One thing was obvious to Jess — aside from sharing conjugal diseases with Lieutenant Monroe, the captain kept pretty much to himself. And he really did have gout, judging by his treatment record, as impossible as that was to imagine for a vegetarian.

Jess' tablet chimed and she looked at it. She had a note.

It was the cook. "Lunch is ready."

Jess looked around, wondering if she'd been so engrossed that cookie had deposited her lunch without her noticing. She saw no sign of food nor smelled any.

"Well, where is it, then?" she asked testily.

Jess' tablet chimed again. "Your lunch is in the galley."

Intrigued, Jess left for the galley, wishing once again that she could avoid the zero-gee lift tube. Maybe she could get some insights on Dr. Metron from the cook.

But the cook wasn't in the galley when she got there. Her lunch was still warm and Jess discovered that she was quite hungry. She had just barely finished when the galley's loudspeaker blared, "Surgeon to the bridge! Surgeon to the bridge!"

Jess gulped, not at all happy at the thought of riding the zero-gee tube from the middle of the ship to the bridge just after she'd filled her stomach.

As she feared, she arrived on the bridge feeling quite as green as… Commander Rock looked. She peered at him for a moment before a cough from another position on the gloomy bridge distracted her.

"Surgeon Cohen, is it?" a querulous voice inquired. Jess turned and found herself looking at the insignia of a ship's captain.

"Yes sir," Jess replied formally, bringing herself to attention.

Captain Cahuyaga waved her salute aside. "Yes, yes, very good," the captain said and then winced. "It's my toe, I've stubbed it and I'm out of medicine."

Jess approached, to see that the captain indeed, had a grossly swollen big toe on his right foot which was bare and surrounded by a protective metal cage. The toe was so red it was painful to look at.

"Captain, you really should be in a dirtside facility," Jess said gingerly as she knelt for a closer look. She could see that his right knee was also abnormally swollen.

"No, Lieutenant, I must remain aboard," the captain replied, his words clipped with pain. "It's my duty."

"Captain, I can —" Rock protested. The captain silenced his first officer with an upraised hand.

"You have done enough, commander," the captain said in a kindly voice. "But the final responsibility is mine."

"I need to get you to sickbay, sir," Jess said, mentally filing their exchange for later review.

"No, I'm needed here," the captain replied. "We're short-handed as you might have noticed."

"I did, sir," Jess replied. "I missed my sick berth attendants immediately."

"With a crew of six, I doubt you'll need them," the captain replied. Before Jess could respond, he added, "Please, could you bring my prescription here? I'm afraid to admit it but this condition is quite painful."

"And bring my prescription, too, lieutenant," Commander Rock added from his console. Then, in an aside to the captain, "I think I have them, sir."

"The aliens?" the captain asked. Rock nodded. "Good."

Jess glanced between the pair wondering if she should bring up thorazine instead. The captain must have caught her look for he smiled, adding, "I'll explain all when you return but — please! — go now."

Jess quickly filled the prescriptions and — just to be safe — two syringes of thorazine.

She gave the captain his pain relievers first and then handed Commander Rock his prescription. She noted that the commander was concentrating his attention on a display unfamiliar to her.

Jess wasn't entirely surprised that she couldn't place the display — she had, after all, only a surgeon's brief training on a ship's controls, so it was quite likely that there would be a console or a display she couldn't easily place.

Except, of course, that Jess was not just a surgeon. She was the daughter of an admiral and an engineer. She gave the display a longer look, checking out the placement of controls, the color and finish of the panel and —

"I suppose you're wondering what we're doing, lieutenant?" the captain said, interrupting her inspection.

Jess turned to him and nodded slowly. "What happened to Dr. Metron? And the rest of the crew?"

"We disembarked the crew at *Rainbow*," the captain told her.

"And Dr. Metron?"

"No one knows," the captain said. "At first we thought he got confused and disembarked with the others but then Mr. Rock —"

"You mean the commander?" Jess asked, confused at the reference.

"I prefer Mr. Rock," the commander said, turning to glance at her. This close Jess could not mistake that his skin was tinged green and his ears were pointed. No, Jess corrected herself, his ears were capped with points. What did the commander think he was?

"When he wears the turtle, he prefers to be called just Rock," the captain added.

"The turtle?" Jess exclaimed. "Sir?"

"I prefer to call it a prosthesis," Commander Rock replied.

They're all crazy, Jess decided, moving her hand unobtrusively to the pocket where she'd hidden the thorazine.

"We're hoping it will convince them," the captain said.

"Who?"

"The aliens, of course," the captain replied steadily.

Who should she get first? Jess wondered frantically. The answer was easy — Commander Rock was clearly the greater threat.

"Sir," Jess said in carefully controlled voice, backing away from the captain and towards the commander. "We've never found any indications of aliens in over three decades of space exploration, what makes you think they exist?"

"Dr. Metron," the captain replied steadily. "He's one of them, after all."

"Dr. Metron is one of them?" Jess repeated. "Why would you say that?"

"We picked him up, of course," the captain continued. "On *Albatross'* maiden flight. That's why we were delayed."

"I see," Jess said. Delusional, they're both delusional. "What is the Commander's involvement in this, sir?"

"I was Ensign Rock on the *Albatross*," the commander said from behind her. "I was responsible for the sideways radar."

"And he tinkered with it," the captain added with a hint of frost in his voice.

"And that's how I spotted him," the commander said.

"Him?" Jess asked, fingering in her pocket for the top of the syringe.

"Dr. Metron," the captain said. "His body was floating in space."

"But then he'd be dead, sir," Jess said. "No one can survive in space for long unless —"

"They're in a spacesuit," the captain finished for her. "And he wasn't. We thought he was dead, too. But when our surgeon started hearing banging coming from the morgue and opened up the crypt we'd placed Metron in, he got the shock of his life."

"He was alive?"

"Quite alive," Commander Rock confirmed.

"But he spoke no known language," the captain said. "We were convinced that he'd suffered severe brain damage but that wasn't the case. In a week he'd mastered all the languages spoken on the ship and was teaching himself anatomy from the ship's computers. We figured he was an android of some sort."

"Really?" Jess asked. She twirled suddenly, syringe raised to Rock's chest and thrust — only to have her wrist caught by his hand. He squeezed tightly and the syringe fell out of her limp fingers.

Still holding her wrist painfully, Commander Rock bent over and retrieved the syringe.

"Thorazine," he said, holding the syringe out for the captain's view. "As I surmised."

"Very good, Mr. Rock," the captain said. He looked at Jess. "I suppose you've got another in your pocket? Would you be so kind as to hand it to Mr. Rock?" He nodded at her admonishingly. "And remember that he can just as easily inject *you* with the thorazine he has now and retrieve the other from your unconscious body."

Jess sighed in defeat, and carefully handed the second syringe to the green-tinged commander.

"It was logical that you would attempt this," Mr. Rock said to her. "I only hope she didn't change your pain medicine as well, captain."

The captain waved the objection aside. "No matter, I didn't take them," he said. He smiled at Jess' surprise. "I still had some from Dr. Metron, of course."

"You didn't trust me?"

"I was right not to, don't you think?" the captain replied. "After all, you must be convinced that we're insane."

"All the evidence you have clearly supports that hypothesis," Mr. Rock added.

Jess found herself thinking rapidly. If they knew that she would suspect their insanity, then why did they allow her aboard the ship? Or was the accident with the boarding tube supposed to be fatal? Or did they just chicken out? It could have just been the engineer, who seemed to have his own personal delusions of vampirism or an act of nascent jealousy on the part of Lieutenant Monroe. But if they knew she would discover their insanity, then why —

"The embryos." Jess said aloud.

"Very good," the captain said encouragingly. He looked back at Mr. Rock. "I told you she would be as quick as her mother."

"You know my mother?"

"Who doesn't know Admiral Cohen?" the captain asked. "She very kindly arranged for me to get this mission."

"Mission."

"Yes," the captain said. "Although the burden of eighty thousand embryos would fall mostly on —"

"Eighty thousand?" Jess interrupted. "There are only forty thousand, sir."

"Forty thousand human embryos, yes," the captain said. "Which we'll exchange for forty thousand alien embryos."

"Captain —" Mr. Rock began reproachfully only to be silenced by the captain's upraised hand.

"Someone will have to go with the human embryos, Mr. Rock," the captain declared. "And someone will have to stay with the alien embryos."

"You're going to trade with the aliens?" Jess exclaimed.

"It was their idea," the captain said.

Suddenly the lights on the bridge went out.

"Oh, damn!" the captain exclaimed. "I was afraid of that."

Jess felt light-headed, couldn't stand, and sank slowly to her knees in a dead faint. Just before she did, she heard a loud hiss and a giggle.

#

She woke up in the sickbay with a splitting headache. It took her only moments to remember what had happened and to make her diagnose — hypoxia. The hiss must have come from Commander MacDowell and the giggle from his new girlfriend, Lieutenant Monroe. The engineer must have cut the supply of oxygen to the bridge.

Apparently the engineer disagreed with the captain's course of action. Jess wasn't sure whether she agreed with him or not.

If Captain Cahuyaga and Commander Rock were correct, then *Brevity* was en route for a rendezvous with the first aliens humans had ever contacted and would exchange an equal amount of embryos. Jess could understand the thinking behind that — to allow each different race to raise the youngsters of the others as their own.

Of course, that meant that the aliens had to have physiologies not too dissimilar from humans, and could thrive in an oxygen-rich atmosphere under the force of one gravity. It also meant that the aliens could communicate or learn to communicate in a manner comprehensible by humans — and vice versa.

Under such circumstances, exchanging young was a good way to build ambassadors for the future — humans and aliens who had grown up with the other's culture and norms.

But forty thousand? There was no way that forty thousand made sense. Jess would have worked with no more than a dozen, probably only three or four at first, until she was sure she understood all the problems of raising aliens in a different world and culture.

What crazy person had — Jess' thought brought her up short. Crazy person indeed. The whole idea was crazy. There were no aliens. There was no Dr. Metron. MacDowell and Monroe were right in capturing the bridge and subduing Commander Rock and Captain Cahuyaga — hadn't that been Jess' plan, too?

Jess put her hand to her head to ease the throbbing that was banging there. Air starvation gave worse hangovers than anything alcohol induced, even though the two were functionally equivalent. Rubbing her head didn't help. In fact, the throbbing got worse. More rhythmic. Boom-boom-boom, boom-boom-boom.

Jess' looked up, turned her head. The noise wasn't in her head at all.

"Oh, no!" she said, lurching to her feet and staggering to the morgue. She opened the first crypt.

There was a body inside.

"Dr. Metron, I presume," Jess said sourly.

The body's eyes popped open, then one winked at her and the doctor raised his hand to his lips in the classic "shh!"

Jess nodded slowly. What else? she thought to herself.

As in answer, Metron turned his head and pointed to the side of his neck.

Puncture wounds. Of course! Jess thought to herself. MacDowell had assaulted Dr. Metron, and was probably responsible for the incident with the docking tube.

Dr. Metron was beckoning her closer. Jess leaned down to him and bent her ear to his lips.

"They're here," he whispered.

Jess leaned back and raised her brows inquiringly. In answer, Dr. Metron put two fingers behind his head and wiggled them suggestively.

The aliens had arrived.

#

Jess locked eyes with Dr. Metron when Commander Rock's voice called over the intercom: "Surgeon to the bridge! Surgeon to the bridge!"

"I'd better go," Jess said.

"Yes," Dr. Metron agreed, fingering the puncture wounds in his neck. "Commander MacDowell probably still believes he killed me."

"MacDowell is a lunatic," Jess growled. She groaned as she stood up and headed for the lift tube.

She felt so bad from the hypoxia-induced hangover that she clamped a hand over her mouth as a precaution as she rode the zero-gee tube to the ship's bridge. Cautiously, she slowed herself before exiting.

The bridge was ablaze with light, so brilliantly lit that Jess squinted.

"Ahh!" A man's voice nearby groaned in pain. "The lights! They burn."

Jess identified the crouching figure as Commander MacDowell. Lieutenant Monroe was trying, with success limited by her short stature and small frame, to shield her lover from the harsh lights.

"I am glad to see you recovered, lieutenant," Mr. Rock said as he saw Jess enter. "The commander here is in some pain, doubtless psychosomatic."

Jess walked over to MacDowell, eyeing him carefully. She furrowed her brow as she noticed small lesions on the engineer's skin — they were smoking.

"Perhaps not," Jess said as she peered more closely. "Mr. Rock, I think perhaps you should dim the lights."

"But Commander MacDowell —"

"I think he's learned his lesson," Jess interrupted. She looked over at the green-skinned pointy-eared first officer. "You can control all the lighting on the ship from here, correct?"

"I can," Mr. Rock agreed dubiously. "But I am sure that Commander MacDowell could devise an override if he were allowed back to engineering."

"I think that will have to do," the captain said decisively. Jess looked over and saw that the captain was seated where she had last seen them. "I am glad to see you no worse for the wear, doctor."

"Thank you, sir," Jess replied.

The captain nodded to Mr. Rock who, reluctantly, dimmed the bridge's lights back down. Immediately Commander MacDowell's groans subsided.

A beeping on the communication console distracted them.

"We're being hailed," Lieutenant Monroe exclaimed in surprise. She looked at MacDowell. "But who we're micro-jumping, aren't we?"

"We are, indeed," Mr. Rock agreed. "And, as you've guessed, no one should be able to send a coherent signal to us."

"The last time this happened was over ten years ago," Captain Cahuyaga added.

"On the *Albatross*?" Jess guessed. She looked from the captain to the first officer and then pointed to the communications console. "The aliens sent you a message?"

"No," the captain replied. "Nothing so sophisticated."

"They strobed us with radar," Mr. Rock explained.

"Which is just as unlikely," Jess declared.

"Exactly," the captain agreed.

"Sir, they're still hailing us," Lieutenant Monroe said, having taken in the exchange with growing surprise mingled with shock.

"Perhaps you'd better answer them, lieutenant," the captain told her.

Jess watched as Monroe crisply took her seat, settled a headset on her head and replied efficiently to the hail. She listened for a moment, then turned to the captain.

"They say that they are ready for the transfer, sir," she reported, eyes wide.

"You're just going to do this?" Commander MacDowell growled from the floor. He pushed himself upright and glanced at the others. "You're going to let the aliens have the embryos? Don't you know what they'll do to them?"

"Raise them as their own," a voice said from the lift tube. Dr. Metron stepped briskly out. He nodded to the captain and Mr. Rock. "In exchange, they will send forty thousand of their embryos to us."

"Forty thousand?" MacDowell repeated, shocked.

"How do you plan to raise forty thousand aliens, Dr. Metron?" Jess asked. "I couldn't imagine raising more than half a dozen humans at a time, myself."

"Indeed," Mr. Rock replied. "Which is why the aliens have kindly agreed to give us their stasis technology."

"And their hypertime technology," the captain added. He looked at Commander MacDowell. "If you think about it, their technology obviously is more advanced than our micro-jump capability."

MacDowell, always the engineer, nodded after a moment, eyes gleaming with anticipation.

"Why would they give us all that?" Jess asked. She could imagine a one-for-one trade but it seemed that the aliens were giving far more than they were receiving.

"Ah," the captain said, "we owe that to Mr. Rock here."

The first officer looked slightly embarrassed.

"You see," the captain continued, "when he first convinced me that we really were in contact with aliens, he also convinced me that we should act like we already *had* been in contact with aliens. That we were, in fact, a part of a federation —"

"You mean the ears and the turtle were part of an act?" Jess blurted.

"A bit more than that," Mr. Rock conceded. "I'm afraid that after ten years, I must confess that I find myself quite accustomed to the methodology." He cocked at eyebrow towards Jess. "I believe you would refer it as directed schizophrenia."

"They're going to name a whole hospital after you," Jess muttered, looking around the bridge in awe of all the psychoses present.

"Indeed they are," Captain Cahuyaga agreed. "A maternity hospital for baby aliens."

"But who is going to raise them?" Jess asked, perplexed. "Even with this stasis technology, they're aliens."

"Which I have always been programmed to rear," Dr. Metron said. He looked over to Lieutenant Monroe as he added, "We had hoped that we might find someone suitable to go with the human embryos but I am afraid I was not the judge of human psychology I'd hoped."

Lieutenant Monroe quailed when she grasped Metron's meaning.

"It would only have been for a little while," he said, trying to sound kindly. "Until the first children were old enough to look after the others."

Jess looked around the cramped bridge, saw Mr. Rock's radar console illuminate the approaching alien ship, and decided that Dr. Metron was perhaps a better judge of human nature than she.

"How long?" she asked, looking directly at Metron.

"Ten years, maybe less," the android replied steadily. "The aliens are really quite like you humans, and you'd be welcomed with —"

Jess cut him off with an upraised hand. Suddenly it seemed to her that every second of her life made perfect sense, that this was *her* moment.

"I'll go."

The Terrorist in My Kitchen

This story scares me. It scares me because of how people might react to it, how they might miss its true meaning and purpose. It was inspired by so many things in our history, including the Troubles in Northern Ireland. It is a resonance story and it will haunt you.

The terrorist in my kitchen has got a bomb strapped around his chest — he showed us. I don't understand, why is he in my kitchen? Why isn't he someplace else? What's so important about my kitchen? About us?

He says he's hungry. I look at him wide-eyed but I don't say anything. I don't want to piss him off. I bend down and write this in my diary. He asks what I'm doing and I tell him. He makes a face but nods.

"Go right ahead," he says. Is there such a thing as a nice terrorist?

My name is Marla and I'm ten. My eleventh birthday is in three weeks. I don't know if I'll be around for it. Why doesn't that bother me more?

"What do you want to eat?" my mother asks him, her voice trembling. Her name is Betty. Why does that matter? I mean, if she's going to be blown up in the next several minutes, who really cares what her name is, right?

One...two..three...four...five...six...seven. I count the questions in my diary. It's funny how many questions I have. Mom says I always ask too many questions.

"Can you make toast?" the terrorist asks. He looks at my mom apologetically. "I'm a bit nervous."

Who wouldn't be with a chest full of explosives? For that matter, why think of eating?

"Why are you hungry?" I blurt out, looking at him. Instantly, I regret it and lower my head back down to my diary.

"What's your name?" he asks.

"Marla," I say, and continue, "What's yours?"

"I used to be Steve but I'm Ahmed now that I've converted to Islam," he says.

"If you're a Muslim, why do you have that bomb?" I ask.

"Don't worry," Steve assures me, "I won't hurt you."

"Then why are you here?" I ask. "And where did they take my father?"

"Marla, hush!" Mom says. She fumbles the toast into the toaster. Her hands are trembling. "You don't want to distract the man."

"I just want to know," I say to my mother. I mean, if we're all gonna die, shouldn't I ask least know why? I turn to Ahmed. "It's okay to talk to you, isn't it?"

"Sure," says Ahmed who was Steve. He's got a long beard and his eyes look like he hasn't slept for days. I notice that his hands are trembling too. That's not so good as one of them's on the trigger that keeps the bomb from going off.

"How are you going to eat your toast?" I ask. I mean, it's hard to eat toast with one hand, isn't it?

Ahmed's eyes widen and he notices the trigger in his hand. He shakes his hand. "I can eat it with one hand."

"So you don't want jam or butter on it, then?" I mean, I can see eating plain toast with one hand but with jam or butter, it's hard to keep it level — some of it will drip off on to the floor.

"Butter would be nice," Ahmed the terrorist says. After a moment he adds, "Maybe some jelly. Do you have any grape jelly?"

"Do you want a PB&J?" I ask. "I like to have them when I'm getting ready for tests."

The terrorist looks a bit green around the gills and shakes his head.

"Sorry," I say hastily because I'm really worried about how he's holding the trigger. I mean, wouldn't it suck to die because you pissed off a terrorist over a PB&J?

"I'm allergic to peanuts," Ahmed the terrorist tells me.

"Really?" I say, surprised. I'd never thought that a terrorist would be allergic to something. I mean, it just doesn't make sense, does it? "They let you be a terrorist and you're allergic to peanuts?"

Okay, stupid question, and I knew it the minute it left my mouth.

"Sorry," I say again.

"Marla!" Mom says at the same time and then she jumps because the toast has popped up. The terrorist jumps because she jumps and I let out a shriek — has his thumb moved off the trigger?

We all drew another breath. Ahmed's thumb is still on the button, the bomb didn't go off.

"Sorry," Mom says now to Ahmed.

"It's okay," Ahmed says. He glances toward his thumb. "I'm holding on, you see."

"Why?" I ask. I mean, really, why? Is he waiting for toast? Why not just lift his thumb and let it all happen?

"What?" Ahmed says, turning his head to me.

"I mean, are you just waiting for the toast?"

"No," Ahmed says as Mom turns to look at him, just as curious as I am. "I told you, if everything goes right, you won't be harmed."

"What about Dad?" I ask. "Will he be alright, too?"

You see, they came in the morning, burst open the front door, roused us out of our beds — all except the baby — and told my Dad that if he didn't come with them, all of them except Ahmed, then Ahmed would blow us all up then and there. All Dad had to do was what they wanted, they said.

After they'd hustled out Dad, mom had heard the baby crying and Ahmed had allowed her to go change his diaper and bring him down here in the kitchen. He's sitting in his bouncey chair, and he looks a little scared.

"Shush, Stevie, it'll be all right!" I say to him. Uh-oh! Ahmed/Steve the terrorist looks at me. "My brother's name is Steven."

"Oh," Ahmed the terrorist says, looking at my brother for a moment. Stevie is just fourteen months old. He's starting to talk. Usually, you can't shut him up but today... well, I guess I should count my favors where I find them.

"Mom and Dad say that he's our little bonus," I say to Ahmed the terrorist. Mom gives me a look but I ignore her. I mean, if we're all gonna die, what's it matter if she's pissed with me, right? "For nine years I was an only child and now we've got him."

"You don't like him?" Ahmed asks.

I make a face. "Not when he's bawling in the middle of the night or when he poops."

"Marla!"

I ignore her. "He's okay, I guess," I say to Ahmed. "I think you're frightening him."

"I am?"

"Yeah, usually he's all chatter and noise, googling and *mmmm*'ing and stuff like that," I say. I look over at Stevie and make a coochie face. "Aren't you widdle Stevie, aren't chu?"

Stevie looks back at me solemnly likes he's not amused.

Mom hands Ahmed the toast on a plate. She looks a bit confused as he reaches for it and grabs the toast off the plate, putting it into his hand.

"Sorry," she mumbles.

Ahmed takes the toast in one hand and starts eating it. A moment later he looks at it. "Could I have some butter?"

Mom gives him another apologetic look and goes to the fridge to pull out the butter. She takes the toast back from him and gets a butter knife — she's careful only to get a butter knife — and tries to slice the butter into thin wedges to slather on the toast. It doesn't work, the butter's too cold and it tears the bread.

"Sorry," my mom says, all big-eyed and fearful. She sounds on the edge of hysteria. "I can make you some more."

"How about some jelly?" I say. They both look at me and I shrug. "It's easier to spread jelly, you know."

"Could you try?" Ahmed the terrorist with the bomb strapped around his chest asks oh so politely. I guess there's nothing wrong with a terrorist with manners — I just never thought of them that way. I mean, aren't they supposed to be all angry and just blowing shit up?

Oops. Well, if Ahmed's thumb slips on the finger it won't matter that I wrote shit. Anyway, this is *my* diary and who are you to be looking in it? Stevie? Of course, that'd be years from now and I've already got a good hiding place, so good luck Stevie.

Mom goes back to the fridge and gets the jelly. She slathers it on the toast which looks worse for the wear. I mean, after the assault with the butter, and now being smeared with jam, it looks really sad, don't you know?

She puts the plate with the sad-looking toast back in front of Ahmed the terrorist.

Ahmed looks at it and sighs.

Baby Stevie makes a sound and suddenly it's a lot less pleasant in the kitchen.

"Mom, Stevie pooped!" I say, enjoying the look on her face when I say 'pooped'. There really isn't a better word but it bugs my Mom and sometimes that's a cool thing, isn't it?

I look over my diary. Twenty-two. That's how many questions I've got in it now. I suppose that's enough. You won't be able to read anything after this. It'll just be all in my head. Is that okay, God?

I get up and go behind mom, around the far side of the table. I grab the toast and bring it toward Ahmed.

"If it's not too gross, I could feed you," I say to him. "I mean, I'd prefer that to getting blown up."

Ahmed thinks about it for a moment. He's a Muslim, right? So shouldn't it be okay to have women feeding him? Even if I'm just a girl? He nods. "Okay."

It's awkward and I smile as he takes a bite. It's a bit like feeding Stevie.

I make a face. "It'd probably be better if Stevie weren't smelling up the place, wouldn't it?"

Ahmed nods, his mouth full of toast. I turn to my mom and say to Ahmed, "How about Mom gets him changed? I'll stay here and feed you the toast."

Ahmed frowns at this, swallows and then says, "Okay."

My mom looks at me. "Go on, Stevie smells!"

She bends over, gives me a slight hug on my shoulders — it feels good but I don't move, I don't want Ahmed to notice. And then she's got Stevie and his bouncer and they're out the kitchen door into the living room. I feed Ahmed another bite of toast and I start talking just to add noise.

"You know, it's a bit weird isn't it, feeding a terrorist toast in my kitchen," I say to him. My ears are straining for the sound and I hear it — the front door closes. It's not so quiet that I can't make it out but I'd be surprised if Ahmed hears it over me, the toast and the usual neighborhood noises. I scrinch my nose at him. "Why'd you become a terrorist anyway?"

"Because Americans are oppressing Islam," Ahmed says, his words a bit muffled as he tries to swallow the toast in time to answer.

"Aren't you an American?" I don't know why I'm talking now, it's just him and me. He might be stupid but I can't see him being so stupid that he'll let me go. I mean, pretty soon he's gonna figure that Mom and Stevie have got away. And then he'll be mad. I can't fake that I've got to go to the bathroom — damn! I *do* have to go! — and hope that he'd let me run away. And — ew! gross! — I'm not letting him go with me!

The front bathroom hasn't got a window, so I couldn't go there and crawl out while he was standing outside. And he's already seen it so I can't pretend to need the upstairs bathroom. Oh, wait! If I peed myself — *eeewww!* — then maybe I could get him to let me take a bath. But then I'd have to crawl out of the bathroom window on the second floor and then figure out how to get down. I don't think I could do that.

"Where's your mother?" Ahmed asks suddenly suspicious. I look at him and he knows. He growls at me and stands up, moving angrily. I rush at him, grappling, trying to force his thumb down over the button, to keep it there and then —

— it slips.

There's a huge sound, so loud my ears pop and I'm in pain, pain, pain! I'm blown away, back up into the air and for a moment I'm flying, flying up and away covered in a fine, thin red mist that is all that remains of Steve the terrorist. And then I hit the top corner of the kitchen and my neck snaps as my head hits the ceiling and there's only pain, pain, pain. And, somehow even worse, the explosion pushed all the pee out of me! Do they let you into heaven if you've wet yourself?

And my last thought, as all the pain overwhelms me, is that Mom has my diary and she's going to see that I wrote 'shit' in it.

I hope she doesn't get too mad.

Coward

> COWARD *was written for Ed Green's anthology,* WHEN THE HERO RETURNS.

Lieutenant Monet eyed his security detail as they fanned out, ensuring that they took exactly the positions he'd prescribed. Overhead, the roar of the dropship grew louder and louder but neither he nor the rest of his platoon paid it the slightest attention even as wisps of dust began stirring on the cement-covered ground beneath their feet.

Wind rose and roared as the dropship hovered for a moment, extending its wide legs and landed. The hardened landing pad seemed to lurch slightly under it weight. The roar of the jets ceased and their sound was replacement by the mechanical noise of the ramp being extended, lowered to the ground.

Monet raised his eyes at that moment, glancing beyond the dropship to the four heavy assault ships arrayed strategically around the edge of the landing field.

Enemy assault ships.

His government had demanded it, had insisted on the protection that it, now demilitarized, could no longer provide.

For the heroes were coming home.

The Star Ranger Division, Rhone's finest, were finally being returned.

Monet was not there for them, however. He and his security platoon had only one purpose, one man: The Coward of Corair.

A noise from inside the dropship caused him to look toward it. The skirl of bagpipes, an honor guard, formed and marched down the ramp, colors flying.

Of all the Divisions of Rhone, only this one had been allowed to keep its colors after their defeat by the Empire.

Behind him, someone cleared his throat loudly. "They're turned out well."

Monet's shoulders stiffened involuntarily. No matter how hard he'd tried, he couldn't prevent the reaction. It was one thing to know that the field was guarded by Imperial assault ships, quite another to have to remember that their commander was standing right behind him.

The honor guard marched clear of the ramp, executed a text-book rear-march and halted, bagpipes still skirling, colors raised high as another troop formed up and marched out of the rust-stained, battered combat dropship.

"Are they disembarking by *platoons*?" Monet cried, the words surprised out of him as he saw the first small group move into sight.

"By battalions," the Imperial general behind him growled, contempt for Monet evident in his tone.

The Star Ranger division was composed of three independent brigades, each composed of three battalions. A spaceforce battalion numbered between six hundred and seven hundred and fifty combatants.

"I'd heard they'd been decimated," Monet said, as he picked out the colors of the first battalion, the 1st of the 1st — the famous Iron Battalion of the equally famous Iron Brigade.

"So your government said," the general replied. Monet turned enough to meet the Imperial general's eyes and saw the cold flint in them.

"This looks more like less than a tenth survived," Monet protested.

"That's correct," General von Kampf agreed, turning his eyes back toward the dropship and the next formation exiting it.

Monet copied him even as more questions began to nag at him.

The government of Rhone had made it very clear that it had been the arrant cowardice of the Star Ranger's commander which had caused the surrender of the wormhole to the Imperium.

At first the news reports had been full of praise for the gallant Star Rangers and General Cowan. This was the premiere division of the Star Army of Rhone, the front-line defense against any aggressor. The Star Rangers had the best of men, the best of training, the best equipment, and the best positions.

As the Imperial attack continued, however, the news reports changed. Fort Clarion had been lost — one of the three largest of the three dozen forts guarding the precious wormhole transit point. Then Fort Alphonse, Fort Beauregard — all of the front-line fortresses.

The Star Rangers, according to the reports, clung bitterly to the remaining forts and even set up special fortifications amongst the asteroid fields surrounding the wormhole. For two weeks the news was good. The government announced that the Star Division, well-supplied, at full strength, was able to hold the enemy up for a month or more — certainly long enough for Rhone to convince the nearby star systems to bring aid.

Then Premiere Algonquin spoke to the planet with terrible news: "*Nous sommes trahis!*" We are betrayed.

Forty-eight hours later, the Imperial battleships entered orbit and the red, white, and green flag of independent Rhone was ignominiously hauled down from the capital.

Shocked, betrayed, and desperate, the government lost no time in assigning blame for this terrible defeat. Clearly, the loss rested in the hands of the one man who commanded the most powerful force in the arsenal of Rhone — General Cowan, now named the Coward of Corair, after the last remaining fortress of the wormhole — the fortress from which he had negotiated the surrender of the Star Rangers.

Monet looked impassively at the ranks of that famous division. If they only knew! Would they turn on their commander? Would they tear him from limb to limb for his treachery?

He made a hand signal to his men as the ninth battalion — another remnant little larger than a platoon — stood to attention and the tone of the bagpipes changed.

At first he did not recognize the tune, he was no favorite of Celtic music, preferring the rich tones of Rhone and the distant symphonies of France but it was one that was familiar and haunting.

Londonderry Air.

As one, the Star Rangers removed their classic black berets, berets adorned with the three stars of their division, raised their hands to their brows and saluted.

They saluted as the Coward of Comair and his headquarters battalion descended the stairs.

The color drained from Monet's face as he saw their numbers. Headquarters battalion for a division numbered no fewer than eight hundred. Eight hundred of the toughest soldiers ever to have donned a spacesuit.

Down the ramp came seven.

In front of the other six was one man, his leg in a cast, his right arm in a sling.

He paused at the top of the ramp and removed his beret. He stood as best his could and saluted, left-handed, holding his salute with a trembling arm until at last, he eyes running with tears, he lowered it again.

Finally! Monet thought to himself. Now we can finish this farce. He nodded toward Chevarre, his trusted adjutant. Chevarre's jaw tightened, his one eyelid lowered fractionally to show that he understood his orders. Good man, Monet thought to himself.

General Cowan spotted Monet and nodded to himself. One of the men behind him rushed forward, pointing toward Monet and spoke quickly in Cowan's ear. Cowan seemed to listen politely, then shook his head, emphasizing it with a hand gesture. The man seemed ready to argue but Cowan shook his head once more. The General's aide or whoever he was, raised his head and called out in a loud voice that carried throughout the field, "Division! Present Arms!"

As one, the twelve hundred and twenty-seven survivors of Rhone's finest division moved with exquisite precision. Even the wounded shifted, raising themselves where possible to sit up and salute while those more wounded raised their arms — those that still had them — to honor their commander.

General Cowan, visibly moved, returned the salute and held it for a long moment before walking down the ramp toward the waiting detachment. He didn't get far as the troops broke ranks and surrounded him, heedless of the calls to order from their superiors.

Slowly, General Cowan moved through the mass of his troops toward Monet and his detachment. When he reached them, Monet stood still, not raising his arm in salute. Behind the General, the troops of the Star Rangers murmured ominously at the dishonor.

"General Cowan, commanding, Star Ranger Division," Cowan said even as his eyes brushed over Lieutenant Monet's nameplate.

"Sir, I am requested and required to inform you that you are under arrest pending a court martial on the handling of your division," Monet told him crisply, signaling to his men who moved toward him.

They did not get far, finding themselves blocked by burly Space Rangers.

"The Division will stand down," General Cowan said loudly, his eyes still on Monet.

Reluctantly, the burly soldiers moved aside, allowing the less intimidating security detachment to surround the General.

Cowan smiled slightly and raised his hands to the Lieutenant. "Sir, I surrender myself into your custody pending the inquiry into my actions."

"Court martial, sir," Monet corrected him harshly. Behind him one of the security men murmured, "Coward."

A movement from behind Monet distracted them at that moment. General van Kampf stepped forward, his hand outstretched.

"General Cowan," the Imperial general said, clicking his heels together sharply as he extended his hand.

"General van Kampf," Cowan said, his lips tight.

"I am sorry for your losses sir," the general said. He nodded to the division beyond. "Your division fought with exceptional gallantry."

Cowan accepted that with a sharp nod. Then he noticed something. "I see that you have the honor of commanding the Imperial's finest."

General van Kampf turned his head to survey the colors of the guard behind him. "Yes, I have the honor to command the Emperor's Own Kashtreya."

Cowan nodded. "Perhaps one day you'll explain their history to the Lieutenant."

General van Kampf clicked his heels together once more. "It would be my honor."

Cowan turned back to the lieutenant. "Very well, Lieutenant, I am your prisoner."

His words flowed back to his troops and there was an immediate cry of outrage.

"Where are you taking the General?"

"Leave him here, with us!"

"They're arresting him!"

"Arresting the General, why?"

"They're going to court martial him!"

Quickly the mood turned ugly, then uglier and Monet motioned for his detachment to form close around the General as they shuffled slowly toward the waiting ground transport.

The discipline of the Star Rangers shattered and they started pummeling the guard detachment. The guards grew scared and drew their weapons. There was a sudden, loud *crack!* — a single shot.

General Cowan slid slowly to the ground.

Monet looked over toward the sound only to see Chevarre, his pistol drawn, with a look of triumph on his face. Without thinking, even before the troops of the Star Rangers could react, Monet drew his own pistol and shot his trooper — a head shot, direct, deadly, final.

Chevarre's body crumpled to the ground beside Cowan's and Monet raised his pistol at the same time as he shouted, "It was an accident! Stand down! Star Division, stand down!"

A wave of shocked silence swept across the field. Slowly, the men of the Star Rangers drew close to their commander. A group of men gently raised the body, raised it high and carried it back toward the dropship's ramp and the remaining staff.

As he regained control, Monet gestured to his men to gather up Chevarre's body, grabbed his comm and tersely relayed the news to his superior.

A hand clapped his shoulder and Monet jumped before he realized it was the Imperial General.

"Well done," General van Kampf said. "That was a difficult situation and you handled it well." He gave the Lieutenant a very bitter smile. "Your superiors will doubtless be pleased."

"I lost my man," Monet said.

General van Kampf shook his head. "You don't fool me, lieutenant."

Monet gave him a sharp look.

"Let me tell you about the Emperor's Own Kashtreyas," General van Kampf said. "After all, I'd promised General Cowan and I'd like to keep my honor."

"I don't see —"

"No, of course not," van Kampf interrupted. "You follow orders, do your duty and hope for promotion." He pursed his lips sourly. "Your superiors tell you that Cowan is a traitor and you believe them."

"But —"

"Do you know how many troops fought against your Star Rangers?"

"A weak, under strength division, everyone knows that!"

"A full corps," van Kampf corrected. "And that was to start. A full, battle-hardened, assault-trained Imperial Guard Corps." He shook his head. "We wanted a quick victory, do you think we'd commit inferior troops or numbers?"

A look of doubt entered Monet's eyes.

"In the end, we had to commit ten full divisions to the assault," van Kampf said. "In the end, it was the Emperor's Own Kashtreyas who broke through the command center, who took the General and his six surviving staff — all the headquarters company had been destroyed."

"But — he surrendered! He never fought! He didn't try!"

"Ten divisions," van Kampf repeated, shaking his head. "And our casualties were appalling.

"This was the worst battle in the history of the Empire," van Kampf said. Monet shook his head, refusing to believe. "It was. This was worse than the Battle of the Forlorn."

"The Forlorn?" Monet repeated, surprised. The Battle of the Forlorn was legendary, more famous even than the ancient battle of Thermopylae.

"The Forlorn: where one battalion held up the Emperor's best for two weeks," van Kampf said in agreement. He waved his hand back at the troops behind him. "The Kashtreya battalion, to be precise."

"Them?" Monet asked in surprise. "They joined the Empire?"

"Naturally," van Kampf said. "Do you recall what happened to their commander?"

Monet shook his head.

"He survived the battle, you know," van Kampf said. "Very much like your General Cowan." He nodded as he saw the growing alarm in the Lieutenant's eyes. "He survived, was charged with cowardice, was shot by someone and died in dishonor."

"So the Kashtreya —"

"The Kashtreya accused their government of assassinating the commander," van Kampf cut across him. "Within three months, members of the Kashtreya had proof, the government collapsed and — naturally, the Emperor moved in to restore order."

"The Kashtreya were cowards."

"No, their government was," van Kampf said. "And the Kashtreya proved it." He gave a quick, short smile and continued, "The Emperor makes many of his acquisitions in this manner, you know. Just letting corrupt governments prove their unworthiness, their willingness to sacrifice not only lives but *honor* for their own ends."

He turned back toward the grieving men of the Star Rangers. "How long, Lieutenant, do you think it will be before I can welcome them as the Emperor's Own Star Rangers?"

Lieutenant Monet made an inarticulate noise, half moan, half gargle.

"Do you think these men will stand by, these men who fought ten divisions to a standstill, do you think these men *won't* demand justice? And do you honestly think that a government that can coerce a mere lieutenant into murdering their best general will long survive?"

General van Kampf shook his head, enjoying the lieutenant's misery. "Six months. Six months at the most and then your planet of Rhone will be another Imperial protectorate." He met the lieutenant's eyes squarely, his lips stretched in a vulpine smile. "And *that's* why I let you assassinate him."

At The Bottom Of The White

> *This story was written for Stellaris: People Of The Stars, a collection of stories celebrating our future in space. The character's name, Cin, is pronounced like the first part of Cynthia.*

YOU ARE LEAVING EDEN.

The words floating in the air rustled as Cin approached them. The letter 'Y' glistened at the top and seemed to be turning itself into some stylized butterfly — bio or software? Cin wondered, her lips twitching briefly on one side as she walked through them.

She craned her neck back over her shoulder for a moment as she confirmed that — once again — the letters had completely rearranged themselves to say:

You are entering Eden.

As she turned back and continued her exit, another set of floating letters asked: *Entering cross-contact area. Clothing required.*

She moved out of the walkway and into the alcove that was the changing area. She went to the dorm's locker and pulled out her shipsuit through the simple expedient of reaching in and pulling out the first thing she felt.

Valrise knew her: she would never get the wrong clothes. She could have reached her hand into another locker and she would still have got the right clothes — and a polite admonition as well as an unvocalized bio-check to be certain that she wasn't suffering from some mentally debilitating malady.

Valrise was an old ship; she had developed some quirks that newer ships might not value but... *Valrise* was an old ship. 'An old ship is one that works' as they said.

Cin was surprised to feel a bulkier sweater among her things. She was going somewhere cold, she surmised, shrugging on the sweater after pulling her on her single-piece shipsuit. The sweater smelled new — clearly something

Valrise had cooked up for the occasion and had Cin's name stencilled over the left breast.

"And some makeup," *Valrise* said. "There are Contacts in the ice rink."

Cin raised an eyebrow in question.

"They aren't used to shaved eyebrows," *Valrise* explained.

"Makeup?"

"Use the dark pencil to mark your eyebrows and the synthetics will do the rest."

Cin felt inside her locker, pulled out a slim case. There was a mirror in it and a thin stick with dark substance on it. Cin had used makeup before — a couple of years back — so she wasn't totally unfamiliar with the notion.

"Lip color?"

"Natural will do."

"Anything else?" Cin asked after using the liner.

"Hair," *Valrise* said. Cin grinned as she looked in the mirror once more and saw that hair had sprouted on the ridge of her eyebrows. "Pull the hood of the sweater up over your head."

Cin complied.

"The young ones are competing," *Valrise* told her. "The Contacts are quite amazed at our gravity control."

"How far back are they?"

"A good 100, 150 years," the ship told her.

"Poor, proud, and paranoid?" Cin asked, repeating the mantra that the crew used when referring to earthers.

"Exactly," the ship replied. "Now, go!"

#

Cin was glad of the sweater when she entered the much cooler confines of the ice rink. She paused as one of the contestants took to the ice, gained speed, and darted toward the low mound in the center. Cin's newly applied eyebrows descended thoughtfully as she judged the positioning of the skater: she was deliberately off the central axis.

Cin's observations were confirmed when the skater shot up the mound, entered a skew loop and neatly landed upside down on the inverted rink, and continued in a curved loop "down" the mound and onto the flat ice on the "ceiling" of the rink. Those of the crew watching applauded mildly while the more obvious Contacts looked on in slack-jawed wonder — anti-gravity was always one of the first technologies to be lost when colonizing new worlds.

Valrise and the other trader ships spent some of their time re-establishing contact — and trade — with lost colonies. It was short-term not as profitable as hauling goods between advanced worlds — the advantage was in establishing long-term trade. *Valrise*, in her hundred years of existence, had built up quite an extensive trading circuit. There was always danger in establishing new trading partners; care was required and friction inevitable as hopelessly outdated planets met up with the latest technology... and culture.

Hence the "dog and pony show" — as *Valrise* called it. Cin had been so intrigued by the phrase that she'd looked it up: she couldn't understand why a sentient starship would communicate with references to various four-legged mammals but she'd long ago come to recognize that the ship had a quirky sense of humor.

A second skater started on the downside rink and made the leap to the upside rink and then the two of them entered into a very precise — and risky — *pas de deux* between the two gravity fields causing not just the Contacts — but also crew to gasp in delight.

The world of the new Contacts was named Arwon. The inhabitants, at least some of them, were Arwonese. The Arwonese had just recently completed a war of integration — another lost world affectation that Cin didn't entirely understand (it was bad for trade, so why?). *Valrise* had provided a news précis which had left Cin mostly bored and slightly informed — she got the impression that the losers were mostly in hiding and an inkling of some dark means of repression being used. Messy.

Cin had learned a number of years ago that the Contacts could be evaluated by how conservatively Valrise had the ship's crew dress: these Arwonese were clearly among the more strait-laced worlders — every crew member visible was fully clothed and wore eyebrows and head coverings or actual hair.

"You are Cin, the bouncer, are you?" a stranger's voice asked from beside her.

"I am," Cin said. She found herself looking down into a pair of intense dark eyes set in a face framed fetchingly by raven locks of hair. There was almost an impish look to the... woman... Cin guessed from the shape of her body. Cin called up her implant and provided it with a feed from her optic interface.

She is the Calmt Prime, Valrise informed her through the link. A quick overview of the governing hierarchy and the woman's place in it caused Cin to blink in surprise: she was talking to the third most powerful person from the planet.

"And what is it like, bouncing?" the Calmt asked her.

Cin closed her eyes for a moment, recalling memories. She smiled as she said, "It is like nothing ever experienced before."

"We have developed sky-diving in recent years," the Calmt informed her.

"That is when one falls in the air until restrained by a high-drag device?" Cin asked, trying to frame the words appropriately.

She must have been not quite right for the Calmt smiled before replying, "Something like that."

Cin nodded. "Bouncing is more involved than that. Our Bouncers are purpose-made to resist high temperatures while giving their occupants complete control over their position and angle of entry."

"And you bounce off the planet's atmosphere?"

"Yes," Cin replied. "We have sensors to feed us and our Bouncers are transparent."

"What do you see?"

"At first, nothing," Cin replied. "But as we get deeper and deeper into the atmosphere, the air around us begins to glow a deep pink with the heat of our transit."

"That must be quite frightening."

"Oh, no!" Cin said, shaking her head. "It is quite beautiful."

"Aren't you in danger of burning up?"

"We control our angle and our bleed," Cin said. "The Bouncers radiate excess heat away every time they leave the atmosphere."

"But it *is* dangerous."

Cin nodded. "Although I imagine it is less so than hoping that a high-drag device deploys on time."

"A parachute?" the Calmt said. "Not opening?" She nodded. "It happens very rarely these days."

"Very rarely for us, too," Cin replied. "And, of course, mostly we use remotes for the momentum exchange."

"And you will train our people to perform this momentum exchange?"

"So I understand," Cin said. When she saw the questioning look in the other's eyes, she added, "It makes more sense to have a trained planetary crew. With momentum exchange, half will end up with only orbital energy while half will have ship energy."

"I'm sorry, I don't understand."

"We use the momentum exchange between our incoming cargo and the outgoing cargo to slow down the incoming and speed up the outgoing — it saves energy and costs."

"And the Bouncers bounce off the planet to change direction," the Calmt added.

"With equal masses, we can slow down and speed up equal cargoes with a 95% per cent efficiency."

"Why not just have the cargo containers bounce themselves?"

Cin shook her head. "There is too little control. It works best when we can provide quantum changes in momentum."

"And it looks cool with all those flames in the atmosphere," the Calmt said with a grin.

"And it looks cool," Cin agreed, choosing not to argue the point.

"All orbital transfers involve momentum exchange in one way or another," the Calmt said. She nodded toward Cin. "Your way is elegant and efficient, if a little odd to those of us from lesser technologies."

"A lot of time was spent developing the momentum exchange," Cin said.

"The advantage of the smaller exchanges is a lower acceleration, less stressful to certain cargo," the Calmt observed.

"Yes."

"The human body can withstand accelerations many times that of normal gravity," the Calmt continued. Arwon was a nearly Standard planet, with a gravity just a bit below that of ancient Earth.

"True," Cin agreed, wondering where the woman was going with the conversation.

"Is the Calmt learning much?" a male voice spoke from Cin's far side. Cin turned to face a taller, handsome man dressed in clothes that were considered fine on the planet below. To Cin's eye, they were boorish and overbearing.

"Yes I am, your Holiness," the Calmt said, speaking around Cin.

"Good," His Holiness replied. To Cin he said, "The Calmt is expected to learn much."

"There are many things in which I am ignorant," the Calmt agreed. To Cin she explained, "My people only recently were integrated into the Greater Whole."

Cin gave her a blank look while sending a silent query to *Valrise*.

The most recent acquisition by the large, unifying government, Valrise explained. *There was fighting and many casualties. The details are suppressed.*

Can you not discover more? Cin asked.

I am trying, Valrise replied. *But I must consider the impact on Trade if my inquires are discovered.*

"In fact, your Holiness, I was hoping that I might participate in the training for our Bouncers," the Calmt said, glancing hopefully to Cin.

"That is not —" from Cin clashed with:

"I don't see —" from His Holiness.

The two exchanged looks of chagrin. Cin motioned for His Holiness to speak with a polite, "I'm sorry."

His Holiness accepted it as no more than his due and continued, "I don't see why you would prosper from such training."

"I am told it is very risky," the Calmt said, "and I should like to know the risks myself so that I can best describe them to others."

Cin bit back her immediate response: it wasn't risky, only delicate. Instead, she said, "Most of us have implants and years of training, your Holiness."

The Calmt gave Cin a half-pleading, half-grateful look. Cin got the impression that the Calmt *wanted* His Holiness to be concerned by the risks.

She is offering to risk death *for the Greater Whole?* Cin asked *Valrise* through their link.

So it would appear, Valrise agreed. Cin was troubled by this notion; *Valrise* seemed just as troubled.

"If you wish it, I will consult with the Council," His Holiness said to the Calmt. To Cin, he said, "Can she learn without your 'implants'?"

"All the recruits will start without implants," *Valrise* spoke up. "I'm sure that, if it is acceptable to you, we would have no difficulty training the Calmt."

His Holiness jerked around, trying to find the owner of the voice.

"That was *Valrise*, our ship," Cin explained.

His Holiness made a warding gesture before quickly composing himself. "I had forgotten that your ship talks. It must be quite alarming."

"We get used to it," Cin said. "She has saved more than one life with her quick warnings."

"Really?" His Holiness said. His brows furrowed. "And why would she?"

"Trained personnel are hard to replace," Cin said.

His Holiness considered that. "I suppose that is so."

He turned his attention to the Calmt. "If you are finished with your interrogation of the technician, we should return to our meeting."

The Calmt gave Cin an apologetic look before nodding to His Holiness. "If you will lead me, your Holiness."

"Always," His Holiness said with a grim smile.

#

The skating event continued. Cin found her appointed seat — some distance from the Arwonese delegation but still close enough that she could see them. There were six members — and the Calmt was the only female among them. She was also the only one of her coloration and ethnic look. The others talked more amongst themselves than they did with the Calmt. She seemed very much the outsider. Cin thought she was both lonely and scared.

You have an observation? Valrise spoke on their link.

Cin relayed what she'd been thinking.

I cannot determine whether their behavior is ostracism because of her race or her gender, Valrise said. *Trade is the best way forward.*

That was what *Valrise* always said. It was what everyone on the ship believed — there were centuries of data to confirm the belief.

Trade always started slowly with a re-contact world. First came raw materials and hand-crafted artefacts; in return for which the ship would trade increased technological abilities. Slowly the re-contact would be brought up to the standards of the rest of the galaxy. *Valrise* would generate goodwill and continue to profit from all trade. It made the ship and her crew independent of any one world for their needs. *Traders to the stars*, that was their credo: Cin believed in it firmly.

This is your first re-contact, Valrise observed. *It is not unusual to have misgivings and concerns.*

Do you also have concerns?

Always, the ship replied in laughing tones. *Will it ease you to train the Calmt yourself?*

Cin thought it over, glanced toward the small woman in the distance and nodded, knowing that *Valrise* would correctly interpret her non-verbal gesture.

The worlders were served lunch. Cin had already eaten and did not get a meal. She saw the Calmt watching her. Cin smiled her way. The Calmt gestured her over.

"Why are you not eating?" His Holiness said when he saw Cin approach.

"I've already eaten, your Holiness," Cin told him.

"We consider it important that we break bread together," His Holiness said.

"If that will please you," Cin said. "My tastes may be different from yours. Would you like me to eat from your plate or get another?"

"I have a taster for that," His Holiness said. He glanced to the Calmt. "You may eat from her plate."

Cin started to object but the Calmt merely broke a piece of her bread and passed it, wordlessly, to Cin. Cin smiled at her, took it and broke it in half, proffering one half back to the Calmt while popping the other half into her mouth.

The Calmt smiled as she took the other half and popped into her mouth.

"There is a hint of cinnamon in the bread," Cin said when she'd finished her piece. "On *Valrise* we often consume cinnamon raisin toast."

"We are not familiar with 'raisins'," the Calmt said. "What are they?"

"They are dried grapes," Cin said. Quickly, she added, "Grapes are grown on vines in moderate climates. Wine is also made from them."

"We have moderate climes but no grapes," the Calmt told her sadly. She gave her a wistful look. "Would it be possible to try some of this bread?"

"Of course," Cin said. She sent in a silent request to *Valrise*. The ship's response made Cin blush. "Oh, I'm so sorry! *Valrise* informs me that we don't know how your metabolism would handle raisins!"

"Are you refusing food to the Calmt?" His Holiness asked in a tone that was more amused than affronted.

"I am merely concerned that your metabolism may not be able to handle it," Cin said. "Your people might have an adverse reaction."

"If anyone should be the judge, it is the Calmt," His Holiness allowed. He turned to the smaller woman. "What say you?"

"I am willing to try," the Calmt said. She gave Cin a reassuring look. "I have recently discovered that I am able to stomach many things, some more unpleasant than others." His Holiness jerked at her last words and glowered at her.

Cin decided that the best way to defuse the tension was to accept the Calmt's assurances. A small tray of sliced bread, some toasted, some not, quickly arrived on Cin's table.

"What servant brought that?" His Holiness asked, glancing around in surprise.

"Our technology allows us to move things easily," Cin lied. She knew it was too early to mention their nanotechnology — it would appear to be too much like magic. And Cin knew that these people had only recently stopped persecuting 'witches'.

The Calmt reached for a slice.

"This is bread, this is toasted bread," Cin said, pointing to the two sides of the tray. She picked up a piece of bread, broke it in half and passed one portion to the Calmt. The Calmt eyed it carefully, sniffed it, and pulled out one of the raisins.

"It smells sweet."

"It is," Cin agreed, taking a bite of her piece. "The raisins are dried grapes. As they dry the sugar content increases."

The Calmt pulled off one raisin. She eyed it for a moment and then popped it into her mouth. "It is soft and squishy," the Calmt said. Cin was surprised at her choice of the word 'squishy', it seemed out of character with her serious expression.

Before swallowing, the Calmt took a small bite of the bread. She smiled at Cin when she swallowed her piece. "This is excellent!"

"I should like to try," His Holiness said, extending a hand toward the tray.

Cin passed it over and shortly, all the bread and toast had been consumed by the emissaries. Another, larger, tray appeared.

"Is this available for trade?" one of the men asked. Cin took in his sharp features and decided that this person was a trader or merchant like herself.

"I am sure something could be arranged," Cin said, using the time-old circumlocution.

Well done, Cin, we'll make a trader out of you, yet! Valrise teased through the implant.

I prefer bouncing, Cin replied with mock-seriousness. The ship's response was a snort of laughter.

Out loud, *Valrise* said, "We have a limited supply of raisins on board this trip. I'm sure we could bring more in the future."

"And how long would that be?" the trader asked. "Also, how much of these 'raisins' do you have for trade?"

"Everything is for trade... at the right price," *Valrise* replied.

His Holiness shot the trader a quelling look. "Our trade is precious, van Domit, as I'm sure you know."

Van Domit gave His Holiness a deep nod. "I meant no disrespect. But I believe a trade in this commodity would be to the profit of all, your Holiness."

His Holiness considered the matter and then said, "And what would be required for this trade?"

He looked toward Captain Merriwether. Cin bit back a smile: the captain was old and not altogether 'there' any more; everyone knew that *Valrise* ran the crew herself.

"I would ask the ship," the captain replied, jerking a finger up toward the ceiling.

"Indeed," His Holiness replied, seeming out of sorts. He took a deep breath, sighed and glanced upwards. "Could we arrange a trade, ship?"

"I believe we could," *Valrise* replied. "In fact, if you desire, we could go one better."

"Better?"

"I understand that you have a large area on your southern continent that has recently become uninhabited," *Valrise* said. Cin saw the Calmt jerk in reaction to her words. "We would be willing to lease part of that land and use it for agricultural purposes. Our sensors indicate that it would be perfect for growing grapes."

"The grapes that become raisins?" The Calmt asked with alacrity.

"The very same."

"And you would trade them to us?" Van Domit asked.

"Of course," *Valrise* replied. "We would train your people in their planting and harvesting, naturally." There was a slight pause. "Would that be acceptable?"

Van Domit looked ready to shout with glee but controlled himself with some effort to give His Holiness a pleading glance. "It could profit the

Church."

"We have some lands there that might serve," His Holiness allowed. He waved the matter aside. "It is a matter for later, perhaps."

"Trade is not best made waiting," Cin said, recalling an old saw among the ship's crew.

His Holiness gave her a sharp look.

"What I mean, your Holiness, is that all too often good ideas are lost in the crush of events," Cin said quickly. "It seems that we have discovered another source of trade and have come to an agreement. Why not settle it now?"

"It would profit to do so," Van Domit said in agreement. Hastily he added, "Your Holiness."

His Holiness pursed his lips. Finally, he nodded. "Very well," he said. He glanced to Van Domit. "I shall leave the matter in your hands. I trust the Church will receive all due accommodation."

"But of course, Your Holiness," Van Domit said obsequiously, clasping his hands in front of him and rendering His Holiness a respectful half-bow. "Your will shall govern our Council."

Cin couldn't tell if the man was being sarcastic. His Holiness seemed not to care, deliberately taking another slice of toast and carefully consuming it.

When he was done, he turned his attention back to the display on ice.

Cin had to admit that the skaters were good — very good. The downsiders had had only a few days to train on the two gravity fields but they were the best of their world — and it showed. The ship's crew had welcomed them openly and they had trained extensively. Now, they worked together in a display of cooperation that spoke well for future efforts, effortlessly teaming up to provide a whip line of five skaters and whirling themselves up and over to the inverted gravity field and then back down again. At one point they flipped the line so that one of them floated in the null gravity while the pair on either side flipped over and over as the central anchor precessed in a circle with them.

"This is amazing!" His Holiness declared. He turned to Cin. "Is this not the greatest wonder your ship can offer?"

"It is one of them, your Holiness," Cin replied.

"One of them," Van Domit repeated in surprise.

"Is there any better?" His Holiness asked.

"Those of us who ride the atmospheres in our bouncers think that this is the best," Cin replied with a dimpled smile.

"*This*, however, shows a reverence for the Lord," His Holiness said, jabbing his hand toward the skaters, "through his gifts of our bodies and our minds."

"Indeed," Cin agreed. "For myself, I often find much to marvel upon as I bounce through the red of another world's air."

"The Calmt, then, shall try this and give us her opinion on the matter," His Holiness said with a curt nod toward the Calmt Prime. The Calmt nodded back, then gave Cin a grateful look. Cin returned it with a smile of her own.

#

Out of the twelve Arwonese assigned to bounce training, only three were women — and all bore the same features as the Calmt Prime. Cin learned that they were Calmterians, named after their continent on Arwon. The Calmt Prime was their acknowledged leader, although Cin caught some strange undertones in the way the other two women, Mira and Sikar, spoke of her. It was like their respect for their Prime was conditional. Whatever it was, it did not affect their training.

It bothered Cin, however, that the three women chose to keep to themselves and were reluctant to train with the men. She and *Valrise* attributed at least part of that to their gender — it was clear that the males considered them of lesser value even when they demonstrated their technical prowess for all to see.

A week out of orbit, they were still too far to practice for real — unless a special transport dragged them closer. *Lewrys* was the name of the craft.

Cin had let Mira take the controls of *Lewrys*, knowing that *Valrise* herself would keep a careful eye on the trainee. Coklon — one of the more sensible men, in Cin's opinion — sat in the co-pilot's chair. They two worked together well, if without any real chemistry.

Chemistry! Cin chided herself. But that was the best way to reflect upon their interactions. Mira and Sikar worked together flawlessly, slightly less well when paired with the Calmt — there was a deference, almost a reluctance in their actions — but excellently when tripled together.

"Today we will practice bouncing," Cin said. "You've all done well in the simulators but now you're going to find that the real thing is an entirely different matter." She paused. "Some of you will discover that bouncing is not for you. There is no shame in that. If you find yourself overwhelmed, we will recover you automatically, you need not fear."

The men all assured her that they would not 'chicken out', as they said on Arwon.

"First up, Coklon and Alvar," Cin said.

Cin followed Coklon and Alvar on her monitors as they performed their preflight checks, nodding as they proceeded normally. She threw in a slight curve for both of them and they caught it — in the case of Coklon it was a failing transceiver, in the case of Alvar it was a low battery. Both 'failures' were acknowledged and corrected.

"Prepare to undock in 3…2…1…go!" Cin called. They were under manual control — more testing. The two men undocked within milliseconds of one another — almost as good as regular crew. The bouncecraft rotated and set up a course toward the atmosphere.

Cin double-checked their vectors. Alvar was slightly off. She frowned, wondering whether she would tell him but before she'd made her decision, his voice chirped, "Vector correction, azimuth increment zero point five."

She checked the trajectory and said, "Vector correction acknowledged and confirmed." A moment later, she added, "Good catch."

A burst of static that might have included a snort of laughter came back to her. Alvar was cool, level-headed, and known for a fairly dry sense of humor.

Coklon, meanwhile, was set up for a textbook insertion. He'd hit his mark and then bounce back up and away toward their rendezvous point with the test cargo vessel. They would impact it, exchange their momentum and return for another bounce back to *Lewrys*.

Cin double-checked with *Valrise* who agreed. Cin told the two bouncers, "You are go for de-orbit and bounce."

"Coklon copies 'go' for de-orbit and bounce."

"Alvar copies 'go' for de-orbit and bounce."

The two bouncecraft slowed and started their descent to the planet's atmosphere. Their velocity and trajectory were too great for re-entry, instead they would bounce off the atmosphere and rebound back into space on a new trajectory with reduced energy. When they hit their cargo target, they would exchange energy and fall back into the atmosphere for another bounce.

"Atmosphere," Coklon reported right on schedule. Cin's brows creased as she looked at Alvar's displays. The man said nothing. She checked his medical readouts: heart rate high, pulse high, breath rate high — he was cracking up.

"Alvar, report," Cin called on her private frequency. She waited seconds beyond his response time. "Alvar, I know what you're feeling. We're on a private connection, no one can hear you but me. Just take a breath. Take a breath and press your transmit button."

"I'm going to burn up!" Alvar shouted a moment later. "It's too hot!"

"Alvar, try a sip of water," Cin replied. She knew that the bouncer's skin temperature was normal, its internal temperature nominal, the 'heat' was Alvar's fear. She waited, hoping he would follow her orders. "Alvar, drink. The water's cool."

A moment later, she saw that he had sipped.

"It's too hot, I'm burning up!"

"Do you want recovery?" Cin said. "Do you want me to bring you back?"

"It's all red outside! Glowing! There are flames! I can see flames!" Cin checked her readouts, brought up visuals from the inside of the Bouncer.

"There are no flames, Alvar," Cin told him calmly. "What you're seeing is normal for your altitude and speed. You are in the green, textbook."

"I'm dying, I'm dying!" Alvar wailed. Readouts showed his heart rate climbing alarmingly.

"I'm going to pull you out, Alvar," Cin said.

"No! No, if you do that, I'll die!" the man's voice roared in her headphones.

"You're completely safe," Cin said. She readied the abort sequence but held off for a moment.

"No, I'm burning up! And if I go back, I'll die! I know it!" He roared. His voice lowered. Pleading. "They'll kill me, don't you see?"

Cin hit the abort. On the all-call channel she reported, "Systems malfunction on Alvar's bouncer, recovery initiated."

"NO, NO, NO!" Alvar cried on their private frequency.

"I said it was a systems malfunction," Cin assured him. "Not your fault."

"No! Let me go!" Alvar cried. "I can handle it!"

An alarm wailed suddenly in the shuttle's cabin. *Manual override! Valrise* warned even as the shuttle's com announced, "Manual override on Bouncer Alvar, manual override."

"Alvar, re-engage the controls," Cin said. She checked her readouts. "You're going off course."

No response.

"Alvar! Alvar, you must let the computer take control, you're off course!" Cin said even as *Lewrys'* telemetry indicated that Alvar had engaged his thrusters... in the wrong direction.

"Warning, systems anomaly, temperature variance increasing," the autonomous telemetry for Alvar's Bouncer reported.

"Initiate emergency recovery," Cin ordered. She knew better — the first thing she'd trained the earthers on was how to disable the automatic systems in case of emergency. While he'd been operating under manual control, he had to purposely pull the circuit breakers to disable the automatics.

"Systems off-line," the bouncer's system reported. Alvar had clearly retained that much knowledge in his panic. "Hull breach imminent."

"Alvar, you've got to change your course!" Cin shouted. "You're burning up!"

"It's beautiful!" Alvar's voice came back. "It's so beautiful!"

"Contact lost," *Lewrys'* tracking systems announced. "Debris detected."

Alvar's bouncer has disintegrated, Valrise reported. Cin pulled immediately checked on Coklon: he was still on profile.

"Coklon, report," Cin said.

"Everything is nominal," the Arwonese man replied laconically. "It's beautiful down here!"

"What happened to Alvar?" Mira shouted loud enough to be heard through Cin's headphones.

Valrise? Cin asked through her link.

The bouncer has disintegrated, Valrise replied. *We shall record it as a malfunction.*

Cin pulled off her headphones and said to Mira, "Something went wrong with his bouncer."

"Wrong? What happened?"

"He didn't make it," Cin told her.

#

Captain Merriwether handled the discussion. "We are too close to change our delivery method," he told His Holiness. "We can abort the transfer."

"And if you do?"

"We will return when we can," Captain Merriwether replied. "Probably in three years or so."

"This is your fault, Captain," His Holiness replied sternly. "You have admitted that there are other ways to deliver cargo and affect trade."

"Not as efficient, therefore more costly," Captain Merriwether said. "We've found that this is the best for long-term trade."

"Perhaps we don't want your long-term trade," His Holiness replied.

"For a fee, we are willing to announce your presence to other traders," Captain Merriwether returned calmly.

"For a fee," His Holiness sneered. Someone off camera spoke in urgent tones but Captain Merriwether did not hear what was said. The expression of His Holiness altered. "How often are your Bouncers destroyed like this? Surely you lose a lot of your own crew in such accidents?"

"We experience a mechanical difficulty about once every one hundred thousand flight hours," Captain Merriwether said. He nodded toward the camera. "You have that information in your initial contact packet and signed the contract acknowledging the possibility."

"One of our *men* died, Captain," His Holiness snapped back. "We now wonder whether your contract has any merit."

"That is your decision, Your Holiness," Captain Merriwether replied calmly. "If you wish us to deliver cargo, we must continue the training immediately."

"And what if we leave the operation solely to your crew?"

"Then we will abort the transfer," Captain Merriwether said. "If it is of any aid, you may contact your remaining personnel. They have assured me that they understand the risks and are willing to continue their training."

"All of them?" His Holiness asked.

"All of them," Captain Merriwether replied.

His Holiness mulled on that. After a moment, he nodded. "I should like to speak with them in private. If they agree, I will approve."

"Very well," Captain Merriwether said.

#

"Now, as we all know, we suffered a loss but we have agreed to continue this mission," the Calmt Prime said as she looked over the Arwonese Bouncers. "We have been training in simulators since the accident; today we are back in real ships." She nodded toward Cin. "Cin here will accompany us on our bounces, while the ship *Valrise* will provide additional support." She paused. She glanced at Mira and Sikar who gave her reassuring nods. Then she looked to the men.

"Let's get to it, time's wasting!" Coklon declared.

"I shall go first," the Calmt declared. The others gave her shocked looks. "It is my right and my duty."

Cin said nothing, gesturing for the Calmt to enter her bouncer. Cin triple-checked the bouncer's systems: as expected, all were perfect. She checked her own unit — one built for her to her specifications. Her bouncer was named *Terra*, after mankind's homeworld. Cin promised herself that, one day, she would bounce on the homeworld itself and the craft's name reflected that promise.

The two undocked from *Lewrys* and commenced their de-orbit burn.

The Calmt is requesting a private channel, Valrise informed Cin.

Fine, Cin replied, toggling a connection. "You wish to speak in private?"

"I did," the Calmt said. "I have been thinking —"

"We could abort, if you wish," Cin said.

"Not that," the Calmt said. "I have been thinking about Alvar."

"We have determined the cause of the error, and I can assure you that your bouncer is operating nominally," Cin told her.

"Of course," the Calmt replied in a smug tone. "I am convinced that the error has been corrected. Alvar is not at the controls."

"What do you mean?"

"He caused the accident, didn't he?" the Calmt said. When Cin didn't immediately reply, she continued, "He panicked and cut out the failsafes."

"What makes you say this?"

"There is something you don't know about our world," the Calmt said.

"There are many things I don't know about your world," Cin replied.

"Alvar panicked, didn't he?"

"*Valrise* reported a systems malfunction," Cin temporized.

"We suffered a major famine and our people are starving," the Calmt said. "Those who were selected for the bouncers were expected to succeed. We need your trade if we are to survive. His Holiness made it quite clear that anyone who did not learn to use your bouncers was a 'mouth wasting food' — his own words. So when Alvar panicked, he knew that he would die. One way or another."

"Why did you not say there was a famine?" Cin said. "*Valrise* is committed to humanitarian aid."

"It is a very *select* famine," the Calmt replied. "Those His Holiness considers unworthy are those that starve."

"Are your people among them?"

"My people are *most* of them," the Calmt said. "We are the ones most recently 'assimilated into the Greater Whole.' Are you familiar with the concept of a 'scorched earth policy'?"

I am, Valrise said to Cin, relaying relevant images. Cin fought an urge to vomit.

"Why did you not contact us directly?"

"We could not, we had no transmitters," the Calmt replied. "I was elected among my people to join the Greater Whole, to renounce my kind in the hope that I might protect them from within." She added bitterly. "In that, I failed."

"So why do you continue to work with His Holiness?"

"Who says I am?" the Calmt replied.

Cin checked her readouts and waited. The Calmt said, "Coming up on bounce in five minutes."

"Watch it, it'll be beautiful," Cin said almost automatically. She'd been watching the outside of her bouncer lighten and had noted the first pink rays of atmospheric heating color the nose of her ship. Unlike the Calmt, Cin wore nothing when she dove. Her body was encased in an air-breathing fluid, it filled her lungs, allowing her to perform higher-gee maneuvers than the normal bouncers could. Like all the bouncers, her ship's hull was transparent, unlike those for the Arwonese, her instrument panel was also transparent, marked only by the small specks of the highly-integrated circuits which comprised her computer controls. Cin's craft had a slightly lower thermal insulation, allowing her to feel the temperature rise as her bouncer sliced through the atmosphere. She — and all the other bouncers in the crew — liked the notion of being able to 'feel' the air around them.

They bounced. Minutes later they impacted the target cargo vessel and reversed course.

"Amazing!" the Calmt declared as they returned to the red depths of the atmosphere. "Absolutely amazing!"

#

Cin met the Calmt as she emerged from her bouncer. Cin had already donned a shipsuit to avoid offending the Arwonese woman.

"Your skin is glowing," the Calmt declared, raising a hand to her own face. "Is mine like that?"

"No," Cin said. "When I bounce, I wear no clothing."

"Isn't that dangerous?"

"My bouncer is all I need to wear," Cin said. "I like to feel the heat of the air on my skin."

The Calmt shook her head in wonder. "I don't think that is too strange for my tastes." She waved the topic aside. "How are the others doing?"

"They are within tolerance," Cin replied, having checked in with *Valrise*.

"I'm sure His Holiness will be pleased," the Calmt observed tartly. "Will we be able to proceed, then, with the transfer?"

"We have to make up for lost training time but I believe, with no further difficulties, it will be possible."

"And the remotes will help," the Calmt said.

"Training with the remotes will become the first priority," Cin said. "The remote bouncers are always the primary form of momentum exchange."

"The human bouncers are just for fun," the Calmt guessed.

"Not just for fun," Cin corrected. "However it is true that we work best in managing the remotes."

"Why couldn't the ship do it herself?"

"It is a question of proximity," Cin said. "*Valrise* will not be close enough to provide immediate responses."

"But isn't this all rather pre-determined?" the Calmt asked. "I mean, isn't it just a matter of physics?"

"Almost," Cin replied. "Atmospheric turbulence means that not even the most advanced calculations will be completely predictive. There is an element of chance that must be managed." Cin added, "And sometimes the masses of the cargo containers are not as accurate as desired. We know how to handle that."

"And will we learn to manage that?"

"Mostly that will be up to the crew bouncers," Cin said. She caught the Calmt's look and added, "As you get more experienced, we will bring you more closely into the operation."

"You mean, the next time you come back."

A week later, Cin still had misgivings about the proficiency of the Arwonese bouncers.

There is something going on, Cin informed *Valrise*. *I see too many strange looks passing between them, particularly the women.*

Their performance is above average, *Valrise* replied. *And we must make the trade, particularly after losing one of their own.*

Cin frowned but nodded in troubled agreement. The integrity of the ship was at stake.

Keep an eye on things, let me know if anything untoward occurs, *Valrise* added.

And you do the same, Cin replied.

They are planning several low-level launches, setting up the GPS system we recommended, *Valrise* reported. *Beyond that, their space efforts are limited strictly to the cargo exchange.*

"We'll know one way or another the next five hours," Cin said aloud, glancing at the automated countdown timer.

Lewrys and *Marys* — both named after revered and long-dead crew members — we prepped for launch.

Cin was aboard *Lewrys*, ferrying the downside crew — mostly the Arwonese — to their destination. Goroba had the rest of the bouncers with him on *Marys*. Cin had no concerns about the crew bouncers, so she'd suggested that she ride with the earthers. *Valrise* had agreed.

With Emery as pilot, the shuttle was cramped with the eleven earthers and the two crew. Its racks carried a full complement of crewed and remote bouncers — forty in all.

Fortunately, they didn't have far to go. Arwon was now a large ball filling their port side almost completely.

"Once again, tell me the drill," Cin said to the collected Arwonese bouncers.

"We drop anti-orbit, hit our cargo, bounce back, and hit the inbound cargo," Coklon said with a grin. "Repeat and continue until sufficient momentum is exchanged, then rendezvous back here."

"Where *Valrise* will place an orbiting station which will include a re-entry vehicle," the Calmt finished, glancing at her two fellow women. Cin's brows creased as she caught their looks: it was that some disturbing look she'd seen before.

"*Arwon I*," Coklon said in agreement. "The Blessing has already been bestowed by His Holiness."

Cin kept her face blank. She'd had little time to learn more about the politics of Arwon but what she had learned — through her training and in conversations with other crew — was enough to make her wary of religious oligarchies.

Coklon snapped his fingers in an expression of the ease of the task facing them.

"Prepare your bouncers," Cin said. To Emery she said, "Deploy the remotes at your discretion."

"I'll deploy 'em when you launch," Emery replied with a chuckle. He and Cin had once been lovers; they still worked with the easy camaraderie of two people who had shared thinking.

"Just don't be late!" Cin teased. She moved down the corridor to the hatch to her bouncer. Out of sight of the Arwonese, she gladly shucked her shipsuit before wriggling through the hatchway and onto her craft.

"Sealing," Cin reported, activity the controls. *Terra* responded eagerly, like some ancient steed awaiting her commands. Cin closed her eyes, engaged the atmospheric controls and waited as the slightly damp, cool gas rose from the reservoirs onboard the *Lewrys* to cover her completely. She took the breath that she always hated as the gas rose to the level of her lips. It rose over her head quickly and Cin forced herself to inhale it. For a moment she fought panic as her lungs instinctively tried to expel it. The gas condensed slowly around her and inside her, turning to a body-temperature liquid that encased her protectively within *Terra's* supertech transparent hull.

"Life support," Cin said.

Life support 105%, *Terra* responded through Cin's link. The bouncer was considered operational with life support as low as 90% but *Valrise* insisted that there be a margin for error in all normal operations. *With bouncers, normal is a rare condition, Valrise* had once explained to Cin, alluding to the general crew belief that anyone who would expose themselves to a hard atmosphere in extreme conditions was very much outside the norm.

Cin completed the rest of her systems checks and turned her attention to the earthers preparing beside her.

She was not surprised to learn that all the women had chosen to leave their shipsuits behind. What did surprise her was that Coklon and Batric had also "gone native." For herself, Cin couldn't imagine bouncing in some as constricting as a suit. The gel-liquid that surrounded her and filled her lungs operated with less friction that a suit, making her movements just that much quicker and efficient. Early in her training — and again in her training of the worlders — she'd had to wear a shipsuit through a bounce; she never liked it.

"All systems nominal, we are coming up on insertion," Emery reported just as Cin had come to the same conclusion.

"Call, Calmt," Cin said. She was letting the Calmt call the orders.

"*Valrise, Valrise*, this is LEO bounce team, request insertion," the Calmt said with the clipped precision of a well-trained professional.

"LEO bounce team, I copy and confirm that you are ready for insertion," *Valrise* replied over the regular comms.

They're good, Cin said, emphasizing only that she thought the team ready.

"LEO team, you are cleared for insertion," *Valrise* said on the comms. "Wait one, I have a transmission from downside."

"Waiting," the Calmt replied, her tone notched up just a little with worry.

"Stand by for His Holiness," a voice, modulated by transmission from the distance of an atmosphere and reflecting somewhat inferior electronics, spoke up.

"We are ready, your Holiness," the Calmt said.

"Godspeed," His Holiness' voice came back. "May this be the beginning of a great new adventure."

"Thank you," *Valrise* replied. "We look forward to continued trade."

"Do we have your permission to commence the operation, Holiness?" Coklon asked.

What? Cin shot to *Valrise*.

"You are authorized to proceed," His Holiness responded. "Godspeed in all your efforts."

"Coming up on insertion," Emery said with a note of worry n his voice. Cin checked her readouts: if they waited too much longer, they'd have to abort to the next orbit.

Cin? Valrise asked.

What if we don't go?

Trade would be impacted, Valrise said.

Then go, Cin said.

"LEO team, separate," *Valrise* spoke over the comm. To Cin, she added, *Keep your eyes open.*

Cin watched as the team separated in order. Cin went last, the Calmt just before her.

"Insertion," the Calmt ordered when everyone confirmed their positions.

"Initiating," Cin responded when her mark showed.

Little pinpricks lit the sky around her as the bouncers began their descent into the planet's gravity well.

"Cargo marks," the Calmt called out.

"Roger, targeting cargo," voices came back in confirmation.

"Drone release," Emery called.

"Roger," the Calmt replied. Cin double-checked the telemetry. "Drones on course."

In addition to the eleven bouncers there were now thirty-three remotes en route — allowing the combined bouncers to manage the eleven upbound cargo containers which were themselves matched by eleven containers coming from *Valrise*. They were not matched for mass, the outbound containers being more massive than those from *Valrise*. That reflected the greater value of the incoming cargo — gram for gram it was worth nearly a thousand times more.

The maneuvers — bounces — were fairly straight forward: Cin and the others would change the initial circular orbits of the containers into highly elliptical orbits, then turn the orbits around — this was possible because at an orbit's apogee the velocity of the object was nothing and the energy required to alter its trajectory equally nothing.

So the LEO crew would bounce the outbound cargo up, then exchange momentum with the inbound cargo — slowing it down by speeding themselves up — and repeat the process.

The process became involved because of the relative masses and the need to make the momentum exchanging impacts at sufficiently low gravities.

Bouncers could safely handle ten gravities — Cin herself had tested to twenty. The containers were often much more fragile: taking only three gees maximum. This was particularly true for the planet-built outbound containers. Included in the value of the exchange was the higher-tech of *Valrise's* containers — containers that were standardized in the Trade.

According to preliminary calculations, it would take twenty-three exchanges to complete the momentum translation.

The first impacts would be glancing blows as the bouncers dropped to the atmosphere.

Cin double-checked the trajectories — the earthers had to hit center of mass in two dimensions to avoid imparting any spin or yaw to the containers. The remotes could help in correcting any errors. And, in this first instance, the rules of physics were the only rules to be considered. Once bouncers hit the turbulent atmosphere of the planet, inconsistencies would be introduced.

"Impact in 3... 2... 1..." Coklon called out. His bouncer and the three remotes were the first scheduled to hit a container. "Impact!"

On profile, Valrise confirmed. Coklon's ship rebounded from the container which seemed unaffected by the multiple impacts. Cin's telemetry showed otherwise and she added her voice to the others congratulating the Arwonese man on his first bounce.

One by one the others hit, all on profile. Cin grunted as *Terra* impacted on the last, and most difficultly placed, container.

Off profile! Valrise reported even as Cin's telemetry flashed red. *There is a mass discrepancy! Center of gravity also does not correspond.*

"We got a bad bounce," Emery reported from *Lewrys*. "Recomputing." On a private channel he said to Cin, "What did you do, woman?"

"Not me," Cin replied. "Something's off."

"Off by a tonne," Emery reported. "The ship's on it, she's talking with the downsiders."

"Re-computing bounce," Cin responded, toggling her computer interface. Fortunately, the bounce was not too far off profile; she could easily correct. She was glad it was her and not one of the worlders: they would have been dismayed by the prospect of a deep bounce.

"Got your Will in order?" Emery teased over their private link.

"Huh!" Cin snorted derisively. It was an old joke common between bouncers and pilots: a part of the rivalry between two 'crazy' professions.

"Cin —" the Calmt called on a private link.

"We have communications from earthside —" Captain Merriwether reported at the same time.

Valrise?

Trouble, the ship responded.

"What is it?" Cin said to the Arwonese woman.

"Missile launch! Multiple missiles inbound!" Emery roared over the link. "Red watch, red watch, red watch! We are under attack! I repeat —"

His voice cut out at the same moment that Cin lost telemetry with *Lewrys*. Instinctively, Cin kicked her thrusters, twisting her vector and velocity at the same moment.

Valrise!

Her comm filled with the voice of His Holiness. "I regret this but it is necessary that the unholy be cleansed," he said.

"What —?"

"The containers, we must save them!" the Calmt cried on her link.

Missile lock, armed, impact in two hundred seconds, Terra warned.

Cin kicked her thrusters to max, setting *Terra* to dive into the atmosphere.

"Follow me!" Cin called over the private link. She sent the same instructions to her remotes but only two responded. A quick check showed her that the other two had been destroyed.

As had all the bouncers save Mira's and the Calmt's.

"What's so important about the containers?" Cin shouted over her comm link.

Communications loss in ninety seconds, Terra warned, referring to the standard atmospheric disturbances that occurred in a bounce into an atmosphere.

"My people," the Calmt replied.

"What?"

"There are two thousand women and girls on your container," the Calmt told her. "They are the last of my people."

"*What?*" Cin checked telemetry: all the other containers had been destroyed.

"Please, you must help us," the Calmt replied. "We had filled four of the containers with our people. This is the last one."

"But —"

"Our people were destroyed, they were going to be eliminated," Mira said on the private circuit. Brokered into the link by the Calmt, Cin surmised.

"We hid them," the Calmt replied.

"I thought you were part of the Greater Whole?"

"I pretended to betray my people," the Calmt said. "I sat on the Council while they were destroyed, trying to find some way to save them."

And now this, Cin thought.

"Why didn't you tell us?"

"And be discovered?" the Calmt asked. "Until my people were in space, there was no surety." She paused. "And even then..."

Debris fields calculated, Valrise added. *Prepare for updates.*

Loss of signal! Cin warned, as her ship started to glow pink with the air rushing around her.

You are own your own, Cin, Valrise told her sadly. *The safety of the ship and crew are paramount.*

I know, Cin said.

Do your best, daughter.

The link went dead: Loss of Signal.

"I'm going to lose your signal," Cin said to the Calmt and her compatriot. "Just take your bounce and we'll talk when we get signal again."

"What are you going to do?"

"Bounce," Cin told her simply. "Bounce your cargo to my ship."

Terra, recompute with maximum gravity impacts for quickest transfer of cargo, Cin ordered her craft. *Ignore safety margins.*

Around her, the air grew brighter. Cin took a moment to bask in the glory that was a world trying to destroy her. The temperature rose as *Terra* hit her perigee and then she bounced off the atmosphere. Back to the stars.

"—almt calling anyone, please respond!" the Calmt's voice came to her, stressed with fear and worry.

"This is Cin, I'm recomputing now," she assured the Calmt. "Is Mira still with you?"

"Yes, I'm here," another voice replied, sounding less stressed and more awed.

"Bounce well?" Cin asked.

"It was beautiful!"

"And all the missiles burnt out trying to follow us," the Calmt remarked.

"That was the plan!" Cin said. "Do they have more?"

"Possibly," the Calmt said. "But it will take them some time to re-arm and launch."

"Okay," Cin said. She was silent for a moment. "Two thousand?"

"Maybe more."

Terra completed the calculations. Cin glanced at them: she'd expected nothing more.

"Mira, would you like to *really* bounce?" Cin asked.

"Will it save my people?"

"It's their only chance," Cin replied. "We're going to have to go deep pink."

"Deep pink?" Mira repeated in confusion.

"She means we're going to dive deep into the atmosphere," the Calmt replied. "How safe is that?"

"Not very," Cin replied. "*Terra* is sending your bouncers the data now."

"Twenty gravities!" Mira swore when she got the download. "Can anyone survive that?"

"I have," Cin said. She didn't mention that it had taken her a week to recover. In this case, it didn't matter.

"If we die —"

"We'll time the highest gees for last," Cin replied. "We should be fine until then."

There was a moment's silence as the other two absorbed her words. They had the calculations: they knew the price.

"Very well," the Calmt said. "I am prepared."

"So am I," Mira said. "My sister is on that container."

"Then we'll give her the best ride we can," Cin said.

I can see no other way, Valrise said through their link. *We will receive your gift, Cin, have no fear.*

Thank you.

I'm launching remotes to aid you, Valrise added. *At the very least they may be able to complete your mission.*

Good, Cin replied. After a moment, she added with a laugh, *Does this qualify as combat?*

Most certainly!

#

They bounced four more times. The third time, a new launch of missiles picked off Mira's bouncer before she could get deep into the atmosphere.

Valrise had launched countermeasures by then so the next array of missiles from the planet were destroyed.

Not that it mattered: there was too little mass to complete the exchange.

"There has to be a way," the Calmt cried over their link. "There has to be!"

"Follow me," Cin said.

"What can we do?"

"Our ships are built better than we are," Cin told her. "They can handle fifty gees. And they can handle higher temperatures. The computers will do it all for us."

"But my people!" the Calmt cried.

"We're exchanging momentum," Cin reminded her. "They'll only get a sharp nudge."

"To do this we must go to the depths of the atmosphere?" the Calmt asked.

"To do this, we must melt," Cin told her grimly.

The Calmt was silent for a long moment. Finally, she said, "It will be a hell of a ride, won't it?"

Cin grinned. "No one will ever see its like."

"And live to tell the tale," the Calmt chuckled in bitter agreement.

"Ready to see the white at the end of the pink?"

"Yes."

#

Valrise recorded it all. She recorded their breaths, their heart rates, their skin temperatures, their pain. Their screams.

From the depths of the atmosphere two fiery, glowing spheroids rose back into the sky to hit the last cargo container with all their light and energy.

It was enough, as Cin had calculated.

"Prepare a grapple and secure that cargo," Captain Merriwether said over the comm.

"Aye aye, sir," the cargomaster replied with a non-traditional military bearing.

"You must return now!" His Holiness called over the link. "You are in grave danger; the people on that container are escaped criminals."

"*You* are in grave danger," Merriwether replied. "You have committed an act of war on a civilian ship." He paused for a moment, glancing at his telemetry. "You have killed four of our crew and thousands of your people."

"Only eleven are mine," His Holiness returned acidly. "The rest are vermin."

"We are taking your 'vermin' with us," Captain Merriwether said. He cut the comm. *Jump,* he ordered *Valrise.*

Alarms sounded as the ship prepared to jump into hyperspace.

A moment later, *Valrise* entered the nothingness.

#

A month had passed since the jump from Arwon. The refugees had been settled on a number of worlds, some had petitioned to join *Valrise* as crew. Some had been accepted.

Captain Merriwether and *Valrise* conferred on the final reports.

"I got good reads on her all the way down," *Valrise* said out loud.

"Cin?" Merriwether asked. His brows furrowed. "What do you propose?"

"I'm going to make another," *Valrise* declared. "We've room in the infirmary, and in the growth tanks, her genetics are on file."

"You're not going to give her all those memories?" Captain Merriwether asked, aghast.

"No, of course not," *Valrise* replied.

"You don't just want to name a shuttle after her?" Captain Merriwether said. "After all, she was just a bouncer. Hardly irreplaceable."

"All five of them," *Valrise* said. Captain Merriwether gave her a questioning look. "We have genetics on the Arwonese."

"They didn't consent," Merriwether protested. Typically, cloning required the progenitor's consent.

"My authority," *Valrise* said.

Captain Merriwether thought for a moment. Nodded. "It's your ship, after all." After a slight pause, he added, "And what was her real name, the Calmt Prime?"

"Sorka," *Valrise* replied. "She'll be Sorka Arwon."

#

Three of the girls were smaller and darker than the fourth. But they were inseparable: born of the same pod at the same time, along with the boy.

Captain Merriwether visited them when he could, *Valrise* was always with them.

"And what's your name?" Captain Merriwether asked the fourth girl.

"I'm Cin," the girl replied proudly. "Cin Valrise the Second!"

Kiss

> *Kiss was written in the early 1990s. It was written when we were still fighting – and losing – the battle against AIDS. When we'd just discovered all the orphans in Rumania, left alone, untended, dying of neglect.*

THEY CALLED HER MOUSE AND SAID SHE WAS BATTY. I COULD SEE WHY 'Mouse' — a wan look, haggard brown eyes, red-rimmed, and string brown hair. A faded Carrie Fisher, sleep starved. I pitied her pimp for scraping the bottom of the barrel but hated him for using such a kid so sorely — no one ever saw her on the street until well after dark, and always with that troubled, trembling lower-lip look. I couldn't see the 'batty' — she wandered among the homeless and the derelicts with a concerned, yearning expression.

Maybe it came from the druggies — they'd always trail her longingly and offer her a hit of whatever they were on. It didn't make sense — that bit of a girl strung out on *anything* — even booze — couldn't possibly make money for her squeeze.

The kids — yeah, they're up that hour on the street; you haven't met the cast out of mankind, have you? — they'd tease her but it was with a reverence and fear that bordered on holy. You'd think, for all my time, that I'd get hardened to it all, but then some wide-eyed waif with ribs showing would look up at me with the eyes of the eternally damned: the street-dwellers, and I'd want to — to scream, to tear a knife through the darkness, to crumble buildings with bare hands, to call down lightning and call up earthquakes to shake people into action; into caring.

"*We care for our own!*" — the medic's credo — would burn through my body, like the burning Willy Pete in 'Nam — they said they cured all that, but they ain't walked the streets at night, seen all the vets line the way with eyes like holes...

And the kids. How do you tell a little kid: get used to the street, you're gonna die there?

Mouse cared — I guess that's why the kids' reverence. I cared, God damn me, but then it was the training, the same training that kept me fixing the grunts in 'Nam when the Willy Pete splashed all over us, burned through my back while I sheltered that guy, got the tourniquet on his leg, closed his bloody open chest with a rag. Willy Pete — White Phosphorous — burns through a man; you can't put it out unless you cover it from open air. They threw mud on my back when the Willy Pete stopped raining down, threw the mud and hauled me back from that grunt, kicking and screaming like a baby from its bottle. *"We care for our own!"* I saw him later, in a body bag. They sent me home, girl spit in my eye when I got off the plane, called me fascist, jabbed me with a peace sign. The brass stuck a medal on me, called me a hero, gave me a check, threw me out on the streets.

"We care for our own!" I'm a medic — can't stop — but how do you cure the future?

So little Mouse did her thing at night and I did mine — can't sleep — passing out clean needles to the druggies, steer vets to the shelter, tell lies to the li'l kids.

When the druggies stopped taking the needles — "Mouse do a better job!" — I got nervous. AIDS is on the street, man, AIDS in every unwashed needle. I've seen people die from AIDS — they die quicker on the street but I've seen 'em die in hospitals, too. I prefer Willy Pete.

I started following her. When I caught up with her, she was with Weird George. Ol' George was a LRP — a member of the special Long Range Patrols they sent out in 'Nam — you never get away from it. He was the worst sort of druggie and sewer shit you could meet. And he was always broke, certainly not the sort to patronize a whore. I watched them around a corner.

What happened next was weirder — Weird George *gave* her some crack. As I watched she lit up, toked deeply and started buzzing. Weird George barked something at her, grabbed her wildly with a lunge but she pulled free. That surprised me, George was mungo strong. She laughed at him; then, all sensuous, like a lover, she leaned over to him. Her head was behind his, so I couldn't see what she did but I guess she must have laid the world's greatest hickey on him 'cause all the sudden ol' George was beaming like he'd got the best hit ever. Come to think of it, she looked kinda down when she pulled back from him.

Whatever it was she did, it was too much for Weird George. His hands started clawing the air and he groaned hoarsely. Mouse stepped back, face in the light, anxious. George grabbed his chest, groaning.

I knew what it was and I came running. By the time I got to them, only a hundred yards, he had already keeled over, rolled to one side, stretched out on the concrete. Mouse was by his side but I motioned her away. I knelt down, loosened his clothing, felt for a pulse.

"Shit!" No breath either — no news. I looked up at her: "Are you okay? Can you help?"

"What do I do?" she asked. Her voice was slurred, like a lover after orgasm.

I figured: she kissed him, she can do his breathing. "Get over by his side. When I tell you, give him one quick breath. I'll do the CPR." I cleared his airway. She knelt beside his head. I pumped his chest fifteen times, then, in a gasp, I told her, "Breathe!"

We worked the corpse for fifteen minutes before I gave up. I swore at the whore who'd helped him on his way, "Sister, you can stop with the breath of life — your kiss finished him."

I could feel her flinch. I got off the corpse, knelt beside it opposite her. "Musta been something," I said to her. In the light I could see his neck where she had kissed him.

"What the - ?" On his neck were two small wounds about an inch apart. "Mouse, what'd ya do to him?"

#

You guessed it: she was gone. Me, I stuck around for the cops. They know me. I rode in the coroner's van when they slabbed him. Figured it was all I could do for a vet. In the van, I felt around his neck: he still had his dogtags.

WALLOPS, GEORGE T., 467-12-2164, NO PREFERENCE, O POS.

The Coroner, Joe Mendez, was another buddy — we'd slabbed too many together. He gave me a 'get out of here' look but I blocked it with a 'family'.

"Run a blood test, Joe," I said after the contest of wills. He frowned. I motioned him over to my side of the body, pointed out the wounds.

"Smitty, what's the mystery?"

"Joe, *please*," I begged, "he was one of ours."

Joe'd been a doctor, fresh out of med school. After 'Nam, he couldn't work on the living no more.

#

"Blood test, right," Joe responded. He looked up at me. "I thought there was no foul play."

I sighed. "Just run the test, huh?" Joe pulled some blood, handed it off to Ernie in the lab. Then he gave me a look, apologizing, and pulled the gurney into the other room. I didn't follow: my job's to fix 'em, Joe's to find out why they broke. He didn't have to do the autopsy, could have saved the county some money but I know Joe — once I'd asked for the blood test, he was sure to take a good look.

He came out an hour later, pulling off bloody gloves and gown. He got some coffee first, I'd made a fresh pot 'cause I knew he'd need it, then wrote up some notes. When he found his voice, he told me, "Stroke. He was coked up, it was too much for him."

I nodded silently but he had his back to me, so I said, "'Figured."

The lab test came back, the technician was excited as he handed the report to Joe. Joe rose and turned to me as he read it. "Did you know he had AIDS? And just about everything else you could imagine? No wonder he croaked — the crack was just too much for his system!"

No news. I figure most of the guys in the night have got AIDS and all the secondary complications by now: they all shared needles — I could never get my hands on clean ones fast enough for them.

Joe looked at me questioningly. "Your office," I said, gesturing with my head. As he entered I stopped him with a hand. I exhaled right into his nose.

He winced.

"Sorry," I apologized, "but I want you to know that I haven't touched anything."

I pulled an eyelid. "Check the eyes — I'm straight."

He looked, nodded, walked by and dropped into the seat behind his desk.

"Okay, you're straight. What's up?"

I told him what I'd seen.

"She musta bit him when I thought they were kissing." He wasn't convinced. "Look, the marks are fresh, who put them there? Her! And the coke: *he* never touched it! How'd it get there? Her!"

Joe digested my news slowly. Wearily, he leaned forward, rested his arms on the desktop, cradled his head in his hands, rubbed his scalp absently. He sighed. "What you're telling me is that she's a vampire and she's been taking drugs off the skiddies on the street and giving them a transfusion in return, is that what you're saying?"

"Okay, so it sounds nuts," I responded, "but think about it. What if she *is* a vampire: she could give a whole bunch of guys a hit for just one toke. And she's immortal — she can't die. So if they get the worst crack on the street it won't hurt her —"

"Then it'd *kill* them," he broke in.

"Maybe not. Maybe she can filter out the crud the dealers cut it with and give them the pure juice."

Joe was willing to play fantasy. "Okay, suppose she can. She gets a bit of their blood, they get a clean high. And no needles." He jerked upright in his chair. "But now she's got AIDS — she's worse than Typhoid Mary — she'll live forever!" He snorted, threw back his head and laughed. "Smitty, that's the best story you've told me in three years!"

"No story, Joe."

He stood up, gestured for me to proceed him. "Go home, get some rest, Smitty. Get some rest before I take a blood sample from *you!*"

I bared my arms. The track marks were old, back from after Cathy died. "Pick a vein!"

Joe smiled and patted my back. "No way, *amigo*. You get some rest, it's been a long night."

I went home. I was sorry to lose Weird George but not too sorry — he was scary even for a vet. But I was glad that he got his last licks in, or rather that that bitch had bit the wrong dog.

Mouse was off the scene for the next several months so she sorta slipped from my mind. Yeah, I know, how can a vampire slip from your mind? Well, I bagged two 'Nam buddies in that time — checked 'em for punctures — helped a couple of new kids stay away from the worst pimps (they wouldn't go home like I told 'em), the usual. I figured she was holed up some place, dying from the stuff that had been killing Weird George. Good riddance!

It was warm, summer had come, when I next bumped into Joe Mendez. Actually, I didn't bump into him. I arrived in a cop car: courtesy of LA's finest. They didn't mess with me, I'm clean and they know me. Instead, they took me up to a special ward.

"Joe! Geez, man, what happened?" I asked as soon as I caught sight of him. He was wasted — ribs showing, hair all fallen out. He didn't have to reply, I knew the answer.

They keep hospitals really clean, you know. Even with all that cleaning, you could still smell the reek. It loitered in the room, cloying at your nose, saying, "I'm death! I'm coming!" AIDS.

"You look great," I lied. Badly. Joe snorted.

"Okay, you look like shit," I admitted. "How long, Joe?"

His next words shook me, coming out of left field like they did. "They stole all the AZT, Smitty."

You know about AZT just as much as I do: slows AIDS, costs a fortune. "Stole it? All of it?"

"The whole LA shipment!" Joe strained to sit up but the IV line held him back.

I shook my head. "I ain't heard nothing on the street, Joe."

"Cops are keeping a lid on it," Joe responded. "They're afraid all the dudes'll go nuts, there's talk some damned religious nuts stole it - *dumped it -*

you know, the will of God."

"Can't they get more?"

"Sure, in a month!" Joe's voice caught on the last word.

I nodded. "And you don't have a month."

"'Sright," he replied, "So I was thinking. I was thinking about your lady friend, you know the one that did George —"

"What, Joe?" I didn't like the way this was going. Not at all.

"Man, I'm in pain. My kidney's are going, my liver's about gone. Without the drugs I'm another cadaver."

I narrowed my eyes. "What do you want, Joe?"

"I was thinking, you know. If she really *is* — is a —"

"Vampire?" I supplied. Joe blinked at the interruption, then nodded.

"Yeah," he agreed, "If she is, maybe she could *save* me."

I spun away, throwing my arms in the air. "Geez! You want to be a vampire!"

"No!" His response was quick, sharp. "I'd just be a vampire with AIDS. I was thinking what she did for George. It wasn't a bad way to go."

I looked at him for a long while. "I ain't heard nuthin' on the streets since that night, dude. She's probably dead."

"Not if she's really what you said —"

"Hell, man, she's got AIDS!"

"Yeah, but she's a vampire. She's immortal," Joe responded softly. There was a hint of sympathy in his voice. He blew out a breath — "God, to be like this forever!"

"You want me to look for her, I'll look for her," I promised him. I regretted it as soon as I left. I mean, where do you go to look for a vampire? The local cemetery? The Yellow Pages? Stop people on the streets — "Excuse me, I'm looking for a vampire?"

#

"Excuse me, I'm looking for a girl." You know, I still asked that question months after they buried Joe. I got started and couldn't stop. It was three months after I'd stood over his grave, Joe had local folks so I could go (they shipped George off to Arlington - only nice thing the country ever did for him), I never expected anyone to give me an answer; other than all the ladies of the night, "I'm a girl, *honey!*"

Tonight, though, I was asking one of the little homeless kids. Big blue eyes, string thin red hair and a blob of a nose. The nose sorta ruined her until you looked again and then it made her — she was pretty in her own way. Young, about eight, though it's hard to tell on the streets 'cause they don't grow that much. One of the eyes was blacked, purple and sore. It was coming on winter - it was pouring cold rain out of the heavens. This kid wore only a short-sleeve shirt and jeans. You could see a welt on her arm where someone had burnt her. People don't treat kids too good on the streets.

I pulled some burn cream out of my pack, caught her arm and rubbed it on before she could cry out. I keep stuff like that in my pack: burn cream, bandages, a can of mace for protection and, well-hidden, a syringe filled with a special concoction guaranteed to sedate anyone — chloral hydrate, sodium pentothal, atropine, muscle relaxants and a few other choice ingredients.

She puckered a little, the burn was still fresh, but she didn't cry out, just gazed at me with those wide eyes. "I'm lookin' for a girl. She might work the streets. She's only around at night. Got brown eyes and hair. Kinda stringy. Seen her?"

The girl nodded mutely. "Recently?" Another nod. "Can you point me?" She jerked her arm back, lifted it close to her face to inspect it, then pointed down an alley. "'Round midnight." She said in a low voice. I nodded. "Thanks."

I spotted her at midnight. She played the same game. This time, though, she had a whole gang. They gave her a vial of horse and she drank it through her tooth. Man, that much should have toasted her, vampire or no! It doubled her over, but shortly she was back on her feet, feeding on the eager crowd. After each guy she gave a low moan, like she was having sex. I watched from around a corner as they all staggered back, higher than kites. She swooned right there in the alley.

I don't know why, but I raced down and grabbed her, threw her over my shoulders like Tarzan. She didn't weigh much at all. I tore out of there before any of the heads clicked to what went down. She just giggled. I stashed her in my apartment.

She was a giggly wreck when I threw her on the bed. She looked up at me and smiled a lazy, druggy, orgasmic smile. "I know you!" she exclaimed, adding, "You're cute."

I stood there, looking down at her. Her hair had fallen about her face and the lazy animation in her eyes made her look fetching, even pretty. Yeah, pretty. I threw my bag off my shoulder onto the chair.

"Ooh." She cooed, eyes closing, body writhing. "My master is calling me." I figured it was just the drugs. She tried to rise, slipped back down. "Oooh, master. I'm coming!" Her voice conveyed more than desire — there was fear and pain as well.

"You're going to stay here, kid," I told her, sitting beside her. I shook my head. "You're a real mess."

She hissed at me, unlidded her eyes and looked up with an indescribable longing.

"Hot! You're hot! I could drink you, you're so warm!"

She rolled to her side close to me, tried to raise up on one hand to caress my neck, failed and slid backwards onto the bed with an "Oh!"

"You're wasted," I told her.

"Master. Master, I'm coming." She arched her neck and flexed her hips. "I'm coming, Master!"

"Geez, Smitty, what a lady you picked," I muttered to myself. I went over to the dresser and pulled out some rope. I've dealt with DTs, withdrawal, you name it. I tied her up tight because she started to get violent. Just to be sure, I gagged her, especially after she tried to bite me.

Just before I gagged her, she looked at me — I mean really looked — and whimpered: "He needs more."

"Yeah, I'm sure he does." I agreed, pushing the gag in.

It was a long night. I must have dozed sometime 'cause when I woke it was to the smell of burning flesh. The whole bed was bouncing up and down as she writhed on it. There, where the sun came through, smoke was rising from her flesh! I pulled the curtains shut, they'd only been open a slit. The flesh stopped burning but she kept writhing in agony. In desperation I cut away her clothing.

The wounds looked just like my Willy Pete holes, only they were thin lines where the rays of the sun had touched. I grabbed my kit off the chair and put some salve on the burns. It must have helped, she stopped writhing and just moaned low. She was exhausted and fell asleep.

I waited by the bedside a while, just to be sure. Then I went to the kitchen and made coffee. I rummaged in the fridge and brought a tray into the bedroom. While I ate breakfast, I thought over everything I knew about vampires. It wasn't much: all I knew came from late night horror movies as a kid. Vampires live in coffins, hate daylight, drink blood. Well, Mouse certainly didn't have to have a coffin; she was doing okay on my bed. Then again, she burnt in daylight.

They could be killed by a stake to the heart; well, I'll hold on that, thank you. They had no shadows. Intrigued, I brought a hand mirror out of the bathroom and looked. Well, *that* was wrong. She looked pretty cute, all relaxed like that. I checked her bonds to be sure.

They don't die; they're immortal. Hell, I couldn't tell if she'd been a vampire for two hundred years or two! They were allergic to holy water, crosses and garlic (or was that werewolves?). Experimentally, I made a cross with my two forefingers. In her sleep she moaned and turned in her bonds. I clapped my hands to my sides hastily, just in case.

They sleep all day. Well, *that* certainly was true. It wasn't until the sun was below the horizon that I caught the glint of her eyes. Carefully, I leaned over her and pulled out the gag. She screamed. I stuck it back in again, wagged a finger at her. Her eyes boiled at me — weren't vampires supposed to be hypnotic or something? I looked away, looked back and smiled at her. She rolled her eyes disgustedly.

"Gonna behave?" I asked. She nodded. I pulled the gag out. No screams. "Good."

She shivered. "How long?"

"You've been out the whole day," I told her.

She shivered again, looked down at the ruin of her dress. I grimaced. "No, I didn't do anything to you. As if *you'd* care. Or know — you were really wired, do you know that?"

"I burnt, I remember," she said, tongue dry. I held up a hand, got some coffee and gave her a sip. She nodded thanks.

"Sorry about that, I didn't really believe and left a bit of curtain open," I told her. "That's why your dress is torn. I put some salve on the burn. Should help."

I looked down at her bare thighs. Not a mark. "Sonuvabitch! It's gone!" She wasn't surprised.

"Have you got a stake?" her voice wasn't resigned, it was relieved.

"Steak?" I asked, deliberately misunderstanding her — I don't kill, I fix.

"Aren't you going to kill me?" she looked at me matter-of-factly. "You'll have to wait until dark, you know."

"You *want* me to kill you?"

"Please. I'll go to *him* otherwise."

"Him?"

"My master," she replied. "Oh, please! The stake!"

I waved my hands over her. "Wait a minute, wait a minute, what's this about a master? Are you a slave?"

Her eyes narrowed. "You don't know, do you?"

I shook my head. Call me ignorant, I didn't know all that much about vampires — not my specialty. "Every vampire has a Master until that Master is destroyed."

I tried humor. "What, like a shop steward or something? You guys got a union?"

She ignored my attempt with a flick of her eyes. "He *made* me. He drained my blood and gave me his. He can *call* me, make me do his bidding."

"So you get too high to know where you are, so you can resist him," I guessed. She nodded. "Smart."

"I can't change form when I'm high, either," she said.

"I've managed to avoid him for a month now." She glanced at me. "I thought I'd lost him after I met up with you."

She coughed. The cough caught in her throat and racked her body. I passed her a tissue. The phlegm she coughed up was green with disease. I could smell it as I went to throw it out, so I looked at it. Closely.

"You've got *pneumonia!*"

"Oh, no, it's going away," she said, "I'm feeling much better now."

Then I remembered. "You got AIDS from Weird George! That was half a year ago! You should be dead!"

"I was *very* sick," she admitted, "We both were."

She made a face. "I was so hoping that he'd die."

Realization shivered down my spine. "The AZT! You took it! You bastards!" I leapt for her, to strike, to do anything. She flinched. That stopped me. I barked — "Are you still taking it? 'Cause if you are, when it runs out you'll all die!"

She blanched. "I never got any. *He* got it all."

That floored me. I dropped to the bed, puzzled. When I finally looked over to her, it was with a strange thought forming in my head — "Do you still drink blood?"

"Yes."

"Do you still *have* to drink blood?"

"I don't know. I did it with all the street people," her eyes lost focus as she plunged into thought. "You know, I never really *took* any of their blood, just a hit of whatever they wanted."

"But you used to, didn't you?" She nodded. "And he still does, doesn't he?" She nodded again.

I grabbed my first aid kit, pulled out a syringe. She shrank back from it. "I want to take a sample." She didn't like the idea. "I need to know something."

Her body tensed. "He's calling me! I'm going to have to go!" Her body started to shimmer, lose its form. "*Do* something!" She pleaded.

I maced her. I keep a can in my med kit. It didn't do much good, she screamed and clawed at her eyes but it gave me enough time to pump her up with my special Mickey Finn concoction. In short order she was the most truthful drunk you've ever met.

"Is that enough?" I asked her.

"Yes." Her body still writhed somewhat as she struggled to answer the call, but it was weak and getting weaker.

"Good. Now tell me where your master lives," I said. She told me. I let out a cackle at the answer — apparently churches don't hold as much protection as advertised or maybe evangelists are in for a rude surprise. I checked her bonds, gagged her again and, for no good reason, kissed her on the cheek. "Later." I took a blood sample just before I left.

#

The lab technician wanted to give me grief. "Look, Ernie, just do it. I swear it's for Joe. You do it and I promise you that the guys that stole those drugs'll pay!"

"Well, okay." Grudgingly he took the sample. "AIDS, and any AIDS-related illnesses?"

I nodded. He shook his head. "I'll see you later," I told him.

"Where ya going?"

I smiled. It wasn't pleasant because he blanched. "Payback time!"

I won't go into details, 'cause it was more Joe's line of work than mine, but Mouse was right, a stake *will* do the job. It was easy, too: that room in the basement of the church was just littered with empty vials of AZT. Vials that coulda kept a hundred guys from checking out. Because of that I was extra thorough: his nibs was as dead as could be when I'd finished.

Back at the lab, the results were what I'd expected. No AIDS, some AIDS-related illnesses, all in remission. She was as healthy as any person recovering from a series of illnesses.

"Thanks, Ernie."

"Will you get the guy?" He asked, hopefully.

I nodded and grinned. "I've already staked him out."

Mouse was still tied up when I got back. She looked different, relaxed, slightly less faded. I pulled the gag out of her mouth.

"He's gone," I told her. She grinned lopsidedly. "Feel better?"

"Feel *great!*" she told me with a leer. "You're a hunk! Let's make love." Truth serum will do that to ya.

I shook my head. "Later, when you're able to say that without a slur."

"Aw!"

She kept me up all night with her babbling. The drugs wore off just before morning. With a yawn, she told me, "I still wanna make love."

I wagged a finger at her. "Still a bit of a slur. See you tonight."

She sighed, rolled a little in her bonds, and drifted into sleep. I got more coffee, made vigil, and thought.

I must have drifted off to sleep.

"I still want to make love." The voice that woke me up was relaxed but hungry. For what? I asked myself.

"You don't even know my name," I returned.

"They call you Smitty." She sounded shy. "I'm Mouse."

I nodded. I got up, walked over to her. I held up an arm, vein down, held it over her nose but not too close. "Mouse, do you want a bite? Do you feel a need to drink blood?"

"You can get a stake," she said, voice flat. Her eyes begged for… for something — trust, love, understanding, I didn't know. I lowered my arm, watching her eyes, her nostrils. Her eyes widened, nostrils flared as my arm lowered. In pain she closed her eyes, turned her head away.

"No, I will *not!*" The words were torn out of her. Then, as if uncontrollably, her head turned back. Before I could react, her neck braced and she raised her head. Her lips touched my bare arm. Tongue caressed it. Teeth brushed over it. Nothing more.

Silently, I unloosed her bonds, lead her to the toilet and turned on the shower. "Food?"

Sheepishly, with lowered eyes, she replied, "I could go for a bloody steak."

We ate together. She washed up prettier than I'd realized, it was hard not to gaze at her longingly. While we ate, I told her what I'd found out — how she must have had AIDS and conquered it. I told her my theory: that AIDS and vampirism counteracted each other; the one cured the other.

"Let's make love." she said. We did. I was tired, she wasn't. Her energy infected me and we were both good.

"I want you to do something for me," I told her as we lay back, resting between love. Her brown eyes focused on me, a languorous smile played on her lips. "I want you to *make* me."

"Why?"

I smiled. "When we're making love, just *make* me." I dallied with one of her trim breasts, slid a hand down her thighs encouragingly. She bit her tongue between her teeth, eyes alight, challenged. Aroused again, we made love to a fever pitch I'd never before imagined. As we both came, I felt hot spikes enter my neck and then the most incredible feeling of burning, of desire, of melting, melding. I moaned in my ecstasy.

Later, much later, after she woke, "Now, I am *your* master!"

"Mistress," I corrected absently, "And I think not."

She lowered a brow. "You're a mutation. Rather, two viruses within you have formed a new symbiosis. You're not quite vampire and certainly not AIDS ridden." She absorbed that mutely. "By the way, how was I?"

Mouse purred in delight. "I meant, how did I taste?"

She made a face. "Chalky, like moldy cheese."

I nodded. "The virus. You don't really need blood anymore. I won't, either."

It took me three weeks of experimentation and midnight visits to Ernie to sort everything out. I was allergic to daylight, my skin would burn in it. But my body healed immediately from any damage. I slept during the day, went out at night. But I didn't need human blood, or any blood. Both of us ate a lot of red meat and I prescribed more B vitamins and Iron. Most importantly, as I had hoped, our blood cured AIDS. Those experiments I did myself.

My last night in Los Angeles came as I was walking back from the hospital. That little girl who'd told me where to find Mouse was playing on the street. I'd learned her name, Sally. Just as I was passing by, she turned to wave at me — her burn had healed nicely.

"*Sally!*" I screamed. Too late. The car hit her, flung her to the side of the road and roared on. I rushed to her side. No breath. Pulse, erratic. Internal organs smashed.

"Oh, kid! There's nothing I can do," I cried to her limp figure. But an answer came as I spoke the words. I looked around and dashed into the alley with the broken body in my arms.

There, in the dark alley, I used my new fangs.

Mouse was waiting for me when we got home. She took one look at the child in my arms, at my expression, made an 'O' of understanding and led the way to the bedroom.

"She'll be okay," I told Mouse as we prepared to sleep for the next day. "She's mending even now."

I looked at my lover. "Tomorrow, we're leaving." Mouse only nodded.

#

And now it is night. Sally was hungry, we fed her rare steak defrosted in the microwave. She is smiling now.

Tonight we leave Los Angeles. Leave the hate, the poverty, the indifference.

Tonight we go home. To Rumania. To all those poor little babies with AIDS.

We care for our own. We'll care for yours, too.

FANTASY

HERE ARE SIX FANTASY STORIES. RHUBARB AND BEETS, THE FIRST IS bookended by RED ROSES, the last.

Rhubarb And Beets

Rhubarb And Beets was written in response to a challenge. The challenge was to write a short story for a charity anthology, Purple Unicorns. So I asked myself, why would a person need purple unicorns? I hope you like the answer!

The elfish girl walked spritely up the path.

"Gran!" she called, stopping for a moment to peer ahead and then starting forward with a skip in her step. "Gran, where are you?"

There was no sign of him in the front of the stone cottage.

"Eilin?" an old voice called in surprise. The doddering old man, steps quick but wobbly, rounded the corner from the back of the cottage. He had a guarded look on his face and then smiled as he spotted the girl. "Eilin, what brings you here?"

"My lady was worried," Eilin replied, peering up at the silver-haired man. "She didn't see you in the garden."

"Oh, I was around back, just pottering."

"Pottering?" Eilin repeated. It was a strange word, like so many of the other words he used.

"Aye, nothing more," Gran replied, gesturing toward the front door. "Come in and I'll put on some tea for ye."

Eilin nodded, not trusting her face. Gran was forever going on about "tea," but it was always hot water poured over strange roots and never quite the amazing brew he made it seem. She glanced back over her shoulder down the path she'd taken. Finding no respite — no signs of her lady mother beckoning her back imperiously — Eilin knew she had no choice but to accept her Gran's offer.

"And what brings you here on such a fair day?" Gran asked as he opened the door to his cottage and bowed her in.

"My lady mother—"

"Ach, lass, that's what *ye said*," Gran interrupted. "I meant the real reason."

The silver-haired man followed her into the cottage, waved her to her favorite seat, bustled about near the stove and came back, beckoning for her to stand again, while he settled in the one plush chair and settled her on his lap.

"Was it the spiders?" Gran asked softly as she lay her head on his warm shoulder.

"No," Eilin said in a half-drowsy voice. Her lady mother said that they kept Gran because he was so good with children. Perhaps it was true: Eilin could never listen to his singsong voice for long before falling asleep on his lap. "Not spiders."

"The prince, then," Gran decided.

"The baby, actually," Eilin allowed. Her brother, the prince, was no longer a pest after she'd discovered that he was more afraid of spiders than she — one night she harvested the worst of them and laid them over him as he slept, curing the prince of any desire to annoy her — which was as it should be.

A whistle from the kettle on the stove disturbed them, and Eilin allowed herself to be manhandled as Gran stood, deposited her gently back on the warm chair, sauntered over to the stove and poured steaming water into a clay pot.

Eilin's nose crinkled as the strange smell came to her. *Another of Gran's terrible brews*, she thought.

How long had it been now? Twenty years? Forty? More? Once his hair had been red, his eyes keen, his face fresh like a new apple. Now it was lined, his eyes were dimming, his hair all white and lanky. Even his body seemed smaller than once it had been, as though time had forced it to curl in obeisance.

Changelings never lasted very long. She'd only just gotten him properly broken in and now he was all worn out and creaky.

The smell shifted and Eilin sniffed again, her eyes open and senses curious. This time Gran's brew did not smell so bad.

Gran came back with two mugs on a tray and set them near the sofa. He scooped Eilin back up, settled himself, and pulled a mug over in one hand.

"If you'd care to try..." Gran offered.

"Of course," Eilin said, never one to refuse a graciousness. She sniffed, took a quick, thin sip and — amazed — her eyebrows rose in pleasant surprise. She took another sip, a bit deeper but only just; the liquid was piping hot.

Gran chuckled at her evident pleasure.

"Rhubarb and beet," Gran said. He took the second mug for himself.

"What's it for?"

"It's for the unicorns," Gran said.

Eilin took another sip. It was always unicorns with Gran. Always the same joke.

"Do you think they'll like it?" Eilin asked, deciding this time to play along.

"We'll see," Gran said, taking another sip. "We'll see."

"Tell me about the unicorns," Eilin said as she'd said most every day she came to the cottage. She sipped her tea and wondered why in the Elvenworld Gran could ever come to the notion that unicorns might drink such brew.

"What's to tell?" Gran teased her.

"No one can see them," Eilin said, repeating his old story. Days and years he'd told her, put her to sleep with his singsong, sad, sorry voice telling her about the unicorns.

"No one can see them," Gran agreed. "Their horns take them from Elvenworld to our world and back."

"They brought you here."

"When I was just a lad," Gran said in agreement.

"And now you're here and you'll never leave," Eilin finished. She leaned back, resting her head on his warm shoulder companionably. "You belong here, with us."

"Forever in Faerie."

"With the Elves and the unicorns, my lady mother, lord father, and the prince, my brother," Eilin concluded. "This is your home and we love you."

"I had a home," Gran reminded her, his voice going soft and a bit hoarse, "and those who loved me."

"Long gone, time slips differently here," Eilin reminded him.

"Drink your tea," Gran said, raising his mug to his lips and draining it impatiently.

For once, Eilin did as he said.

"No one can ever see a unicorn," Gran said to her as she drifted off into pleasant slumber.

#

It was weeks later when Eilin came again. The prince, her brother, had discovered the thorny roses and had tormented her by presenting them to her as a gift, then hiding them in her bed as she slept.

The pricks and pains of the thorns had sent her, crying, to the comfort of Gran's cottage in the distance.

"Gran!" she cried. He had the greatest cures and poultices, perhaps he could pull the sting out of her. "Gran!"

No answer, no movement from the cottage. Alarmed, Eilin picked up her pace.

No sign.

She ran around the cottage to the back, crying, "Gran!"

"Shh!" Gran called from the far end of the garden. "I'm here, no need to shout!"

"What are you doing?" Eilin asked, eyeing the green growth and dirty ground in surprise.

"Just tending my garden, princess," Gran told her, rising from his knees to stand and then bow in front of her.

"My brother, the prince, used thorns!" Eilin cried, raising her pricked palms toward him and then pointed to the gash in her neck and the others on her arms. "He put roses in my bed."

"I can help you," Gran said, nodding toward his cottage. "A bit of brew, some cold water, and you'll be right as rain."

"And how is rain right?"

"It's right when there's a rainbow and the air is clear of dirt and full of freshness."

Eilin nodded. Rainbows were expensive outside of Faerie; her father had the drudges work until they expired to find the treasure required for each rainbow. Gran had once called him too vain for his own good, but Eilin could only think of the pride of the kingdom and the bounty of the Elvenworld. The drudges were only human, lured by the same gold they died to provide, and of no matter to her father, the king, nor even to Eilin herself.

Gracefully, Gran followed her to the cottage and bowed her inside, gesturing toward his comfortable chair. She sat, waiting in pain while he pottered over the stove and set potions to brew.

Presently he was back and had her in his lap again, gently applying his hot brew and holding pressure on her pale white skin until the thorn-punctures closed and the pain went once more.

"Do have you more tea, Gran?" Eilin asked as the last of the pain faded into dim memory.

"Tea?" Gran asked as he put his potions and clothes to one side.

"The purple tea you made," Eilin said.

"Unicorn tea," Gran said in a questioning tone.

"Yes."

"No one can see unicorns," Gran said, half-teasing her.

"The tea was good," Eilin said, feeling her eyelids drooping as the rise and fall of his chest and the warmth of him calmed her.

"The tea will make your stings come back," Gran said. He took a breath, then continued, "Let me tell you about the rainbows."

"There were three that day," Eilin said, recalling his words from so many times before. It was a marvelous story, Gran told it so well, and Eilin always filled with pride at the brilliant trick her father had played.

"Three rainbows and only one with gold," Gran said by way of agreement.

"Fool's gold," Eilin remembered, a smile playing on her lips.

"Fool's gold," Gran agreed. "And the fool was me, parted from friend and family by the faint hope that I could find enough gold to save them —"

"— from the famine," Eilin finished, her eyes now closing. "The unicorn ripped through that day, ripped from our world to yours three times."

"Ripped indeed," Gran agreed, his tone tightly neutral. "But no one saw them."

"Unicorns are invisible," Eilin agreed, closing her mouth at last and snoring gently on the old man's chest.

"Clear as the water they drink," Gran said softly to himself while the little elvish girl slept on.

#

"Gran!" Eilin shouted as she traipsed up the path to the cottage. Drat the man, where was he? "Gran!"

He usually replied by now, doddering out from his cottage or around from the silly garden on which he so doted. He was being slow, and she'd make him bow so long in penance that his back would hurt.

Well... maybe not *that* long.

"Gran!"

No sign of him in the cottage. He was old, Eilin remembered and picked up her pace. Disposing of bodies was something she never liked, and then there'd be the bother of having to find a new human. She sprinted around the corner, looking for him kneeling over some of his silly rhubarb or his beets, but he wasn't there.

His garden opened up on the fields of cloudgrass — the favorite food of unicorns. Gran had insisted on it as inspiration and best location for the sun his plants required.

Every now and then over the years, she'd find him looking at the fields of cloudgrass, waving white and brilliant, watching as clumps were eaten by invisible grazing unicorns.

"What do unicorns eat?" Gran had asked early on when he still dreamed of escape from the Elvenworld.

"They eat cloudgrass and drink clear water," Eilin had told him expansively. "That's why they're invisible."

"And how they can cut between the worlds," Gran guessed.

Eilin didn't know and, as it was inappropriate for a princess to be ignorant, she said nothing, pretending that he was correct.

Eilin gazed from Gran's garden to the field, and her jaw dropped as she spotted the path. She followed it with her eyes, even as she willed her feet into action.

"Gran!" she cried, racing into the cloudgrass fields. She couldn't see him, the grass was nearly taller than her. She'd forgotten that most days when they'd gone into the fields she'd been riding on his shoulders — Gran being her very own special two-legged beast of burden.

"Gran!"

In the distance she heard thunder. Unicorns were racing. She saw lightning where their hooves struck hard ground.

They were stampeding. Soon enough they'd bolt and tear holes between the Elvenworld and the slow world of humans.

Was Gran hoping to catch one? How could he, they were invisible!

"Get on!" a thin reedy voice came to her over the winds and the thunders. "Ride on, go on!"

"Gran!" Eilin cried. "No, Gran, you'll never catch one!" He'd be trampled for certain, unable to see the unicorns, unable to dodge their panicked flight.

"On with you! Thunder and lightning!" Gran's voice, exultant, came over the noises and the cloudgrass.

Eilin remembered a knoll nearby and raced toward it. It was only a few quick strides for Gran but for the little elvish girl it was nearly a hill.

At the top she could see over the cloudgrass, across the fields and — there!

"Gran!" Eilin cried. Oh, the fool, the fool!

He was riding a unicorn, his weak old arms tightly clasped around its neck, his bony legs gripping its withers tightly, and in one hand he held a long-stemmed rose, waving it wildly, striking the unicorn's hindquarters — the unicorn's *purple* hindquarters.

Rhubarb and beets, Eilin thought to herself with sudden clarity. All those years he hadn't given up hope, he'd merely been planning. Oh, clever human!

He'd raised the beets and the rhubarb for the unicorns. Fed enough, the usually invisible hide took on a faint, purple hue. Coaxed with a gentle voice and the sweet and the sour of the rhubarb, it was no trouble to bring one of the unicorns to within hand's reach.

"Gran!" Eilin cried, her thin voice dying in the winds. "Oh, Gran, take me with you!"

The old man didn't hear her.

"Gran!" Eilin cried at the top of her lungs, realizing at last how much she loved the old human. How he'd been the only one to hug her to him, the only one to ever care the slightest about her as a person. "Gran!"

Thunder. Lightning tore through the sky and, suddenly, another strike of wicked electric-blue glow of lightning burst from the purple-veined horn of the unicorn Gran rode.

In an instant, the Void was torn and the far human world sprang into view. The unicorn, goaded unerringly by Gran, leaped through and the tear closed.

A final burst of lightning and thunder rolled through the skies — unicorn and rider were only a dimming memory in the elvish girl's eyes.

Golden

I wrote this story in two parts – on the way up to Seattle and on the way down. I challenged myself to write a story that upheld the notion that "the meek shall inherit the earth."

"How does this sound? *It can never be stressed sufficiently: to anger a dragon is to die. To steal a dragon's gold is to die, to covet a dragon's mate is to die. Death by dragon is swift but not painless, usually involving flames which can melt steel.*"

"I think you could have stopped with the first sentence, Daddy," Golden said. "The rest are merely illustrations of how to anger a dragon."

"And you forgot to mention challenging a dragon to a joust," Elveth said.

"If I mention that then you'll get fewer jousts and less gold," Simon replied. "I thought the idea was to create more challenges."

"The idea is to get more gold," Elveth corrected testily. She smiled at her daughter, adding, "Golden isn't getting younger and she'll need a horde of her own." Her smile faded as she added pointedly, "You're certainly not getting any of mine."

"Of course, mother," Golden said demurely. When Elveth wasn't looking, she shot a pleading look toward her father who shrugged sympathetically.

"Your mother left you quite a nice pile, if I remember," Simon said.

"That's because I killed her," Elveth reminded him waspishly. She flicked a finger at her daughter. "You're not to get any ideas, little miss gold scales."

"Yes mother," Golden replied, dipping her head and avoiding eye contact. Elveth was the sort of mother who would literally rip your head off if she got too angry: Golden had seen it once and needed no reminders — in this she was like her mortal and human father.

In most other things she was the exact replica of her mother. Only where Elveth was a mottled copper color when a dragon, Golden was pure gold —

hence her name. Even when born, she had a beautiful head of fine golden hair and there was no contention over her name.

"She is Golden because she is my gold child," Elveth had said and Simon had wisely kept silent, particularly as, according to his studies, he was the first human dragon-mate to survive through the rigors of a childbirth with a head still upon his shoulders.

Simon and Elveth had often conversed on their daughter's coloring: Simon was convinced that it was protective in nature while Elveth held to the old dragon lore that color predicted flame.

"A pure gold like that will mark the hottest of fires," Elveth had declared with much warranted maternal pride.

At the time, Golden had yet to have her first molt and was still clinging to the forlorn hope that she was not a dragon but, rather, a normal human child. She loved her father as fiercely as all girls — perhaps a bit more so because of her draconish heritage. Simon, because he loved his daughter, hoped that her wish would come true but deep down he was convinced — and secretly relieved — that she would molt and turn into a dragon when she was of age.

There were tears all around when that day finally came and Golden found herself molted into the slim body of a young dragon princess.

"Oh, my dear, you are so beautiful!" Elveth had cried with tears of joy.

"I'm a dragon!" Golden had cried with tears of despair.

"You shall live forever," Simon had said with tears of relief.

"As a dragon!" Golden had wailed. "I don't want to be a dragon!"

"Well, you are," Elveth had snapped, her copper color eyes warming dangerously.

"Ixnay on the agon-dray," Simon had muttered warningly to his daughter.

"But it's true!" Golden cried, flouncing out of their small house and accidentally destroying the staircase, the good dining table, and three large iron pots.

When they had found her later, she was lying on her mother's horde in the deep cavern that was hidden behind their house.

Elveth growled and looked ready to change but Simon put an arm on hers. "She must have a terrible headache."

"Golden, how do you feel?" Elveth asked, primed by her mate.

"My head feels like it's going to explode!" Golden had cried.

"Oh, dear! It's all the magic going around," Elveth had said sympathetically. She turned to Simon. "I should go out and kill more mages to ease the pain of my poor little girl."

"Now, dear, we've had this conversation before," Simon told her soothingly. "The evidence is that magic flows from the sun. The mages merely tame and use it. Ridding yourself of them leaves more magic to pain you."

"At least I've got my gold," Elveth said, moving to join her dragon daughter in the huge pile that spilled from its mound in the center of the cavern. She turned back to smile at her mate. "And I've got you to thank for it."

Simon blushed but said nothing.

"How's that, mother?" Golden asked, her talons digging deep into the pile and spilling it over her like a torrent of pebbles — although these pebbles were mostly gold doubloons mixed with the occasional broken crown or necklace.

"Well, it was your father who realized that knights and princes would wager much to fight against a dragon," Elveth said, glancing slyly at her mate. "And so he arranged it and I've been successfully ridding the countryside of useless knights and worthless princes."

"But I thought Daddy was —"

"Your father, a knight?" Elveth asked with a laugh. She eyed Simon thoughtfully. "Well, he is of the nobility or he would not be a suitable consort for one such as myself but he was a squire when we met and much more scholarly than most." She smiled at him. "The bashful boy was completely taken with me after I'd scorched that useless knight of his into mere ash."

"Sir Girwhed was noble and brave," Simon said in defense of his long lost knight, "but he would not listen to my counsel."

"And that was?" Golden prompted, lifting her snout through a pile of treasure and letting it spill to either side.

"I told him if he fought the dragon, she'd burn him to a crisp," Simon said with a shrug.

"See!" Elveth cried, giving her mate a look of adoration. "He's one of the smartest humans I'd ever met."

"Of course it took a while for our courtship to mature," Simon reminded her.

Elveth laughed long and brassily. "Yes, I recall telling you every night that while I enjoyed our conversations, I was never going to be foolish to transform into a woman just so you could kill me."

"Actually," Simon said, "I seem to recall endless nights of your telling me how quick and painful my demise would be."

"Only after you beat me at chess!" Elveth said, her expression slipping.

"And then she changed into human form," Simon said with a smile that bordered on a leer. To Elveth, he added, "I always knew that you'd be the most beautiful of women."

"Flatterer!" Elveth chuckled. "And, of course, well, Golden dear, you came along."

"And now I'm a dragon!" Golden cried. "And I'll horde gold and flame useless knights to ash just to build my horde!"

"And it had never get bigger than mine, missy," Elveth added warningly.

"Of course, momma," Golden replied shyly.

"How's your headache?" Simon asked.

"Better."

"Then maybe you can change back," Simon suggested.

"Change back?" Golden repeated in wonder. "How do I do that?"

"Close your eyes," Elveth told her. "Close your eyes and think your wings away. Think your pretty scales gone and your beautiful slitted eyes turned back into small golden round orbs. Feel your hair on your shoulders and your body shrink as you become a mere human shape."

It took more coaxing but in twenty minutes, Golden was once again in human form.

"Later, dear, we'll teach you how to build clothes," Elveth promised as

Simon lent his daughter the jacket he'd worn just for the occasion.

#

That had been the beginning of dark days all around.

"Well, I'm learning a lot," Simon had quipped when challenged to find the good in the emotional stew that was two dragon-queens in the same house — one daughter of the other.

Golden would wail about her mother, Elveth would shriek about her daughter, and Simon would spend most of his time trying to perfect his flameproof armor and — naturally — work on creative ways to keep one or the other from escalating things into a firestorm.

"The house is made of wood!" Simon had cried hopelessly at the beginning of their first mother-daughter, dragon-dragon spat.

Not long after the ruins were made of ash.

A year later, Simon was saying, "I didn't know your flame was hot enough to melt brick."

It had been Golden's flame which had reduced their second home to glowing glass slag — much to the surprise of all.

Simon had taken to spending much time in the village tavern — they knew nothing of his home life; thinking him merely a farmer with a wife and daughter but to no avail. It had ended the night Golden had run into the inn crying and a copper dragon had flamed off the roof.

Simon had, at least, earned much respect from the villagers when he'd stood up to the copper dragon and had sent it packing.

Of course, as he knew, the whole family was shortly packing to find some new dwelling — not just because of Elveth's flame tantrum but also because the villagers decided that they were better off without the services of a farmer who spoke to dragons.

They settled many hundreds of miles away in an entirely new kingdom far in the south where, after not too much time, Simon had begun convincing princes in other lands that their greatest glory lay in challenging a flaming dragon in a duel to the death.

Simon also learned much of the ways of daughters and mothers from those willing to share their knowledge — and there were many — and grew more and more despairing for the survival of not just his dwelling, or his hide but of his family.

It seemed like it would all end when Golden, just barely fifteen and far too young for a dragon to go a-roaming, fled the house in a flaming huff which set the far mountains alight.

With the flames marking a clear path back to their home, Simon knew that he and Elveth would also have to move or face uncomfortable questions and other such things — like pitchforks.

"Pitchforks won't hurt me!" Elveth had exclaimed when Simon brought them up.

"I, on the other hand, am not so sturdy," Simon reminded her. She had not been so distracted by the loss of her daughter as to consider the impending loss of her husband unworthy of her concern and so, as Simon had urged, they fled for healthier parts.

Fortunately, Simon was a wise man and had their destination long-planned — when living with two strong-minded dragons, it was practically inevitable that one way or the other they would find themselves relocating — so, even though her family fled in her wake, Simon had the comfort of knowing that Golden would know where to find them.

They were settled into the cold, wet north that was safely far away from their other homes for over two years before Elveth started pining for her missing daughter.

"She's old enough to take care of herself, dear," Simon had staunchly assured her — trying to believe the words that he'd been telling himself for the past twenty-four months.

"A dragon isn't mature until her fiftieth year!" Elveth cried.

"You were forty-five when you ate your mother," Simon reminded her.

"Exactly!" Elveth said. "I'm glad you take my side in this, Simon. If only you had been quicker, she would still be with us."

Simon wisely kept silent. The only result of his reminding his dragon-wife of her part in their daughter's departure would be to have her grieving over the ashes of her husband... and, doubtless, complaining that that was her daughter's fault.

When Elveth had finally dissolved into a flood of heart-broken tears, Simon said, "There, dear, we'll find her. She'll be back, you'll see."

"She'd better," Elveth hiccupped, pushing herself away from her husband, her eyes slitting as she speared him with her gaze. "After all, it's all your fault."

"Yes dear," Simon had said wisely. He then excused himself on the grounds that he needed to get some water. He did not say that he intended to douse himself in it for protection. He was away long enough that Elveth was asleep when he returned, her human body slumped in her chair, head on the table. With a sigh, Simon gently pulled the chair back, lifted her up, and carried her to their bed.

He was still drying himself off, having covered her in their blankets, when he heard wings rustling. He dropped the towel and tore out the front door.

Out of the darkness a golden-haired girl emerged hesitantly.

"Daddy?" Golden asked in a small quiet voice.

Simon raced to her, grabbed her and twirled with her in his arms, his head pressed firmly against her shoulder, his tears flowing unabashed. "Baby!"

They stood, entwined, for the moment that was forever. Then, because even eternity must end, Simon pulled away from her.

"Are you staying?" he said, glancing back to their newest home and wondering how to manage the re-union and its aftermath.

Golden shook her head and her fine blond hair shimmered around her like a gold waterfall. "I can't."

Simon heard another noise rustle in the darkness and quickly pushed her behind him, ready to defend her with his life.

A small, dark-haired, green-eyed woman shrank back from his motions.

"This is Erayshin," Golden said, grabbing his arm and pulling him to a halt. She beckoned with her other hand for the girl to approach.

"Is she —?" Simon asked, his eyes wide in fear.

Golden shook her head.

"Does she —?"

"Yes," Golden said. She gestured again for the girl to join them. The girl stepped forward. She was smaller than Simon, short, and lithe. Her eyes were on his daughter. They flicked to him with worry and then back to Golden with determination. Golden's voice hardened as she said, "They wanted her to marry a prince and she didn't."

"She saved me," Erayshin said, her voice fluid with words learned far away.

"He brought a dowry," Golden said, her voice filled with the sharpness and longing that Simon had first heard so many years before from his dragon wife — the voice of dragon lust.

"There have been twelve more," Erayshin said. An impish look crossed her green eyes and gave Simon the distinct impression that the foreign girl was just as devilish as his daughter.

"I've got a rather nice horde," Golden agreed.

"I asked to come here," Erayshin said, giving Simon a frank — and somewhat terrified look.

Simon had rarely seen that look but he knew all the muscles that caused it. He waved to his daughter. "Why don't you let me talk with your friend for a bit, Golden?"

"I need to stretch my wings," Golden said agreeably.

"There are some nice places to the north — the far north," Simon suggested.

"Thirty minutes?" Golden asked.

"That would be plenty," Simon agreed. His daughter smiled at him, waved at her friend and walked off into the dark. Not long after a beautiful gold dragon erupted into the skies above them and raced away northwards.

"She's been gone two years," Simon said in the silence.

"I met her about six months after," Erayshin said, moving closer to him so that she could look up into his eyes in the gloomy dark.

"My wife — her mother — is inside, sleeping," Simon said, waving toward the house. "I'd invite you in but… well, Elveth is jealous."

Erayshin smiled. "So is your daughter."

"She learned it from the best of teachers," Simon told her with an answering smile. A moment later he said, "Will there be a prince who claims your heart?"

"Will there be a woman who claims yours?" Erayshin responded. When Simon shook his head, she nodded. "I came to ask you how you managed."

"It will be easier for you," Simon told her. "Without a daughter to argue with, all you'll have to —"

"There will be a child," Erayshin said, her hand going to her belly. "I wanted to know —"

"A child?" Simon interrupted in amazement. "How?"

"Golden told me: 'Where there is a heart, there is a way'," Erayshin said. "It took her many months but we found a way."

"The child is hers?" Simon cried.

"Ours," Erayshin said. Her smiled turned inward for a moment. "Just once, she became a male."

"I must write of this," Simon said, preparing to run back to the house for pen and paper.

"Please," Erayshin said, reaching forward and touching his arm for the first time. "I must know — how, what, how —?"

Simon put his other hand over hers. "You have to say yes if you say anything," he said, glad to have this one chance to share his hard-won knowledge with someone. "You must be silent when you want to scream, be obeisant when you want to fight —"

"I can do that," Erayshin said, trying to sound certain.

"You should be ready to move often," Simon warned.

"She has a horde, we know where to go," Erayshin affirmed.

"And you must never stop loving the both of them," Simon said finally.

"How do you do that?" Erayshin said as they heard wings in the distance flapping back toward them. "She's been gone all this time — how did you —"

"And you have to love them more than life itself, love them enough to let them go when they need, love who they want," Simon told her. He moved and brought her close against him, wrapping her into a tight embrace.

Erayshin looked up at him, her eyes wet with tears. "Will you forgive me? For taking her love from you?"

Simon shook his head, his lips quilting upwards. "You could never do that. I will honor you."

"For what?"

"For having the courage to love her."

The wings hovered near the forest, stopped, and Simon turned them to face the darkness.

Golden rushed out into the light, paused fearfully, and then rushed into their open arms.

#

Twenty minutes later, Simon returned to his home, pausing just long enough to watch the gold dragon and her rider wheel overhead and then disappear into the dark night.

He sighed and quietly entered the house, went to the bedroom and crawled into bed with his wife.

Elveth nuzzled against him and murmured sleepily in a combination accusation and comfort with a plain meaning: Where have you been? I missed you.

"Golden came back," Simon told her softly. She tensed against him. "She has a partner, a horde, and a home."

Copper-colored eyes opened and peered up at him.

"They are with child," Simon said, choosing his words as carefully as always. "You're going to be a grandmother."

Elveth was silent for a long while, her eyes closed tightly. When she opened them again, tears streaked from them. "There has never been a dragon who knew her grandchild!"

Simon leaned forward and kissed her tears away. "I know."

Elveth was silent for a moment, then snuggled herself against Simon.

"She's a good child," Elveth murmured before turning to face him directly. "Let's make another."

Simon, wisely, said nothing.

Red

RED is the sequel to Golden.

Drat it all, Simon thought as the copper dragon plunged from the sky, swooped, grabbed him in its forelimbs and soared off into the midday sky in full view of the small village and the farmers in their fields. *We're going to have to move again!*

Elveth knew better.

Elveth was a dragon. She could shape-shift into a human, but at the cost of some very nasty migraines, the pain of which could only be soothed by immersion in a large horde of nice, cool gold—something Elveth seemed to be abandoning as swiftly as their home.

That was the first inkling Simon had that something was very wrong. Dragons spent most of their days collecting gold; they were not known for abandoning it.

Simon's surprise gave away to alarm as Elveth climbed higher and higher, working with all her might to fly as fast as she could. The air thinned; Simon felt himself getting colder and colder. After a while, he realized he couldn't feel his toes . . . or his fingers. Not much later, he suddenly felt very warm and lost all consciousness, his last memory being the sound of wings beating in furious effort.

#

"Simon, Simon!" Elveth cried. "Simon, wake up! This is no time to dillydally."

Dillydally? Elveth never used that word.

"I am afraid that he needs his rest," a suave male's voice intoned slowly. "As I have told you before."

"Well, he has to wake up now!" Elveth said.

At her best, Elveth resolved her anger management with flames and claws. Now, halfway through her pregnancy, her temper was so far beyond control that it could only be measured in astrological proportions. In this case, Elveth's proportions exceeded both the realm of the gods of war and of chaos, nearing half the sky in Simon's internal scale of measure.

"Esteemed Mother, it grieves me to see you so careworn," a young woman's voice spoke soothingly from the doorway. Erayshin: their dragon-daughter Golden's mate.

She approached Simon. He tried to move his arms to embrace her, but they seemed not to work.

Erayshin seemed to sense his movement and pushed herself away from him, leaving one tear falling on his cheek, as she said, "You must rest; you nearly died."

"He didn't," Elveth growled with all the hallmarks of a mortally frayed temper.

"Esteemed Mother, it was not criticism, merely fact," Erayshin said in a quiet voice. "Again, I must give you my deepest thanks that you came here, unbidden, on the instinct that my beloved was in grievous pain."

"Golden?" Simon cried. Something had happened to his daughter, Golden? Something Elveth had felt half a world away?

"She lives, Father," Erayshin said. He felt her small, thin hand grip his wrist comfortingly. "Her heart is broken, as is mine."

"Aleen?" Simon blurted, forcing his eyes to open. Had something happened to his grandson?

In all his years of research, Simon had discovered no other human father who had survived the birth of his dragon child, let alone his child's adolescence. And here he was, not only alive and a grandfather but he hadn't even had to perfect his flameproof armor.

The room spun in his vision, with the brilliant green eyes of Princess Erayshin, his daughter's lover, the only steady thing in the whole panorama.

Forcing himself to focus solely on the red-rimmed whites of Erayshin's eyes, Simon noted the hunger-induced pallor in her skin, saw how her brilliant cheekbones had sharpened with overlong worry and heartbreak.

"Water," Simon croaked.

Elveth was beside him a moment later with a cup of water. She somehow managed to pass it to Erayshin while at the same time moving to one side to raise Simon's torso upright.

Erayshin smiled wanly at Simon, flicked her eyes in gratitude to Elveth, and then tipped the cup against Simon's lips so that he could get a sip of the cool, clear, utterly marvelous water.

The water soothed his parched lips, wet his dry tongue, eased his raw throat. Encouraged, Erayshin tipped the cup more and more until Simon had drained it entirely.

As Erayshin moved away with the empty cup, Simon leaned forward to grip Elveth's forearm.

"Take me to her," Simon said, ignoring the pain in his throat.

"We will have to fly," Elveth warned.

"We cannot fly too high or too long or you will take ill again," Erayshin said.

"Take me now."

#

Not argument but prudence required that Simon be suitably clothed and wrapped warmly, held tightly in Erayshin's arms as Elveth lifted them both into the night sky much later than Simon would have preferred.

Elveth flew lower than her wont but, fortunately, the distance was not great. A mere twenty minutes later, they descended toward a line of hills in the distance, veered sharply around several alarming peaks, and plunged into a clearing that only a dragon could reach. Elveth's great eyes spied a small glow in the distance that no human eye could ever see. She issued a high, piercing, trumpeting cry that echoed throughout the valley and the stars.

No cry answered, but Erayshin was not worried, insisting that before Elveth changed form, she use her dragon's flame to warm up a large flask of prepared wine, which the princess served before they moved to the glowing entranceway of the cave.

The cave's mouth was large enough to accommodate a full-grown dragon, but there were several switchbacks to be negotiated before the glow resolved itself into a large pile of charred coal glittering in the midst of a valley of gold in all forms.

In the center of the yellow valley lay Golden, her brilliant scales dimmed and muted, her eyes closed, breathing ragged.

As the three caught sight of her, they halted in shock.

"Is this any way to greet your mother?" Elveth demanded sourly, recovering first. "You will change to human form immediately and tell us what happened."

The golden dragon lifted her head, gave a pitiful whimper, and burrowed deeper into the gold.

Elveth's lungs heaved as she readied an irate roar, but Simon's hand on her arm startled her.

"Perhaps I'd best talk to her," Simon said, moving in front of his wife and climbing down into the valley of loose gold doubloons, pots, vases, scabbards, crowns, and other hard-won trinkets.

#

"We're here, baby, we're here," Simon said softly as he knelt down near her head. "Your mother knew something was wrong, and she just grabbed me and flew straight here—"

Coins clinked and the ground shifted enough that Golden's eyes peered up through the mound of gold. They flicked toward him, and then there was a cascade of sound and movement as the shapely form of a golden-haired young woman emerged. She threw herself onto her father's lap, arms clutching his waist as she bawled uncontrollably.

Simon leaned forward to wrap his arms around her, patting her tenderly.

The sound of falling coins attracted his attention; he caught sight of Erayshin marching toward him with Elveth only a few paces behind.

Golden heard and raised her head from Simon's lap. Seeing her human mate, she threw herself at her, crying, "'Shin! 'Shin, I'm sorry!"

"Shush, shush now, love, it's okay," Erayshin said as she clasped her arms around her dragon lover. "We'll make it. We'll make it somehow."

Golden's hair shook as she nodded her head against Erayshin's belly.

"I came as soon as I could," Elveth said in a voice that held none of her usual temper, none of her rage, none of her terrible bluster. "Something told me—"

"Mother!" And Golden shot from her lover into her mother's waiting arms. "Mother, please help me!"

"Yes, dear," Elveth said, bowing to touch her chin to the crown of Golden's head, "anything, baby, anything at all."

Golden stopped mid-sob and pushed herself away from her mother, eyes wide with alarm. She glanced down to her mother's swollen belly and then up again, jaws agape until she managed, "You're pregnant?"

"Yes," Elveth said, a small glow of happiness surrounding her, "but—"

"You shouldn't have come!" Golden roared as fiercely as the fiercest of her mother's roars. She pushed Elveth toward the door. "What if something happened to the baby?"

"Then, dear, it would be my fault," Elveth said softly. She did not see the amazed looks on the faces of Simon and Erayshin. No dragon—especially Elveth—ever admitted to fault. In fact, Elveth had spent many years assigning blame to everyone but herself. "But I couldn't stay away when I felt that pain." She paused for a moment and raised her hands, palms up, toward Golden. "You're my daughter."

"Mother!" Golden blurted in gratitude and buried herself once more against her mother's swollen belly.

Simon and Erayshin watched, awed by the fantastic sight of a dragon mother and her dragon daughter united so closely in their love—a sight that none had ever beheld in all the history of the ages. Dragon-children killed their parents to steal their gold, as Elveth had done to her mother when she was less than half a century old.

"Tell me, when you're ready," Elveth said softly to the weeping daughter who clutched at her so desperately.

Simon reached a hand toward Erayshin, who met it halfway with her own, and, together, they moved toward their dragon lovers.

Mother and daughter were enveloped between husband and wife and, slowly, Golden's sobs eased and she began her tale.

"He's only f-f-four," Golden said. "He's always running around, tripping servants, driving everyone nuts and—"

"Shh, that's normal in a child, boy or girl, human or dragon," Elveth said with more wisdom than experience.

"But I yelled at him!" Golden cried miserably. She turned to face Erayshin, her lips quivering as she confessed, "He pulled my hair and I yelled at him and he ran away and . . ."

She buried her head against her lover and broke into tears once again.

"Don't worry, dear," Elveth said, turning a gimlet-eyed glare to Simon. "Your father will find him."

"We've looked everywhere," Erayshin said, turning her head toward Simon.

"Simon is good at thinking of novel solutions," Elveth said, her tone turning closer to her usual prickly snarl.

"And he's been a boy," Golden added, lifting her head to give her father a wan, hopeful smile. "He might be able to follow Aleen where we can't."

Simon, wisely, kept silent.

#

"Your place is beautiful," Simon said as Erayshin showed them around the palace thirty minutes later after a more sedate flight a-dragonback—Simon riding Elveth and Erayshin perched on Golden's sinuous neck.

"It's expensive to keep, but the people expect it of me," Erayshin said demurely.

Golden nudged her in the side. "Don't lie, 'Shin, you love it!"

Erayshin's lips twitched, and she ducked her head in a brief admission.

"Twenty bedrooms, ten chamber rooms—not counting the ballroom or the throne room—two dungeons, a treasury, various offices—and even indoor plumbing," Golden rushed on, grabbing her princess around the waist and giving her a playful hug.

"How come we don't live like this?" Elveth said, casting a fuming look toward Simon.

"I'm afraid, dear, that you failed to marry a prince," Simon reminded her. He did not add that she'd never complained before, being more worried about the size of her gold horde.

"And, of course, Daddy, I think you'll really like this," Golden said as they paused outside a large pair of gilded doors. She waited for a nod from Erayshin and then pushed the doors open with a strength not common in small, golden-haired women—but not at all out of place in grown dragons.

"I'm sure—" Simon began as the doors opened, but he ground to a halt as he caught sight of the well-lit contents. There were windows on two sides with plenty of clear glass to illuminate the room, but it was the other two walls—floor to ceiling—that caused his jaw to drop.

"Books?" Elveth said, her lips twitching in disdain. "By the way you went on, dear, I thought you were talking jewels."

"More than jewels," Simon said in low voice full of awe and desire. "These are treasures beyond compare."

"Mother, you and I may crave gold, but you must not know Daddy if you don't know how much he hordes books," Golden said as she waved them inside.

"Well, I always knew he was a little strange," Elveth allowed, "but I don't recall all that many books—"

"That, dear, is because books burn," Simon said absently, completely oblivious to Elveth's shocked snort. He left her behind as he strolled to the first row of books, his hands outstretched longingly but touching none. He paused to move one misplaced red book onto a shelf and then continued, very much like a gold-struck dragon, from one end to the other, eyes scanning up and down. His stride broke briefly as he caught sight of the rolling ladder that was braced into a metal railing that allowed it to swing to any location on the two walls.

"My father was thinking of adding a set of shelves in the middle of the room but . . ." Erayshin said, her voice breaking in a sniff. Golden's hand went to her, and the princess took it.

"Did Aleen like it here?" Simon asked.

"Oh, Father, he did! There is absolutely no doubt that he has your love of words," Golden told him.

Erayshin confirmed this with a watery-eyed nod of her own.

"Perhaps he'll turn out human," Elveth murmured in what she thought was a quiet voice—at least, until she found herself under the baleful watch of three pairs of eyes. She met them unflinchingly, adding, "Well, I never heard of a dragon who reads."

"There are not so many male dragons that one would know," Simon said mildly, his eyes going back to the books and then to Erayshin. "Would you, princess, happen to know how extensive this collection is?"

Erayshin smiled. "I've read about half of the books here."

"I used to read her to sleep when she was pregnant with . . ." Golden's voice broke, and her lower lip trembled in recollection. She collected herself, and her eyes shone as she said to her father, "I thought maybe the baby would like them."

"I read to you when you were in your mother's womb," Simon recalled, giving his daughter a fond look.

"I thought that was to keep me from eating you!" Elveth complained. She glanced toward her daughter and then back to her husband. "Did you pervert my child with knowledge?"

"You, too, dear," Simon agreed calmly, reaching for her hand and grabbing it with both of his. "I started reading to you long before you were willing to get pregnant."

"And you're going to read to me again," Elveth declared, her eyes straying toward the bookshelves with a different expression.

"Gladly," Simon said. He turned toward Erayshin again. "Perhaps you would lend me some of these marvelous tomes?"

Erayshin glanced nervously between him and fire-breathing Elveth before sending an appealing glance toward her lover.

Simon snorted and nodded. "Don't worry, dear, I completely understand. Books are special places, some of them full of people we would never otherwise meet." He glanced one more time around the library and then pulled himself back to his task. "And, speaking of special people, perhaps we should return to Aleen's bedroom?"

Aleen's room was full of wooden toys, intricate metal men, a comfy, bouncy bed, a wardrobe, an attached commode, and a small shelf filled with books and half-jumbled toys.

"I thought it would be bigger," Elveth sniffed.

"He's only four," Simon guessed. "He doesn't need that much space."

A snort of disagreement came from the boy's two mothers. Simon and Elveth turned to look at them.

"He's a boy!" Golden cried. "He runs all over the place!"

"The other day he was in the market, all covered in dirt," Erayshin added with equal measures horror and pride. "He was playing dragon with the boys in the market."

"We need to find my grandson," Elveth reminded them pointedly.

"So, princess, you were under a great deal of pressure to acquire a prince and produce an heir, and . . ." Simon said, bringing himself back to the problem of the moment.

"And then the dragon came," Erayshin said, smiling at Golden.

"Ah," Simon said. "And then?"

"When we discovered that we—" Golden said, breaking off with a troubled glance at her partner.

"When you discovered that you were in love," Simon said for her, "what then?"

"Well . . ." Golden began.

"It was her idea," Erayshin said. She grabbed Golden's arm and turned her toward her parents, adding with pride, "Tell them."

"Well, when we decided that we were going to stay together," Golden began slowly, "we talked a lot about all the problems that created."

"A dragon with a human?" Simon guessed.

"A princess without a prince," Erayshin corrected. "Or an heir."

"Ah," Simon said, deflated. Her gestured for them to go on.

"Well, Golden figured it out," Erayshin said. "We were lying together one night—"

"I'm not sure I want to hear this," Elveth protested.

"We were in my lair, and I was a dragon," Golden said. A tear appeared in the corner of her eye. "I'd decided that I had to tell Erayshin everything."

"I'd met her first in human form, of course," Erayshin agreed.

"I had a migraine and was in a terrible mood," Golden admitted. "Nothing we could think of would work and, of course, with my gold lust, things were only worse."

"We have a very nice treasury," Erayshin informed them. "Lots of gold."

Elveth's eyes grew bigger.

"So, Daddy," Golden said, turning to her father, "I thought about how you taught me to break down a problem."

Simon smiled.

"And I said: 'We've got to convince them that you had a lover, get you with child, and somehow keep them from being worried about me,'" Golden recounted. "And that was that!"

"Pardon?" Elveth said.

"Well, Mother, it was simple," Golden said. "All I had to do was become a man."

"That's all?"

"After that, well . . . Erayshin and I could . . . you know . . . and then once she was pregnant, we could introduce her prince and then have the dragon slay him," Golden said in a flow that halted and rushed as her face reddened with embarrassment.

"So you were a man twice?" Simon asked, brows knotted as he absorbed her words.

"More than twice," Golden admitted reluctantly. She glanced toward Erayshin. "She didn't catch the first time, so we had to try again."

"I much prefer you in your natural form, love," Erayshin told her.

"But how did the dragon slay you?" Elveth asked. "You couldn't be both."

"Oh, that was easy!" Golden said. "Erayshin and her prince went out to the countryside, and the dragon descended upon them there."

"So Erayshin came back with a tale . . . ?" Simon guessed.

"Erayshin came back with the two horses, chased by a flaming dragon, and told the tale of how her love, the prince, was devoured trying to save her," Golden corrected with a smug look.

"Ooh, nice!" Elveth crowed, glancing toward her husband as if to ask why he had never come up with such great deceptions.

"So, after that, with the princess pregnant, what happened?" Simon gently prompted.

"Well, since I was known to be the late prince's sister, I stayed to console his bride, and we were shocked to discover that she had been blessed before his savage loss." Golden practically preened with pride. "She begged me, as her only contact with his memory, to stay at her side through her confinement."

"And since then, what with Aleen being such a handful, there was no question that I would need help raising him," Erayshin added in conclusion.

"I see," Simon said. "But are there those who would prefer a stronger throne?"

"Oh, no!" Erayshin said. "You see, they fear the dragon."

"Pardon?"

"Oh, that was Erayshin's idea," Golden said, beaming, "she gets to tell."

"Well, we knew that there would be a dragon seen from time to time—"

"There had to be; I had to get to my horde," Golden quipped.

"—so we decided that I would consult my library to learn the best way to deal with the problem," Erayshin continued.

"And what was that?" Elveth demanded.

"I discovered a way to bind the dragon to me," Erayshin said with a sidelong look toward her lover. Golden snorted in agreement. "And so now, I have demonstrated that I have control of the dragon and that it guards our borders—"

"A lot of hard work, too," Golden put in with feeling.

"—in return for which, we leave it to its devices," Erayshin said.

Simon frowned in thought then nodded. "That will work as long as no one discovers that dragons can take different forms."

"You have to be careful that no one sees you change," Elveth agreed.

"Most of the time, we tell people that I go to visit relatives in my homeland," Golden said. "Once, though, we had Erayshin ride me over the palace to show her control over me."

"Wise," Simon said. "So, who else is in your palace?"

"The servants," Erayshin allowed with a dismissive shrug. "Cleaners, cooks, chambermaids, the like."

"And the guard?"

"We have a small guard which reports directly to me," Erayshin said, drawing her small, lithe frame upwards in a noble stance. "The captain served my father and his father before him. His honor is impeccable. Besides," she added with a sad smile, "he loved Aleen like his own."

"Did everyone love Aleen?" Elveth asked.

"Yes!" Golden retorted hotly. Simon raised an eyebrow and her fierce look cooled. "Oh, he could drive the staff to swearing with his antics, but he had the sweetest green eyes—"

"Green eyes?" Simon repeated.

"Very green and very mischievous."

"Green eyes are uncommon here, aren't they?" Simon said, pressing forward over his undiplomatic blunder. "Are there enough guards to search the town?"

"No," Erayshin said, her shoulders slumping. "Our guard is small to save on expenses. Mostly my people are happy, cheerful, and well-fed. And they have a dragon guarding them." Erayshin smiled at her lover. "Golden's been a wonder in bringing pirates and brigands to bay."

"And my horde's increased accordingly," Golden said with a larcenous smile.

"My people are not the sort to revolt," Erayshin continued, "and I work hard to keep it that way."

"Especially now," Golden agreed. "They've got a handsome prince with lively green eyes, his mother's dusky skin, and her dark, straight her. He's got a slim frame, like his mother, but we're hoping he'll fill out to a handsome man."

"If we can find him," Elveth murmured, but only Simon heard her.

"And you're hoping that Aleen will inherit his father's abilities?" Simon asked. "A dragon prince?"

"We don't know," Golden admitted with a troubled look. "He might just be a normal, human boy."

"But we're hoping," Erayshin chimed in loudly.

"A dragon prince," Simon repeated softly to himself. "It would be difficult," he said at last, "but, with the right upbringing, not impossible."

"Are we the right parents?" Golden said with a whimper. "Is that why he ran away?"

"He asked us about his father," Erayshin noted.

"What did you tell him?" Simon asked.

"He would hear it from the servants," Golden said, "so we told him the story of the dragon and the prince."

"What?" Elveth demanded hotly, eyes once again glowing with fire. "Whatever possessed you?"

"But—but—" Golden said, her troubled eyes turning in appeal toward her father.

"I'm afraid your mother is right," Simon said. "Any young boy—particularly a prince—would insist upon avenging his father, finding his killer and destroying him."

Princess and lover turned to each other and said, "Oh."

"So he ran out of the city?" Elveth said.

"Where would he go?" Golden shook her head. "We never told him where the battle took place."

"He could have learned in the market," Erayshin allowed in a miserable tone.

"But no one said that they'd seen him that day in the market!" Golden protested.

"Tell me where!" Elveth demanded.

"What?" Golden replied, confused.

"To the east, in the valley beyond the hills, just by the river," Erayshin said. "There's a tree and a shady spot."

"I'll go look," Elveth declared, moving swiftly toward the nearest door.

"You'll be seen!" Simon cried.

"Think of something," Elveth told him. "I'm going to find my grandson." As she sprinted away, she could be heard muttering, "Poor boy! Alone for days! And thinking that dragons . . ."

"Should I go after her?" Golden said, glancing toward the exit.

"Alone for days," Erayshin repeated miserably to herself. "He must be hungry, starving!"

"Little boys do eat," Simon agreed, trying to think of some way to sound comforting.

"He was always leaving food around," Golden said with a sniff. "The ants were everywhere."

"Ants?" Simon said. "There were ants in the library."

"Of course," Golden agreed. "He'd never clean up so there were ants everywhere."

"Who fed him?"

"We did," Golden said. "And he was always getting treats from the cooks, or anyone else he could wheedle."

"Ants in the library," Simon said to himself. He turned his head in that direction. "Ants!" His tone changed and he raced out of the room.

"Father!" Golden cried, scurrying to catch up with him. "What is it?"

"The ants!" Simon said. "I saw some on the shelves when I put that book back!" He was racing now.

Golden could keep up with him, but Erayshin was smaller, her legs shorter, so Golden slowed to match her. "Drat the man!"

"Actually," Erayshin said in a thoughtful tone, "he might be on to something."

#

Simon was way ahead of them when they arrived, his eyes scanning the library in the dimming light of late afternoon.

"Father—?" Golden began just as Simon let out an exalted shout and pulled a red book off the shelf.

"Ants!" Simon said, scanning the shelf where the book had lain. "I knew it!"

"But, Father," Golden began slowly. "I don't see—"

"Come here, both of you," Simon commanded. Golden's spine stiffened but she moved to his side, the result of years of parental influence. Simon gingerly turned toward them, the book cradled in his arms. He looked at Erayshin. "Princess, have you ever seen this book before?"

"It's beautiful," Erayshin said with a gasp, extending her arms in an invitation to take the red book.

Simon passed it to her with a slight bow and the under-voiced imprecation, "Careful."

"The eye!" Golden cried as she caught sight of the book, leaning over Erayshin's right shoulder. "Look at the eye!"

In the center of the red book was one, wide, green eye.

"Aleen?" Golden breathed in wonder. "Aleen, is that you?"

"Can he do that?" Erayshin said, glancing up to Simon and then over her shoulder to Golden. "Can you do that?"

"No," Golden said, shaking her head. "I couldn't change until I reached maturity."

"I know of no dragon in the second generation," Simon said slowly. He pursed his lips firmly. "It is not beyond possibility."

"So what do we do?" Golden demanded.

Simon shook his head.

Erayshin, with a sob, clasped the leather—soft leather with deep grooves as though of dragon scales, warm leather as though blood flowed through it to provide heat—tightly to her chest. "Baby, my baby!"

#

"Do something!" Elveth demanded of Simon when, hours later, she returned from her fruitless journey and met them at the entrance. "He's your grandson, do something!"

"He must be starving," Simon said to himself.

"He must have a terrible headache," Erayshin said. She saw Golden start and explained, "You always get them when you transform and, worse, he's starving."

"And scared," Golden added in a small voice. "He must be very scared."

The green eye on the cover of the book was stuck open.

"We need to bring him to your horde," Elveth said. "The gold will soothe him."

"Now?" Golden asked.

"Right now," Simon said. "And get something for him to eat."

"As a dragon?" Erayshin asked, her dusky skin going lighter.

"As a boy," Simon said.

"Um . . . my horde?" Golden said, casting a worried glance toward her mother, then seeing the look on Erayshin's face, she said, swallowing her worry, "Okay."

#

They took off from the top of the palace in the dark of the night, two dragons—one gold and one copper—with two riders and one red book.

Golden's horde was not far away. Simon brought a sack of fruit and nuts. Erayshin held the book tightly to her chest the whole way.

"I'll start a fire," Simon said as they entered the darkened cavern with its floor gleaming of dull, cold gold. Surprisingly, Elveth moved to help him.

"You must keep him warm," Elveth said as they left princess and daughter clutching the book.

Simon noted that her orders were superfluous; Erayshin would not let the book out of her grasp.

They found a nice dell in the mountains of gold, and Simon quickly got a small fire going, which they surrounded, hands outstretched for warmth.

"I feel better," Elveth said, leaning against her husband with a sigh. "Gold is so friendly."

"I didn't understand," Erayshin said, "until Golden showed me."

"The effects of gold on genus draco is understood more apocryphally than in reality," Simon agreed.

"Well," Golden said, moving closer to her lover, "we're here. My mother, who killed her mother for her gold, is here in my secret domain."

"I was here before," Elveth reminded her waspishly. "And you never met my mother."

"Elveth, Golden," Simon said in a warning tone, "we're here for Aleen."

"Yes," Golden agreed, her eyes flashing briefly toward her mother before dimming again as she looked toward Erayshin and the book. "Now what?"

"I think we need to understand a very confused little boy," Simon said slowly. "Aleen is only four. He was told that his father was killed by a dragon." Golden's eyebrow arched in warning. Simon ignored her and moved away from Elveth, closer to Erayshin. He beckoned for the book. Reluctantly, the princess relinquished it.

"Aleen, how did it feel to ride on a dragon?" Simon asked, addressing his words to the book. "Were you afraid? Your mother was holding you tightly, so I know you weren't cold."

"Daddy—" Golden started, but Simon silenced her with a raised hand.

"Would you like to be a dragon, Aleen?" Simon said. "I know that your mothers said that your father was killed by a dragon." He paused a moment. "That's a lie. You know it now, because you saw your mother change into a dragon and back."

"Simon—" Elveth's tone was nearing anger, but Simon glared at her and she subsided, muttering, "I hope you know what you're doing."

"No one knows what I'm doing," Simon said. He turned his attention back to the red book with the green eye. "My name is Simon, and I'm your grandfather. The copper dragon, Elveth, is mother to your mother, Golden. Your mother turns into a beautiful, golden dragon with white flaming breath. Your mothers are very much in love with each other. So much so that your dragon mother, Golden, turned herself into a man so that they could have you.

"Think on that, Aleen," Simon continued. "Your dragon mother loves your human mother so much that she would change in any way to please her."

Golden sniffed.

"They want to be together for as long they live," Simon said. "But people fear dragons, and people think that a princess can only marry a prince." Simon's tone made it clear how silly he thought both of those notions were. "They love you very much. They want to be your parents for as long as they live, too."

Simon felt a twitch in the lump he held.

"It's scary, being human," Simon said. "It's just as scary—in a different way—being a dragon."

The book twitched. In the dim light, Simon thought he saw the green eye go wider.

"Your mothers think that you decided to slay the dragon that killed your father," Simon continued. "They thought that you had run away to do that. So your dragon grandmother flew off to see if she could find you." Simon glanced toward Elveth with a smile. "She cared so much for you that she risked being found or even killed."

The book quivered. It definitely quivered.

Simon stroked it soothingly.

"But you are smarter than that, aren't you?" Simon said with a touch of pride in his voice. "You wanted to learn how to slay a dragon before you went after it, didn't you?"

The green eye twitched.

"So you went to the library," Simon continued, "and you looked at all the books and you ate and you got tired and you fell asleep."

Silence.

"You fell asleep and dreamed about killing dragons," Simon guessed. "Something scared you, and you dreamed about the books—about the book that would tell you what you wanted to know."

"He did?" Erayshin said in a small voice. "Oh, baby!"

"And when you woke, you found yourself in this book," Simon said, his voice growing warm with awe and sorrow. "You were the book that had all the answers to your questions."

The book quivered.

"But you're scared," Simon said. "You're scared because you can't read the words written on the pages. You can't learn how to slay dragons because you've learned that you really are a dragon."

"A red dragon?" Elveth cried. "He's a red dragon!"

"A red dragon with green eyes," Simon agreed, stroking the leather cover gently. "A hungry, scared, red dragon with green eyes."

"But I couldn't change until I was twelve!" Golden protested.

"That," Simon said, "is because you are not your son." He smiled down into the green eye. "Because even though, my daughter, you are a most beautiful golden dragon and a sweet, golden-haired girl, you were never nearly half as mischievous as your green-eyed son."

Simon leaned down and stroked the red book lightly. It quivered. Simon suddenly looked up at his daughter and his eyes were gleaming.

"But you're just as ticklish!" Simon cried with joy. He ran his fingers all over the red book, and it was suddenly quivering and shivering and giggling and—

—then there was a little boy wriggling in his lap, his face contorted with laughter.

"Ah!" Simon said. "Aleen, I believe!"

"Am I really a dragon?" Aleen asked, trying to recover from his giggles.

"A very ticklish dragon," Simon assured him, leaning in to tickle the green-eyed boy into another uncontrollable bout of laughter.

"With two mothers?" Aleen said, gasping for breath. "I have two mothers?"

"Indeed, my prince, you do," Simon said. He handed the giggling boy over to his parents, adding, "And they love you very much."

Golden and Erayshin raced to him. Golden was the first, but she paused to let Erayshin grab him and then wrapped herself around the two of them.

"You know," Elveth said as she looked happily on the reunited family, "this is rather nice place." Her eyes glinted as she glanced around the gold-filled cavern. "I could get used to it."

Golden turned her head toward her mother. "This is my gold, Mother."

"You can share," Erayshin told her firmly.

Golden turned back to her lover, eyes wide.

"I'm afraid—" Simon began, but Erayshin cut him off.

"They need the gold to shelter from the magic and help their headaches," Erayshin reminded him, glancing toward Elveth and then back to Golden. She said again, firmly, "They can share."

"You heard her, Golden," Elveth said, squatting down to grab a handful of coins and let them spill slowly through her fingers. "We share."

"Yes, Mother," Golden said, leaning across her son to kiss her lover on the lips. When they broke free, she added, "I learned long ago that Erayshin is always right."

"Which makes her nothing like your father," Elveth observed with her usual waspish tone.

Simon suppressed a smile, nodded in gratitude toward Erayshin, and—wisely—said nothing.

The Dragon Killer's Daughter

The Dragon Killer's Daughter was a story I wrote for an illustration by the amazing Larry Elmore for The Writers Of The Future, Volume 33

Paksa was ten when the painter brought it: it was a grand painting with Calbert in his dark armor and the dragon in her red scales. Calbert paid for it handsomely, grumbling as he passed over the gold piece even though Paksa knew he was rich.

"Is it not a good painting, Father?" Paksa asked.

Calbert hung it over the mantelpiece and stood back, admiring it. He shook his head. "No, it's very good."

"Then why grumble so over the price?"

Calbert made a face which Paksa matched with big eyes of her own. She was old enough to know that Calbert could rarely resist her big eyes.

"All this will be yours one day," he told her, spreading his arms expansively to include the house and lands. "This and all the gold you need."

Paksa couldn't understand why they needed gold. Oh, it was useful to buy things—even pretty things—and all the villagers were eager to get their hands on it. Of course, there were fewer villagers these days than there had been. That had been another of Calbert's grumbles. He had said it after calling her in late in the afternoon and she'd found him watching another family, their belongings loaded on their cart, trudging next to their oxen, own their way out of the valley.

"Pretty soon, no one will be left," he had muttered. It had been a grumble but Paksa wasn't sure if he'd sounded unhappy or pleased. He'd glanced at Paksa when he'd said it and then had shaken himself, as if to dislodge whatever thought was troubling him. It must have worked because he called for Cook the next moment and ordered their dinner.

After a few weeks, Paksa started noticing some odd things about the painting.

"Didn't you say that it was all green here in the valley?" Paksa asked her father one day. She pointed at the painting. "That painting makes it look like the village is today, all brown and dusty."

"The painting is exactly what I asked for, child," Calbert grumbled at her.

"But the green –"

"Exactly as I asked for," Calbert cut across her. He turned away from her as though afraid to meet her eyes. Paksa barely heard him as he continued, "One day, you'll know."

Paksa wasn't sure but she knew her father well enough to know when to stop. She resumed her playing. Father had given her a pile of gold pieces of her own to play with. She rarely did anything with them, preferring instead the battered old dolly that her nurse had left her so many years ago. If she ever did play with the gold, it was only to build a castle in which she would put the dolly.

"Why make a castle?" Calbert had asked when he noticed.

"To protect her from the dragon," Paksa had told him easily. "That way, the dragon will eat the gold and not her."

"Dragons don't eat gold, child," Calbert had said.

"What do they eat, Father?" Paksa asked.

Calbert's eyes grew dim, wary. "They eat people when they've no other choice."

"And when they have a choice?"

"They thrive on the raksha," Calbert said, gesturing to the outside of their sturdy stone-built keep. Paksa knew that he would have preferred something smaller but the villagers had insisted on building it for him. It really wasn't much of a keep: a house with two stories, four bedrooms (two unused), a wall around the enclosure against which the stables were nestled and an archway leading into the bare courtyard. The house itself fronted on the main street–the only street of the village.

"Why don't they come here then?" Paksa asked. "Everyone says that the raksha are driving out our cattle and destroying our land. There must be plenty for a dragon to eat!"

Calbert nodded. "Plenty."

Paksa returned to her game.

#

On her eleventh birthday, Calbert told her the story. He told it to her every year but this was the first year he told it to her in the dining room, gesturing toward the painting.

"The dragon came after the raksha," Calbert said. "But we'd driven most of the raksha out of the valley so it soon had nothing to eat."

"And you fought it," Paksa said, pointing up to the painting. "You rode your horse, Monique, and wore your armor and carried your sharp sword, Vengeance."

"But first the villagers had to send away for a warrior," Calbert said, bringing them back to the start of the story.

"And they had to send far away because no one had fought a dragon before," Paksa said.

"No one had fought a dragon and lived," Calbert corrected her.

"Where did they send first?" Paksa asked. She knew the answer but there was a marvelous cake waiting for her for dessert and she knew that the story had to be finished before the cake was cut. If she didn't ask, there was a good chance that Calbert would spend ages before getting to the point.

"They first sent to the city of Varoir—"

"The nearest city."

"The nearest city," Calbert agreed. He smiled and wagged a finger at her. "You know this story too well. Just remember, one day you will have to tell it to others."

A chill ran down Paksa's back. Calbert had never said that before.

"Why, Father?"

"Because I won't be here forever," he told her, his eyes warm with affection. "You'll have to take care of yourself then."

"Shouldn't I marry?" Paksa asked.

"I don't know if that's what you want, child," Calbert said. He seemed about to say more but, with another firm shake of his head, dismissed it.

"What happened at Varoir, then?" Paksa asked, deciding that the story was safer than what had caused her father's shudder.

"The squire of the city told them to go to the duke," Calbert replied.

"And the duke was found in Suvre by the sea," Paksa said, her mouth breaking into a grin as she saw her father's eyes glow with approval.

"So you can tell the story yourself, can you?" Calbert teased.

"Please, it's better when you do it," Paksa said. She thought she might have to use her big eyes on him but he merely snorted and nodded in acceptance.

"Next year, maybe, you'll tell me the story," Calbert said. He took a breath and continued, "The Duke, His Grace Davignon, sent me."

"He sent his best warrior," Paksa said.

Calbert shook his head. "I wish I could say so."

"You are the best, Father!" Paksa proclaimed stoutly.

Calbert smiled at her and reached over, tousling her fine black hair. For a moment they were both still in surprise–rarely had Calbert shown such affection. He pulled his hand back, as if burnt and examined it as if it were a stranger's.

"Why did His Grace send you, then, father?" Paksa asked when the silence grew too severe.

"He sent me because he could afford to lose me," Calbert told her brusquely.

"But you were his son!" Paksa protested.

"I was his youngest son, the last of seven and the death of my mother," Calbert said, his eyes going moist.

"Your father was mean!"

"He was strict," Calbert said. "He was fair as well. He gave me my horse, my saddle, my armor, my sword. He told me that what I earned I could keep."

"He expected you to die," Paksa declared. She was old enough to hold her own opinions. Calbert gave her a sharp look. She'd never said that before.

"He expected me to die," he agreed.

"But you didn't," Paksa said.

A smiled twitched Calbert's lips. "No, I did not."

"What did you do, Father?"

"I rode here to little Levinar, and met the townsfolk," Calbert told her.

"They fed you a great feast, more than they could afford," Paksa said.

"They did, for they wanted to show their gratitude to His Grace for having sent one of his own sons to protect them," Calbert agreed.

"And there was a young lass, one of the prettiest–"

"What?" Calbert exclaimed. "Wherever did you hear that?"

"And you lay with her–"

"Paksa!" Calbert burst forth from his great chair, eyes flaring with anger, face contorted in rage. "What made you say that?"

"It must have happened," Paksa said in small voice. "Else how did I get here?"

Calbert slowly sat back into his chair. He dropped his head to his hands and said nothing for a long while. When he looked up again, he said to Paksa, "Enough of the story. This is your birthday, let us cut the cake and get you to bed."

"Yes sir," Paksa said numbly. They ate but she couldn't remember the taste of the cake afterward.

#

Paksa was careful around her father for the next few months, as they neared winter, fleeing when she could, remaining respectful and silent when she couldn't.

One morning, however, Calbert asked her, "Why did you say that?"

"What, Father?" Paksa asked as dread certainty supplied the answer.

"That I'd lain with a woman?"

"Well, that's how children are made," Paksa said with a shrug. "So I thought that–"

"Never mind," Calbert told her. He finished his plate and rose from the table. "It didn't happen like that."

Paksa wondered why he lied to her. Everyone in the village–except for those still in diapers–knew how children were made. They saw the same thing with horses, cattle, pigs, dogs, even the rare cat. Paksa had learned about it from the nurse before she'd left.

So Paksa was born, like all the others in the village. And that meant that Father had been with a woman—married her in all proper ceremony, Paksa was sure–and the result was herself.

There were so many unanswered questions! What was she like? Did she die in childbirth? Paksa could imagine a raven-haired woman like herself, with piercing green eyes and a ready smile, her face beaming with pride as she wed the famous dragon killer–no, wait! Father hadn't killed the dragon when they were wed. Babies, Paksa knew, took nine months to grow. But father hadn't come to the village more than a fortnight before he'd killed the dragon. Did he bring someone with him? No one had ever said so. Maybe because it was all too sad. Where *had* he meet her mother?

#

There was hardly anyone left in the village. The wild raksha, insatiable, had ravaged the herds. The herds themselves had stampeded too often and destroyed the few crops that had been planted. The village was no longer green. Soon it would be abandoned.

"We have gold," Calbert had told her when she'd mentioned it. "Gold is all you need."

You? Paksa thought. Perhaps Father meant the two of them but Paksa was worried. She went to her room, with her dolly and the castle of gold.

Dolly–little Nina–was not very interesting that afternoon. For once, Paksa felt drawn to the gold. It would protect her, Father had said. It was all she needed. She ran her fingers through the pieces, feeling their coolness, smiling as the pieces were warmed by her touch. Idly she stacked them, pushed them down, rearranged the pieces into a lattice-work; spread them out in a mosaic across the wood floor. She stepped on them, feeling their coolness on her bare feet in contrast to the warmth of the wood.

Father was right! Why did she ever want to play with a silly dolly anyway when she had gold to comfort her?

#

"Father, can I have more gold?" Paksa asked that evening. Calbert gave her a probing look. "It's just that there's not enough to build a proper fort."

"I will see what I can do," Calbert said. "I have some set aside in the storeroom."

Paksa smiled at him sweetly, dimples and all. "Thank you, Father."

The gold, a small casket, thrilled her for the rest of the month. But by month's end, Paksa was asking for more.

"Your birthday," Calbert told her. "I'll get more for your birthday."

"But that's months away!" Paksa whined. She flounced up from her chair at dinner and raced up the stairs to her room.

Calbert found her later, lying on her bed. It was covered with coins.

"Please, father, I need more!" Paksa told him, making her eyes as big as they could get.

"You'll have all you need come your birthday," Calbert promised.

"But that's two months away and I need it now!"

"It won't be ready," Calbert said. "You must wait."

Paksa pouted at him. Sighing, Calbert left her.

#

Monique, Calbert's aging horse, died the next morning. She'd been ravaged in her stall by a raksha. Calbert spent all day digging a huge ditch in which he placed her corpse; dragging it there with two oxen he'd borrowed from the last farmer. He came in to dinner covered in sweat and mud.

"We'll have to start making our own dinners," Calbert said when they'd finished. "The Marquettes are leaving."

"They are?" Paksa said. "But who else is there?" Her eyes got wide. "Couldn't you pay them more, Father?"

Calbert shook his head. "The raksha killed their last cow; they want to leave before it kills their oxen, too."

"Can't you do something about the raksha?" Paksha shuddered at the thought of them: teeth, claws, fangs–leathery killing machines that tore, ripped, savaged.

Calbert shook his head. "There are too many of them. If I were even to find a lair and kill the dam, I'd only be killing one of many families here in the valley."

"Maybe we should leave, too," Paksa said.

Calbert shook his head. "No, I promised to steward over this land. My brother gave it to me when my father died."

"How will we survive, then?"

"We've a few hens and some crops," Calbert told her. "We'll manage."

"The raksha eat hens. The raksha eat horses. They eat cows. What eats raksha?" Paksa mused.

Calbert's eyes lit for a brief moment and then he shook his head. "The only thing I know that eats raksha is a dragon."

For a moment, Paksa wondered what it would be like–to be a dragon.

#

The village was a ghost town. Paksa had the full run of it but she stayed in her room. Calbert worked in the fields most days and they ate, if sparingly, on his produce. He seemed older, frailer, than Paksa had ever seen him.

He seemed as if he were ready to die. He was waiting only for her.

"We should leave," Paksa said on the night before her birthday. "There's no one here and the raksha will kill the last of our hens soon enough."

"We'll stay," Calbert said. "It is the least I can do." He met her eyes. "Tomorrow is your twelfth birthday. You are growing into a fine young woman." Paksa felt her cheeks flush red. "We will go for a walk, tomorrow. It is time I showed you."

"Showed me what, Father?" Paksa asked. But Calbert shook his head and refused to meet her eyes.

That evening, as she was in her bed, Calbert knocked and entered. He knelt beside her and stroked her shoulders. "I hope I have been a good father to you."

"You have, Father," Paksa assured him, trying to hide her alarm at his actions, clenching her blankets tightly. Calbert rarely touched her and never came to her when she was in bed.

"Tomorrow we will get your gold," Calbert told her. With that, he rose and strode out of her room.

Your gold.

It was a long time before Paksa fell asleep.

#

Paksa was up with the first rays of the dawning sun. Even so, she found father dressed and sweaty from his morning's labors. He gestured her to the table which was bare except for a small handful of hard boiled eggs and a pitcher of water.

"It will be enough," he told her when he caught her eyeing it warily. After a moment, he added, "Today you are twelve."

"And we get to see my gold," Paksa said, her heart suddenly beating faster in her chest.

Calbert nodded and closed his eyes, seeming weary from his labors.

Paksa jumped out of her seat and hugged him. "It will be all right, Father."

"I hope so," Calbert replied, raising one hand to cover hers. After a moment he moved it away again and made to leave his seat. When he was standing, he looked down at her – but not so far down as he had done years before – and said, "Are you ready?"

He was answered with a bob of her head and a huge smile. He gestured toward the hall and the front door. Before they left, he strapped on his sword, Vengeance.

#

"How far is it, father?" Paksa asked, eyes darting around on her swiveling neck to seek into all the nooks and crannies they passed. The land was parched, dusty, barren. Paksa knew they were going to where Calbert had slain the dragon. Sometimes she would skip ahead and then come racing back, one hand extended as though she would grab him and tug him forward.

"Not much further," Calbert said. He was breathing heavily. His eyes seemed full of sorrow.

"This is from the painting!" Paksa exclaimed as they crested a small ridge and took in the distant cliff. She twirled back. "This is where you killed the dragon!"

"Aye," Calbert said, pausing to take in the view with pain etched on his face. "This is where I did the evil deed."

"You saved the village!" Paksa cried in fervent defense. "What else could you do?"

Calbert did not reply, trudging along to a point halfway to the cliff where he found a boulder and sat on it. Paksa came back to him. She stood, looking up expectantly.

"This is where I tell you everything," Calbert said wearily. He gave her a troubled look. "It was a terrible thing I did."

In the distance a raksha's cry echoed against the hills.

"It was a dragon!" Paksa cried. "It was killing villagers!"

"Aye, it did," Calbert agreed. "There were no more raksha to eat."

"You did what you had to do, what you were commanded to do," Paksa said, stoutly defending him. Her eyes wandered over the terrain and, in a lower voice, added, "Where is the gold?"

Calbert stirred and moved away from her uneasily. "Close."

"It was the dragon's gold, right?" Paksa said, moving closer, her eyes gleaming with passion.

"It was," Calbert said. "I took a little afterward but the rest is there, in her lair."

"Her lair?"

Calbert nodded. His eyes grew clouded as he remembered. "I met her here on this field. She didn't flame me when we fought." He snorted. "If she had, I would not be here talking to you."

"Not all dragons breathe fire, right father?"

Calbert narrowed his eyes at her. "How did you know that?"

Paksa shrank away from him for a moment before regaining her courage and saying, "I heard you talking with that bard."

"Bard?" Calbert repeated to himself, brows furrowed as he strained to recall. Then, he said, "That was years ago!"

Paksa nodded. "I wanted to know all about dragons and you and that bard were so secretive."

"I didn't want you to know," Calbert said. "I wanted to keep you innocent until..." he shook himself. "It's time now."

"So she didn't flame and that saved you," Paksa prodded.

"She could flame but she chose not to," Calbert said. He paused as a pair of rakes called in the distance. They were getting closer. He judged them still far away. Even so, he loosened the strap on his sword. He smiled at her. "Did you know that dragons can change their shapes?"

"They appear as old hags and try to steal gold," Paksa said, repeating the stories she heard from the other village children when they were trying to scare each other. "And when they get it, they eat the children."

"The bard told me many things," Calbert said vaguely. "He sent me parchments and scrolls over the years and I learned much about dragons." He smiled secretively and met her eyes. "I know more about dragons than anyone in this kingdom, maybe even others."

"Why, father?" Paksa wondered. "You killed the dragon."

"I killed a dragon," Calbert said. A ripping, tearing roar cut through the air and Calbert turned in alarm. "Raksha! Run, child, run!"

"Where?"

"Follow your heart!" Calbert called after her, climbing to the top of the rock and drawing his sword. He gestured toward a place in the distance. "It's not far!"

Paksa could have stayed, could have argued but ... she had no sword. And Calbert had given her an order.

If there was one thing she was good at, it was running. And Paksa ran, ran with all her might. The wind tore at her, pulled her hair out in a stream behind her. She was nearly flying.

The sound of the raksha dimmed behind her but not before she heard one of them give a yip of pain. Calbert had got one!

There was a small opening in the hill. Paksa made for it. As she neared, she discovered that it had been disguised, cleverly hidden by stones rolled in front of it. The opening was much larger, large enough for a horse when all the rocks were removed. Paksa had no time to ponder on that before she was inside. She ran around one twist in the track and then stopped dead.

Gold! Mountains and hills of gold! More gold than she could imagine. The sounds of the raksha were distant in her mind as she climbed up the nearest pile. It was cool, it was brilliant—and it was all hers!

With a laugh, Paksa poured the gold over her head, rolled in it, buried her body under it. It was marvelous! It was wonderful!

And suddenly Paksa was scared. Her body felt different, wrong. She was hungry. Terribly, terribly hungry. She was ravaged by the hunger. She wanted meat, bloody and red, she wanted to tear into it, gorge on it and–

A raksha's cry startled her. She replied with a roar of her own. She burst out of her gold cocoon and raced down the pathway.

Only ... she didn't run-she flew!

She glanced toward her arms and found wings. Wings!

She was out into the daylight now, out of the cave, even as the gold called to her. The raksha had cornered something, someone.

Father! She tried to call out but produced only a roar. The raksha paused in surprise and she was upon them, tearing, rending, destroying. She would protect him. She would save her father.

Two, three, four raksha fell to her fierce onslaught. One snagged its claws in her wing she roared with pain but a moment later, she had darted her neck toward it and impaled it on her sharp teeth. She landed then and chewed the dying beast off her, pausing only to swallow hastily before turning back toward the others.

She could find none. She turned again, her hunger sated, to the crumpled mass on the top of the boulder.

"Father!" And suddenly Paksa could talk again, she could run toward him.

He was broken and bleeding. His sword was broken in half: one part was sticking out of a dead raksha; the other was still in his hand.

She reached him and knelt beside him, cradling his head in her arms.

He opened his eyes at her touch. "Daughter," he croaked. He raised a hand up toward her but was too weak to reach her. She grabbed the hand with one of her own and dragged it to her breast.

"Here," she told him. "I'm here."

He smiled. "I saw you fight. You were magnificent. As gorgeous and deadly as your mother." His smile faded and he coughed once, with blood flowing freely from his lips. "I gave you this valley. It is free from humans. It is full of raksha. You have your gold. It is all I can do to make amends."

"Father!"

But Calbert did not answer.

In the distance, Paksa heard the cry of raksha gathering for another assault. Gently, she lay his head back on the ground. She stood for a long moment, staring at him before rising to her feet.

Her belly grumbled. She was hungry. The raksha howled again. A feral smile crossed her lips. Good! Let them come! She was hungry for revenge, and thirsting for blood.

Paksa leaped from the boulder and in an instant was airborne, her wings flapping strongly toward her dinner. Later, she would bathe in her gold and cry for her parents.

But that was for later. Now, Paksa, dragon-daughter, reveled in her newfound wings.

Small Bird's Plea

I wrote this story for Jonathan Strahan's marvelous anthology, The Book Of Dragons.

Jing-Wei told her stomach not to bother her. She would feed it when she could. It rumbled in discontent and she gave it a sour look: *Stupid stomach! Did I not say I would feed you when I* could?

But I'm hungry noowwww! her stomach seemed to grumble.

Jing-Wei shook her head and pressed on, convinced that in a few moments her legs would voice their woes. Probably, they would say: "We've been walking for aaages!"

If it is not for me to complain, it is not for you to complain, either, Jing-Wei told her organs. She pressed on. The path was climbing upwards. Perhaps that was a good thing.

Jing-Wei was not the largest person in her village – indeed, her name meant "small bird" – but she was the only one who went. She was the only one who could go – the rest were fighting the demons or had already lost the battle.

She rehearsed what she would say: Oh, great masters! Please hear my plea! My village and valley are beset by demons and without your aid all will die!

No, that wasn't good enough, she thought to herself, absently wiping a bead of sweat from her brow. The air was thick with steam, but at least it was not the freezing hail that had battered the valley's crops and driven the bravest men to cry at the torture inflicted by the demons. Of course, the demons liked to hear such things; it encouraged them.

Lau De had warned the others not to moan so but they had paid no attention to her. When the hail beat her down and they found her body in a ditch, they had said, "See! The witch is dead! She was no match for the demons!" Why they hadn't said "Oh, we are such fools! Here was a wise woman and we did not heed her!" Jing-Wei didn't know, except perhaps that they were such fools.

And so, the last witch in the village had perished along with their crops. As if in celebration, the freezing hail had stopped and the harsh heat had begun. The village went from sopping, icy wetness to hot, crackling dryness.

The villagers were starving, the valley was dying. The demons were winning. And soon they would feast on the corpses of those too weak to move.

Unless Jing-Wei could get help. She tried to get others to come with her; she begged her best friend, Mei-Xing, whose name meant Beautiful Star, but she was too afraid. "My parents say I can't play with you," Mei-Xing had told her in a small voice, her eyes cast to the ground.

"I don't want to play!" Jing-Wei had snapped back. "I want you to come with me, so we can free the village of demons!"

"If I can't play, what makes you think I can come with you?" Mei-Xing asked crossly. "My parents say there are no demons. It is just the weather. They are going to pray to the god of spring for aid and we will be saved."

"I saw the demons, Mei-Xing!" Jing-Wei told her. "I saw them just like Lau De herself!"

"My parents say Lau De was moon touched," Mei-Xing said with a frown. "They say that she was touched by all the moons in the sky and that was why she was blinded at night and fell into the ditch, hit her head, and drowned."

"There was a hailstone the size of her fist right where they found her!" Jing-Wei exclaimed, unable to believe that her friend hadn't understood the import of that. "It was the hailstone that killed her. The hailstone sent by the demons because she knew them for what they were."

Mei-Xing absorbed this silently. Finally, she repeated, "My parents say I can't play with you."

She had even less luck with the boys, but she only asked them because everyone said a little girl was not supposed to travel alone.

"You are a silly girl, go away!" Zhang Chen told her, grabbing a clump of cold, wet dirt from the drying river and throwing it at her. Jing-Wei was small but she was fast and dodged the clumsy boy's clod easily.

"I must help my parents in the field," Yang Dingbang apologized.

"Your name means 'protect the country' and yet you won't help?" Jing-Wei asked in astonishment.

"It's just a name," he said with a melancholy shrug. He made a shooing gesture at her and smiled, "Fly away, little bird!"

"Small bird!" Jing-Wei corrected. "Get it right, you oaf!"

Yang Dingbang's smile remain fixed. "Fly away!"

In the end, Jing-Wei had not flown, although she could easily imagine how her arms would have complained if they were wings: I have to lift all of you up into the sky and you won't even feed me? How horrible is that?

Fortunately, Jing-Wei had only arms and they weren't complaining . . . much.

#

Her arms started to complain not long after because the climb had become so steep that she had to use them to haul herself up the densely wooded hillside.

I will not cry! I will not break! she told herself forcefully, as her legs tried to stop moving and her chest couldn't stop heaving with the effort and her stomach was an empty hole inside her.

Another step. Another foot.

The air was wispy with fog as she climbed higher. She shivered, realizing that she had left the dense humid jungle beneath her, leaving the sweat to chill on her skin. There were fewer and fewer trees and no undergrowth to slow her down. Now all she had were rocks and a steady drizzle of cold rain falling over her through the breaks in the treetops.

But there! Just above her she could see the pass, flanked by two mountains. Soon she would see what was on the other side. And she knew, just knew that this time she would find what she was looking for.

Oh, great masters! Please hear my plea! My village and valley are beset by demons and without your aid all will die!

She reached the crest of the hill, crawled through the saddle between the mountaintops and stopped, looking down at the expanse spread before her.

It was beautiful: the valley unfolding below her. Beautiful with verdant grasses and tall trees.

Jing-Wei's heart fell – it was just like the last three valleys she had seen. She would have to go through it and climb the mountains beyond. Her lips trembled at the thought. Wasn't there a limit to how far she could go?

She forced her legs to carry her forward, looking for any signs of something she might put in her mouth to silence her stomach.

As she reached the end of the saddle and prepared to descend into the valley below, a shape moved in front of her. It was a lion, and it looked just big enough to eat a small bird like herself.

It sat on its haunches and regarded her silently. It was a girl lion. Jing-Wei knew that the males had manes – "just like peacocks, always strutting!" the Lau De had told her when she had spoken of far off places and strange creatures.

At least it isn't an elephant, Jing-Wei thought. As if to torment her, behind the lion a large shape loomed up. She saw the large ears, heard the slow lumbering thud of its movement, and her eyes grew wide. "Lions will eat an elephant if they can," Lau De had told her once on a dark night when they were guarding the village. "But sometimes they become friends."

Friends. The word echoed in her head. She started moving forward, her hands open but by her side. She looked up to the elephant and back to the lion.

"It's only me," Jing-Wei said. "I'm a little girl from a village beset by demons and I need to ask for help in the cave of miracles."

The lion took two steps toward her. The elephant thumped up a moment later.

"I heard a song about you," Jing-Wei offered, telling her heart to stop racing, her lungs to stop pulling in air so fast. "Would you like to hear it?"

The lion took two more steps forward.

Jing-Wie licked her lips.

"Lion, lion, eyes so bright

What do you see in the night?

Elephant, elephant far away

Do you hear what we all say?"

They looked unimpressed.

"Okay," Jing-Wei said, "I made that up just now." She looked at the lion. "Did you like it?"

The lion took two more steps forward.

"My surname is Li and my personal name is Jing-Wei and I am far from home, looking to help my village as it is beset by demons," Jing-Wei told them, her lips trembling with sorrow. She looked at the lion. "I am only little and I haven't eaten in three days, so I would make a very poor meal, if that's what you are thinking." She looked at the elephant. "I don't know how you got so high but you walk further with each step than I can run and I envy you that." She glanced down at her legs and gestured toward them. "I have only these little sticks of legs and they are very, very tired from all the walking." She looked up at them again and, tired as she was, her eyes filled with tears. "But can't you see, my village needs help? I am the only one who can still see the demons. The others are all lost, praying to the wrong gods or they've just given up and are preparing to die." She took a ragged breath. "Please, won't you let me pass? Please let me find the cave of miracles?"

The lion moved to one side and the elephant stepped forward. Jing-Wei's eyes widened in growing horror as the elephant grew larger and larger as it came up to her. She closed her eyes in fright.

"Please! I have to help my village!" she mumbled in terror. The lion roared and Jing-Wei trembled. She heard the soft thuds of the lion flowing toward her.

And something inside her snapped. She opened her eyes, crouched down, brought her hands in front of her, ready to fight. "If you eat me, I will claw you from the inside!" she roared. "I will fight my way out of your belly, rip you asunder, and then I will find the cave of miracles and save my village!"

"Or you could just climb on my shoulder so that I can lift you up to the back of my friend," the lion said.

Eyes wide with wonder, Jing-Wei did as the lion said. She found herself comfortably perched between the wide shoulders of the huge beast which turned and began lumbering down into the valley below them. The lion with a growl that might have been a chuckle, loped off to disappear in the forest.

"The lion talked," Jing-Wei said to herself in surprise. "I didn't know lions can talk."

"They can't," the elephant replied. "Only demons can talk."

Demons? Jing-Wei's mind trembled at the notion. "Where did she go?" Jing-Wei said allowed.

"She went to get you some food," the elephant replied.

"If only demons can talk . . ?"

"Yes," the elephant replied, "I'm a demon."

I'm riding a demon! Jing-Wei wailed. She made herself as small as possible on the top of the elephant's huge back, waiting for whatever end would come. Tears streaked her face but she did not cry out loud for she would not give the demons the pleasure of knowing they had destroyed her.

A soft sound caused her to open her eyes and she looked around to see the lion with a wicker basket in its mouth standing behind her on the elephant's back.

"You must eat," the lion said after she lowered the basket onto the elephant's back near Jing-Wei.

"So you can eat me?" Jing-Wei asked in a small voice, all she could muster in her despair.

"Well, certainly if you do not succeed in your quest," the lion allowed. "But you'll need food for strength. Your journey was long and the longest part is in front of you."

"In front of me?"

"In the cave of miracles," the lion said. "You are here to plead for your village, are you not?"

"Yes," Jing-Wei admitted. Suddenly beyond all caution, she added, "But you're a demon, why should you care?"

"Not all demons are the same," the lion told her. "Isn't that true with people?"

"Yes," Jing-Wei agreed slowly. Her stomach rumbled loudly and the lion chuckled.

"Eat, little bird!" she said, nudging to the basket toward her. "You're no good to either of us, starving."

"Small bird," Jing-Wei corrected absently, looking at the basket and eyeing the contents warily. "Is the food poisoned?" The lion shook her head. "Or enspelled?"

"It is safe and good for humans to eat," the lion told her. "Chicken and ginger over rice."

"Any garlic?" Jing-Wei asked, moving carefully to grab the handle of bag and creep it toward her.

"Of course," the lion agreed. "And vegetables. Fresh." The lion nudged the basket closer the child. "There's warm tea, too."

Jing-Wei opened the cloth that wrapped the insides of the basket and discovered that the contents were exactly what the lion had said.

"Lion, what should I call you?" Jing-Wei asked in a small voice.

"I am a lion, why do you ask?"

"Demons have names and I have manners," Jing-Wei told her primly.

"Well then, well-mannered child, you may call me ATO Nightingale," the lion replied.

"ATO? Is that Japanese?"

"It's an old, old word that has no meaning anymore," the lion replied, mouth wide displaying many bright white teeth. "It means Assistant Tactical Officer."

"It is important?" Jing-Wei asked. When the lion shook her head, Jing-Wei persisted, "To you, at least?"

"Very much so," the bass voice of the elephant snorted. "She'll never let me forget it, not even after a thousand years!"

"And you, kind elephant, what should I call you?"

"I am PO Knightsbridge, little one," the bass voice replied. "PO means Petty Officer which means the ATO – who holds the rank of lieutenant – outranks me."

"She tells you what to do?" Jing-Wei said. The elephant bobbed his head up and down.

"Well," the lion –ATO Nightingale – mumbled, "I do ask for your opinion, Brandon."

"Oh, we're on a first name basis again, are we Paula?" the elephant said.

The lion said nothing, looking meaningfully at Jing-Wei. "Eat, child. We'll be there soon enough."

"I asked your names that I might thank you for showing such kindness to one so lowly as my poor self," Jing-Wei said, bowing her head to touch the rough skin of the elephant's back. "I, Li Jing-Wei, do give you thanks for this fine meal."

"Taste it first, before you say that," the elephant said with a deep rumble.

"You are welcome, little one," said the lion. "Eat up, life's always best on a full stomach."

Jing-Wei bowed once more and sat, cross-legged on the elephant's back, untying the bundled cloth and laying the meal out in front of her. The rice was in a separate bowl. There was a strange container which held the hot tea and had a cup on top. The hot chicken, ginger, garlic, and vegetables were in another container. She found some odd metal things but fortunately had no trouble identifying some very nicely fashioned chopsticks.

She drank a sip of tea – it was heaven! And then she could hardly contain herself as she transferred warm ginger chicken to the rice and gobbled it down.

She burped – and blushed – not certain if she was being rude to her animal hosts or expressing the highest of praise. She raised the last of her tea in the cup in a salute to the lion and drained it gratefully.

"I'm ready to die now," she said quietly. "My stomach thanks you for this last meal."

"Don't be so quick to plan your funeral," the lion told her. "The valley is wide and we've got hours yet before you get to the cave of miracles."

"Have you been there?" Jing-Wei asked in amazement. "Do they let animals inside?"

"It'd be hard to stop us," the elephant said with another bass chuckle. "And humans are animals too."

"Really?" Jing-Wei asked. "Are we just like chickens and pigs?"

"No more than an old man is just like a baby," the lion chided her.

"Are demons human, too?"

"That depends on the demon," the elephant rumbled.

"Most aren't," the lion said. "They're native to Jade."

"Our planet under the Jade Emperor?" Jing-Wei said.

The elephant snorted and lion looked amused, her amber eyes gleaming. "Something like that," the lion allowed. After a moment, she continued, "What do you know of how you came here?"

Jing-Wei blushed. "I am told that my father and mother wanted a child and they did–" she found she couldn't continue, she was so embarrassed.

"Not that!" the elephant rumbled loudly. "She's asking how humans came to this planet, do you know that, child?"

"Lau De said that long ago the Emperor flew in a sky chariot across the night sky and brought our forefathers here," Jing-Wei said, glad to be on less worldly matters. "But the chariot was assaulted by the lesser demons and the demon Murphy—"

"Murphy!" the elephant bugled. "Poor lad never gets a break!"

"Go on," the lion urged Jing-Wei.

"—and crashed in the mountains," Jing-Wei said, pointing to the distance and then frowning as she realized that they were now in those mountains.

"Here, in fact," the lion agreed.

"The Emperor and all the lesser gods were grievously injured, beset by the greater demons but they managed to fight them off and plant man on the planet, blessed be their memories," Jing-Wei finished.

"We would have left if we could have," the lion added in sad voice. "We didn't want to fight with another intelligent species."

"It was their planet. If they had just let us leave, we could have found another," the elephant agreed.

"We made a peace—"

"Hmph!"

"—and we honored it," the lion said.

"But the people forgot and expanded wherever they could," the elephant said. "And so, broke the treaty."

"Both sides broke the treaty, there is blame on both sides," the lion said.

"Are you saying that my ancestors were wrong?" Jing-Wei asked, trying to hide her horror at the thought. "That they stole our valley from others?"

"That's what we'll find out," the lion said.

"And we'll punish their children and their children's children for their deeds?" the elephant asked, shaking his head. "Is that the right way?"

"Should we continue to break the treaty instead?" the lion asked. "And if we do, how will we survive?"

"You're a demon, aren't you?" Jing-Wei asked. "How can you die?"

"We can be killed, just as easily as a human," the elephant said sadly. "There used to be hundreds of us. Most of us died protecting the treaty or defending humans."

"And now?" Jing-Wei asked. "How many are there now?"

"A few," the lion said in a whisper.

Jing-Wei's eyes grew wide. "Just you two?"

The elephant shook his head.

"Look up," the lion said. Jing-Wei did just as a giant shadow crashed toward her. With a shriek she flung herself into a small ball on the elephant's back.

"Shahbaz!" the lion cried. "You didn't have to scare her so!"

"But it's fun," a voice replied.

"You can look up, child," the lion said, "it's just Shahbaz."

"The bird?" Jing-Wei said, daring to open her eyes. A giant bird was perched on the back of the lion. Who was sitting on the top of the elephant. Beside Jing-Wei.

"An eagle," Shahbaz corrected, grooming his feathers with his beak.

"And you're a demon, too?"

"I'm no demon, child," the eagle scolded. "I'm just as human as the other two."

"So, you're a demon," Jing-Wei concluded.

"Words, just words," Shahbaz grumbled.

"But if you are all demons, then what is in the cave of miracles?" Jing-Wei asked in a small voice.

"Memories," the lion said. "Just memories."

"And power," the elephant added. "Lots of power."

"At least until the captain returns," the eagle said.

"If he returns!" the elephant rumbled.

"PO! You shouldn't say such things!" the lion chided.

"With all respect sir, it's been what—nearly a thousand years?" the elephant said. "They could have gone to Earth and back five times or more!"

"The ship was damaged," the eagle said judiciously.

"And the demons attacked when it took off," the lion said. "It could have slowed them down. They could have stopped for repairs."

"Or they could have been lost and will never return," the elephant said.

"We agreed on all that already, I don't see why we're rehashing it," the lion said.

"Because it's one thing waiting for help and another taking care of our descendants," the elephant said. A moment later, he added, "Sir."

"What else can we do?" the lion said miserably.

"We lost Sens fifty years ago," the elephant said. "By the law of averages, we won't last another two hundred years. And what then?"

"This is a conversation that should not involve a child's ears," the eagle said to the others.

"My ears are just as good as yours!" Jing-Wei protested to the eagle. She peered closely at the bird. "Where are your ears?"

"He doesn't have any," the elephant rumbled. "Which means that your ears are better than his."

"And your ears are the best," the lion said testily. "But the point remains."

"How many people have come to the cave of miracles?" the eagle asked. "How many since Sens?"

"In my village, the cave of miracles is a myth," Jing-Wei said. "I only know about it because Lau De told me."

"Who is Lau De?"

"She is the witch who took me in when my parents died," Jing-Wei said, trying her best to sound matter-of-fact. "She was the last witch of our village."

"I told you that witch idea wasn't going to work!" the elephant rumbled.

"And what would you say?" the lion asked. "That we're the avatars of lost astronauts?"

"First you'd have to explain avatars, then astronauts, and by the time you're done they've either died of old age or fled in fright," the eagle said.

"You talk a lot," Jing-Wei said. Silence fell and she bowed her head. "I mean, it seems so to me."

"Out of the mouths of babes!" the eagle cackled.

"I am not a babe!" Jing-Wei protested. "I am small for my size."

"And how old are you, little one?" the lion asked.

"I'll soon have seen the five seasons six times," Jing-Wei said.

"That'd make her coming up on seven," the eagle said after a moment. "And she walked all the way here on her own."

The three demons were quiet for a long while. Finally, the lion said, "You should rest now, child. We'll wake you when it's time to eat again."

"Tomorrow?" Jing-Wei asked in surprise. She didn't think that the cave of miracles was all that far away—particularly as fast as the great elephant was striding.

"No," the lion said with a chuckle.

"How many meals do you eat in a day?" the eagle asked, peering down at her.

"One," Jing-Wei said.

"Most people eat three," the elephant said.

"They must be huge to eat so much!" Jing-Wei cried in awe.

"Well, at least bigger than you, that's for certain," the elephant agreed.

"Rest," the lion said. "And when you wake, if you're hungry, we'll feed you."

"I'll keep watch," the eagle said.

"And check on our guest," the lion said. "I don't like leaving it alone for long."

"It?" Jing-Wei asked, sitting up and suddenly alert.

"You are not the only guest to come in to our valley," the elephant rumbled.

"You caught a demon?" Jing-Wei guessed. The lion nodded while the eagle leaped into the sky and flapped quickly out of sight. "You caught a demon and you didn't kill it?"

"It is hard to talk to the dead," the lion said.

"You can talk to the dead?" Jing-Wei said in awe.

"No, child, the LT is just being humorous," the elephant told her.

"'LT'?" Jing-Wei repeated.

"It's short for lieutenant," the elephant explained. "Have you heard that word before?"

"The king's men, some of them are lieutenants," Jing-Wei said, eyeing the lion warily.

"When did you see them?" the lion asked.

"They come to collect tithes for the king," Jing-Wei said in small voice. "Once a year. And sometimes they take people, too, to the war."

"And you don't like them," the elephant guessed.

"When they come, we don't eat," Jing-Wei said. "And the prettiest girls and the strongest boys—we try to hide them."

"Lovely," the lion murmured.

"You can't be everywhere, LT," the elephant said. "And at least they've still got monarchy."

"About what we'd expect, given everything," the lion agreed. "Still . . ."

"Like you said, sir, you can't talk to the dead," the elephant said.

"Things were better when the Emperor ruled?" Jing-Wei guessed.

"The captain was never—" the lion began patiently.

"Things were better," the elephant said. The lion's amber eyes glowed with a fire that was quickly extinguished.

"Sleep, child, you need your rest," the lion said. She moved to the side of the elephant. "I'll patrol." And she leapt off to the jungle below.

"She's right, you know," the elephant said. "You should rest."

Jing-Wei curled up into a ball, settled herself between the elephants slowly moving shoulders, and closed her eyes.

Sleep overwhelmed her and brought her wondrous dreams.

#

"Have you figured out where this valley is, then?" a voice echoed in her ears.

"It is about thirty klics from our base," another voice, the lion's, replied.

"Thirty klics, no matter which way, is within the treaty," another voice—the elephant's—said.

"If it's to the east, that'd put it at the front lines," the eagle's voice said.

She was in the cave of miracles. Lights like rare jewels surrounded her, lighting ghostly images of people dressed in strange clothes. There were hundreds of them. Most looked like ghosts. Were they all ghosts?

"And our guest?" the first voice asked.

"We're trying to communicate but we've had no luck so far," the lion replied.

"Which is odd, considering that we had no trouble communicating before," the first voice said.

"Captain, if I may—" the eagle spoke up.

"Yes, Chief Buhari?"

"We still don't know much about their organization, about how they communicate among themselves," the eagle said. "It's possible that this demon never learned our language."

"Which means that it knows nothing of the treaty," the 'captain' said.

"Exactly, sir," the eagle agreed.

"Which means we've got a whole new ballgame," the elephant rumbled.

"And the plan of 'educating' observers seems to have failed," the captain said.

"I don't know, sir," the lion said. "I know it was my plan but I think that the fact that this child tells us that the demons targeted the village witch may mean that they've been more effective than we imagined."

"It's not their effectiveness I question, lieutenant, it's their survival," the captain said.

"Yes, sir," the lion said. "I see your point."

"There has only ever been a few of the colonists we could ever trust with the truth," the captain said.

"Sir, we never really told them everything," the eagle said.

"I know," the captain's voice agreed. "But we had good reason."

"You mean that if we told them that their best hope is to rely on the avatars of dead spacers, I'm sure we all agree," the eagle replied.

"That doesn't change the fact that we're failing," the elephant said. "We're down to three functionals and we don't know how much longer we'll last."

"So you're saying that we must recruit more," the captain said. "From among the population."

"From the witches and those we can hope to trust with the truth," the elephant said.

"I think we should start them young, when they're not set in their ways," the eagle said.

"You want to start with this child," the captain said.

"She's the only one who made it here in the last century," the elephant said. "If we're going to recruit, she's our only candidate."

"Except for the demon," the lion said.

"Yes," the captain's voice was frosty with disapproval. "Keeping it is a treaty violation, lieutenant."

"We haven't decided on keeping it, sir," the lion defended herself.

"But until we can communicate with it, we think it's dangerous to just let it go," the eagle said. "After all, it knows where our base is."

"And if we lose this, we've lost everything," the lion said in agreement.

"I agree," the captain said.

"Sir, sir!" a new voice cried out in alarm.

"What is it?"

"The girl—she can hear us! She's about to—"

\#

Jing-Wei opened her eyes and remembered her dream. "We're here, aren't we?"

"How—?" the lion said.

"Where's the captain?" Jing-Wei asked, looking around a huge cavern that was just as she'd dreamed it. Except there were no ghosts, only the three animals. In the distance she spied a large ball of blue light which flickered to brilliant whiteness in a pattern that seemed like ripples on the water when a stone was bounced on it. She pointed to the ball. "The demon's in there, isn't it?"

"Lieutenant, how'n hell does she know so much?" the elephant asked.

Jing-Wei ignored him, realizing that she was on the ground, on soft blankets just as she'd dreamed. She got up and moved toward the blue bubble. She approached it and reached out a hand.

"Wait!"

"I've never touched a demon," Jing-Wei said. To the bubble she said, "Are you the one who killed our witch, Lau De, my teacher?"

"It can't be," the eagle said. "We captured it weeks before you arrived."

"How many weeks?" Jing-Wei asked. "The demons started their worst attacks about two weeks ago."

"About two weeks ago," the elephant said, nodding toward the demon.

"That's data we didn't have," Shahbaz the eagle said to the lion who had a horrified look on her face.

"So, is this demon important to them?" the elephant asked.

"And how is it important?" the eagle added. "It could as easily be an escapee as an envoy."

"Did you kill Lau De?" Jing-Wei said, looking through the blue luminosity that held the demon to the dark shadow that was the demon itself. Her face hardened as she continued, "Let me tell you about Lau De. She raised me when my parents died. She raised me like her own. She raised me to know about peacocks and lions and elephants. She told me the stories of the great dragons, the most powerful beasts in the sky. She taught me to look up to the stars and wonder at the beauty that surrounds us all.

"And then you demons killed her," Jing-Wei finished, surprised by her own tears. "You murdered her with a hailstone and left her to drown in a ditch by the shivelrat weed.

"Is that all you demons are? Murderers?" Jing-Wei asked. "Do you care about us at all?"

"Child–" the lion said slowly.

Jing-Wei shushed her with a backwards flung hand and a shake of her head. "Demons have taken my laughter, my happiness, and given me in return only bitter tears."

Inside the blue jail, the demon turned a shadowy green. Was that remorse or exultation?

"You want to kill us all?" Jing-Wei shouted at the thing. "Very well," she said, thrusting her hand through the blue barrier. "Start with me. I am no one now. You have taken all that I ever was."

"Wait!"

"No!"

"Lieutenant, she's breached the barrier!"

The words were flung at Jing-Wei but she did not hear them as she entered the blue energy that held the demon.

"Kill me," Jing-Wei said, now peering at the green ball shape that was the demon. "Because I have sworn to kill you. You killed Lau De, you destroyed my village. You should die!"

Life, the word sprang in her head. Kill ends life?

"Yes," Jing-Wei said. She did not stop to wonder how she could hear the demon in her head. She moved toward it, wishing she had a knife or something that could kill demons. Lau De had said there were ways but that no one in the village had the tools.

Life is good, the demon thought inside her. No more life is bad. We want more life.

"You killed Lau De," Jing-Wei said. "Do you take our lives for your own?"

Some do, the demon thought. Are afraid. Don't know. Don't want to try.

To change.

"Jing-Wei?" the lion's voice came muffled through the energy barrier. She sounded worried. "Are you all right?"

"The demon speaks in my head," Jing-Wei said.

"It does?" the elephant boomed in amazement. "And you understand it?"

"Of course!" Jing-Wei shouted back.

End life bad. Life forever. End . . . Jing-Wei got the impression that the demon was looking for a word and could not find it, finishing instead with: not life.

"When you kill, people are gone forever," Jing-Wei said.

Gone forever, when kill? The demon said in her head. She got the impression that the demon meant that it would be gone forever when Jing-Wei killed it and that people were gone forever when the demons killed them.

"Gone forever," Jing-Wei agreed.

Forever is now, the demon said.

"Stupid demon!" Jing-Wei swore, diving toward it. She hit it and flew backwards, stung by something that bit her and left her skin feeling odd.

"What did it say?" the lion cried loud enough that Jing-Wei heard her.

"It said that 'forever is now'," Jing-Wei repeated.

"That doesn't make sense," the eagle muttered. "How can that be?"

"Sounds rather Zen," the elephant said. "Like everything is in the moment."

"Did it say anything else?" the lion asked.

"And why did you fly back like that?" the elephant added.

"Are you okay?" the eagle said.

"It said lots of things about life and death," Jing-Wei said. "And I flew back because it bit me. And I'm going to kill it."

"Bit you?" the lion repeated.

"We read a surge of static electricity," the eagle reported. "It might have just zapped her."

"Why didn't you kill me?" Jing-Wei asked, flexing her hand where the 'bite' had hurt the worst.

No kill. Kill is forever. Life is forever.

"Life isn't forever," Jing-Wei said. "People die."

Not we people.

"We've killed you, I know we can," Jing-Wei said, wondering if, perhaps, there was no way she just on her own could kill this demon.

Yes, the demon agreed. Many people are dead.

"You killed my people," Jing-Wei said.

Your people? We people. The demon seemed confused.

"We're people," Jing-Wei said.

"Oh! Semantic mismatch!" the lion cried. "Jing-Wei, it may be that the demons think that they're the only people!"

"Well then, they're stupid!" Jing-Wei snapped back. "Tell me how to kill it."

"We don't want to kill it," the eagle told her.

"That's because you're demons too," Jing-Wei shouted, showing her despair. She was trapped with a demon she couldn't kill and she'd been led here by demons who were going to eat her. She was doomed, her village was doomed—Yan Jingbang, his brothers, sister, and parents; Zhou Mei-Xing her only friend and her stupid parents; Zhang Chen and all the others . . . doomed.

"This is supposed to be the cave of miracles! Why won't you help me?" Jing-Wei sobbed. She drew a deep breath and shouted with all her might: "Oh, great masters! Please hear my plea! My village and valley are beset by demons and without your aid all will die!"

"Oh, great masters!" the demon cried in a young boy's voice. "Hear my plea! I am the last child and I have no one to play with. The solid ones come and destroy my friends, dig up my plants, destroy my toys, and they won't listen! My parents are gone, lost in a battle I don't remember. My sisters are weeping for there can be no more children and the solid ones will overpower us. We are dying. We want peace. They will not listen. Oh, great masters! I call on you for justice! For compassion! For love!"

"What?" the three animals cried from outside.

"Do you have a name?" Jing-Wei said, turning to the shape now wreathed in blue and looking like the shadow of a very dirty boy. "I am called Li Jing-Wei. My name means small bird."

"I have many names," the boy shape replied. "So many that I don't remember them all. But your words . . . they are strange and hard to repeat. What name would you give me?"

"What name do you want?" Jing-Wei asked. "I was not given a choice, I was too little when I was born."

"I was little, too," the boy shape replied. "But I need a name that you can use, a new one. One that your mouths can shape and I can distinguish from the others."

"Did you kill anyone in my village?"

"No," the boy shape replied. "The others, when they thought you took me, they would have attacked."

"Why didn't they attack here?" Jing-Wei demanded. She turned to the shapes outside the bubble. "Did you cause the demons to attack my village?"

"No," the lion said. "We didn't knew about it until you came here."

"My people would have gone for the nearest solid ones," the demon said. In a different tone, it continued, "Are there many who have died?"

"More than I can count!" Jing-Wei said, waving her hands at him twice.

"What does that mean?" the boy shape asked.

"Many," the lion said. "We count each finger of our hands and each toe of our feet and we get twenty."

The blue boy looked ill. Kill is forever.

"Yes," Jing-Wei agreed. "Forever."

"You would kill this one?" the blue boy asked, waving at hand at himself.

"You didn't kill any of my people, did you?"

"No, I did not," the boy said. "But if I hadn't come here, they wouldn't have died. I'm sorry."

"Sorry won't bring them back!" Jing-Wei cried, her hands balled into tight little fists.

"We can't bring them back," the lion called. "But we can make sure that no more die."

Forever? No.

"Why not?" Jing-Wei asked. "You say you live forever, why can't we make this last forever?"

You do not last forever, the boy said. You are solid. You will stop one day, entropy will destroy you.

"Is that what happened before?" Jing-Wei asked. "The ones who signed the treaty, are they all dead?"

We fight. We forget. We can die. We cannot be reborn.

"No one can be reborn," Jing-Wei said.

"So, not a practicing Buddhist, then," the elephant rumbled softly to himself.

No new ones. No 'children.'

"You said you were a child!" Jing-Wei protested.

Last child. Last in forever. No new children. Soon all will be gone.

"He says he's the last child," Jing-Wei said. "How can that be?"

"They seem to be beings of pure energy," the lion said. "They may have forgotten how they created themselves."

"Their numbers are dwindling, they're dying out," the eagle said.

"And we're helping them along," the elephant rumbled sadly.

"You're dying?" Jing-Wei said to the blue boy.

Can't die. Can't be born.

"What the animals said," Jing-Wei said irritably. "There are no new people for you?"

I am the last child.

"So why did you come here?" Jing-Wei asked.

To ask for help. Cave of miracles.

"He came to the cave of miracles to ask for help," Jing-Wei said. "He wants us to help them learn how to make new baby energy people, like him."

"We don't know how!" the eagle cried in anger and frustration.

"Can't you learn?" Jing-Wei asked. She turned to the blue boy. "We don't know right now. We could learn over time."

"People die," the boy said. "Ending is forever."

"How about I call you Fai?" Jing-Wei said suddenly. "It means 'beginning' because we must begin something new."

"I can be Fai," the blue boy agreed. "Can I be Li Fai, so that we are related?"

"How does he know that?" the elephant asked from asked the blue energy bubble.

"He's accessing our databases," the eagle replied. "Check your monitors."

"Can we stop him?" the lion asked.

"It's probably already too late," the elephant said after a moment. "It looks like he's accessed about fifty per cent of our records."

"It tickles," Fai, the blue demon, said. "Most of the memories fade. I was looking to see if I could remember . . ."

"How to make more of your people?" Jing-Wei guessed.

"No," Li Fai said. "I wanted to know if we could touch."

"Touch?" Jing-Wei repeated. She looked at the blue boy, flinched in memory of the strange pain she'd felt when she'd reached out for him earlier and shook her head.

"Would you try?" Li Fai asked. He reached a blue hand toward her, stretching his fingers out until the index finger was closest. "Just a finger?"

Jing-Wei bit her lip. "Welll . . ." she reached forward. Her finger touched his and suddenly—

This is what it is like to breathe! This is what it is like to feel blood flowing, a heart pumping! Li Fai exclaimed in wonder.

You are like the lightning, like the flash and the boom! Jing-Wei responded. She moved forward, grabbed his hand in hers and pulled him tight against her. *You are power! You are—* words failed her. She doubted anyone, no matter how old, could find them.

And suddenly Li Jing-Wei was no more. Li Fai was no more.

Together, Jing-Wei told the boy. *We do this together.*

Yes! Yes! The boy cried eagerly.

We tell my people and your people what will be, Jing-Wei said. *Harshly*, she added, *those who don't listen will be destroyed.*

Destroyed? A note of doubt.

No one can hurt another.

But us? the boy didn't like that.

Only if they don't listen, Jing-Wei said. We will make them listen.

How?

We must become the biggest, scariest, most powerful being. We will listen, we will love, but we will not allow harm, murder.

You can do this?

No. We can.

How?

My name means Small Bird, the Jing-Wei half responded. We will become the largest beast in the sky, the most powerful.

What beast is that? the Fai half asked, accessing the databanks and bringing forth images and facts on known flying creatures.

I will show you.

"Lieutenant!" the elephant rumbled. "The field is collapsing!"

"We're taking a huge energy hit," the eagle added. They could hear the generators in the back of the cave whine with an immense strain.

And then the noise was gone.

"What happened?" the lion demanded. She glanced to the force field but it was gone. So was the demon and the girl. "Where are they?"

"Look up!" a voice called down to them. The three animals looked up.

"Oh… my… stars!" the lion cried in awe. "You're so beautiful."

"Why thank you," the beast said. In a slightly different voice it added with a note of wonder, "Am I?"

"You're a dragon!" the elephant rumbled.

"A dragon is a mystical creature of great power," the beast replied in a stilted tone. Again, in the different tone, it added, "Of course, silly!"

"Jing-Wei?" the lion asked.

"And Fai," the beast said in a boy's voice. In Jing-Wei's voice it continued, "We are here."

"What are you going to do?" the lion asked glancing up at the gossamer rainbow-shaded wings of the dragon as it hovered elegantly above them.

"Learn," the boy's voice answered. Jing-Wei's voice continued, "But first we're going to my village and telling your people to stop!"

"Of course," Li Fai agreed. "We will tell your people that the mamokh grass and the kerdveydza bush are where we store our memories and keep our connection to the planet. They must stop rooting them up and destroying them, so that we can remember that we are at peace."

"I never knew that!" Jing-Wei's voice exclaimed. "I'm sorry that we took away your memory."

"We could not tell you, we'd lost the grass and the bushes that kept those memories," Li Fair replied.

"So we will tell the villagers and they will stop," Jing-Wei said.

"With your permission," Li Fai said, the great dragon head bowing to the animals beneath it.

"How can we stop you?" the elephant wondered.

"Words work," Jing-Wei's voice said with a hint of her usual irritation.

"Can I come along?" the eagle asked.

"Only if you can keep up!" Jing-Wei's voice cried. And the dragon was gone, darting out of the cave of miracles into the night sky. Its luminescent body lit the night and it gave a strange cry—the two chorus of two voices echoing perfect joy.

We have to eat soon! Jing-Wei thought even as the ground disappeared beneath them. Oh, my wings! They're going to start complaining any moment now!

The demon Li Fai snorted in amusement but said nothing. Together, the two beings in a dragon's body raced the moons to the village of the small bird.

Red Roses

Here to cap it all off, is the sequel to Rhubarb And Beets.

Padraig paused to wipe the sweat from his brow and then leaned back into the dirty job. She deserved better but an unmarked grave was all he could give her. She'd been so small, so fragile, so fair, so beautiful, but she'd lasted no longer than the rose she'd borne.

It was dark, it was raining, the winds causing the drops to sheet in on top of him. Fortunately, he'd managed to get the digger in and had hollowed open the grave with no effort. He hadn't gone the whole depth, fearful that he'd uncover the casket, and he had no idea how he'd explain the digging or the fresh dirt when anyone came to ask.

But it was all she asked for in the end, and he had decided to give it to her, church and police be damned.

He had no box for her, of course. In the end, he'd hacked up some bracken and a bunch of roses. The bracken lined the bottom and the roses he put on top of her. He couldn't bear the thought of piling dirt on her bare beautiful face, so he'd stripped off his shirt, jumped down into the hole, and had gently placed it over her, pausing only to kiss her impossibly white face one more time and say, "There, now you're back on his lap."

More dirt, another shovelful. The first had been the hardest. He'd thrown it on her feet even as he thought, *Maybe she isn't dead. Maybe she's just sleeping or in some weird trance.*

Maybe she was tricking him, he thought as he dropped a heavy load on her chest, hoping to startle some response from her under the bed of roses. He stopped then, thinking that perhaps she had moved but, after standing in the rain until he started shivering, he decided it had just been the dead roses settling.

He'd covered her head last, all the same. Even under his smelly shirt, he wanted to give her one last chance to be alive. He paused and waited, the rain battering him, mixing with his tears, but there was no movement, no single sign of life in the dirt below.

So he continued. And now, he was almost done. He thought back to how it had all started.

#

"Are you Padraig Murray?" the man had called as he trudged over the fields.

Padraig hadn't seen him at first, he'd been too busy with the tractor. As soon as he did, he put the tractor in neutral and turned it off. Petrol — even diesel — was too dear to waste on nothing. Not that his farm or his crop were all that much. Padraig had been fighting a losing battle for the past decade to preserve the small patch of land that had been his family's for countless generations.

"And what if I am?" Padraig had called back, scowling at the man in a neat suit bearing a smart leather briefcase. Back over the fences, Padraig could see a new Jaguar car parked in the drive, slightly dusty from the long way on the back roads, looking just as out of place as the man who shouted.

"I need to talk to you," the man said, hefting his briefcase.

A moment of panic, followed by heated anger, flashed through Padraig. Dammit, he'd paid them the money!

"The loan's paid off!" Padraig shouted. "Get off my land and don't bother me at my work."

"Loan?" the man said, looking confused. "I'm here about your great-uncle."

#

In the small house, Padraig served the man tea and what biscuits weren't stale.

"The only great-uncle I ever heard about was named Joseph and he disappeared back in the famine," Padraig said as he slid milk and sugar toward the man.

"That's the one," the man said with a nod. "Joseph Murray."

"Are you a historian, then?"

"No, I'm with the county council," the man replied. He held out his hand. Padraig took it. "Gregory Paxton. I'm here to ask what you want to do about the remains."

"What? You found his body?"

Mr. Paxton looked away. "Well, we think so. In fact, we were hoping that you'd provide us with some DNA so we can verify it."

"Did he fall in a bog or something?" Padraig asked. He'd heard of bodies pulled out of the bog still well-preserved after thousands of years. There were no bogs within a hundred miles of here but perhaps his great-uncle had gone wandering or off to Galway hoping to get on one of the ships bound for America. That's what the family had all thought. He remembered something about it: how everyone had been counting on him, how he'd left a family behind that mostly starved in his absence. In Padraig's family, his memory was associated with traitors and blackguards. Perhaps he'd merely been unlucky.

"Bog?" Paxton repeated. "Near as the coroner can tell, he died of a blow to the head."

"And after nearly two hundred years you've found his bones?"

Mr. Paxton licked his lips and looked away. "Well, we'd like the DNA to be certain."

"And how much will that cost me?" Padraig demanded, thinking he'd found the rat in the whole affair: the council was looking to get money off him to identify the remains of a no-account, long-dead relative.

"Actually, Mr. Murray, we'd pay you," Mr. Paxton said, raising his head and meeting his eyes. "For your time and any light you can shed on this mystery."

"What mystery?"

"Why is it that a man who should be dead over a hundred years ago only died last week?"

It was all true. Oh, the council didn't pay all that much but Padraig didn't have to worry about petrol or food for a week and the dead man truly was his long-lost great-uncle Joseph Murray.

He'd been found wearing a shirt and breeches. His head was bashed in but he'd been found on a rock. The police were convinced that he'd hit his head in a fall but were clueless as to how that happened. Inside his pockets there'd been some greens, which the farmer who found him identified as a rhubarb stalk and the top of a beet.

"He had a smile on his lips, like he was happy," the farmer had told Padraig shyly as though trying to ease his pain.

"Anything else?" Padraig had asked. The farmer had flinched and hastily shook his head, saying that he had to go home, glancing at Mr. Paxton for permission.

"So, Mr. Murray, do you have any ideas?" Mr. Paxton had asked.

Padraig shook his head. He'd never met this long-lost relative, how should he know anything?

"It's just that he didn't look a day over seventy," Mr. Paxton said to himself. "Like he'd found a way to drink from the fountain of youth or something."

Padraig said nothing. The city folk were always giving farmers shite about fairies and fairy rings. He would do nothing to add to it.

"We can arrange a plot in town, if you'd like," Mr. Paxton offered, seeming ready to forget the whole issue.

"No," Padraig said. "No, I'll take Gran home. I'll bury him near the church."

Outside the police station, Padraig stalked across to the nearest pub. It wasn't that he really wanted a drink — contrary to all opinion, Padraig wasn't much of a drinker — but he was certain he'd meet the farmer inside.

"Mr. Murray!" Sure enough, he was waved over to a table. The farmer had a beer in front of him and the empty glass of another pint on the side. "Tom Mahony."

"I'm grateful for all that you did for my kin," Padraig said as the farmer rose and shook his hand.

"Will you be having any?" Mr. Mahony said, waving toward the drink.

"No thanks, I've a fair drive and things to set in order," Padraig told him. "But I'll sit with you for a bit, if you don't mind."

The farmer waved him to the seat opposite and Padraig took it. They chatted about the weather, what crops they had in and how the markets looked and then lapsed into a companionable, if charged, silence.

Finally, the farmer spoke. "There was lightning just before."

Padraig raised his head, meeting the other's eyes.

"Lightning and then a flash of rain, just a mist and a rainbow," Tom continued. His voice dropped as he added, "You know what they say about rainbows."

Padraig smiled and nodded. There wasn't a lad in all of Ireland nor Scotland nor Wales nor even England that hadn't once gone trying to follow the rainbow — just in case there was a pot of gold at the end. "Did you find any?"

"No," the farmer allowed sullenly. "But just at the last, I saw your man — great-uncle, isn't it? — I saw him out of the corner of my eye."

Padraig waited silently.

"It must have been a trick of the light or something," the farmer said, taking a deep draught of his beer, "but it looked like he was on a horse."

"What color?"

"Purple," the farmer said. He drained his glass and rose abruptly, heading toward the door. "My sympathies to you and yours."

#

And so Joseph Murray had been laid in the family plot in the local church. Father Connelly had decided to mark the date of his death as the day he'd disappeared from the family's reckoning and so, even though the grave was brand-new, the last year on the stone was 1848.

Padraig had visited from time to time just as he'd once managed to be near Tom Mahony's farm and dropped in "just to thank him" as he'd said. But sure enough, neither was fooled, and they spent several hours going over the site where Tom had first spotted great-uncle Joseph. Neither said anything but both were uncomfortable.

Back at Tom's house, over a cup of tea, Padraig got up the courage to ask, "Are there many fairy rings near?"

"A few," Tom allowed, crossing himself. "They're pretty things and don't seem any harm."

"We've no less than six on my farm," Padraig said musingly. After a moment, he added, "I always wondered about them."

"There was one no less than a hundred yards from where I found your kin," Tom allowed.

They finished their tea in silence. Padraig drove home in silence and that had been that.

#

The days had passed into weeks and the weeks into months. Padraig had taken to visiting the grave once a week. It wasn't a great burden as the great-uncle was laid in the family plot so Padraig would take time from talking with his mother and father, his brother lost in far-off wars, and his wee sister who never had her third birthday, to talk with the great-uncle no one had ever known.

And when it wasn't Sunday, Padraig would work the farm, fighting to keep crops and kill weeds, keep the damned tractor running — even though it was nearly as old as his lost kin — and never wonder beyond how he would cope with tomorrow.

When the rains came, they were vicious. And there was lightning, not all that common in that part of the country.

Padraig found himself starting out one morning in brilliant sunlight and trudging back in the afternoon in the dark of clouds and spitting deluge. The weather was always like that, changing from one moment to the next. But this day was different, almost malevolent in its ferocity.

Lightning cracked right behind him and Padraig jumped, turning back in fear that the barn had been hit.

Out of the corner of his eye he saw a flash and movement. He turned to look at it fully and then jumped to one side as a fierce beast clattered past him. He tried to get up but was thrown back to the ground by the weight of a bundle, seemingly thrown from the horse now long gone.

"Where is he?" a voice demanded from inside the bundle. Before Padraig could realise that the bundle was a cloak and the voice was a girl's, a pair of hands grabbed his throat and clenched tight with more strength than he imagined. "Where is he?"

Padraig scrambled with one hand to push the girl off even as he said, "Who?"

Either he was lucky with his hand or the question caused the girl confusion but he suddenly found himself able to scramble away far enough to be out of her grasp and able to look at her in the dim light that was left of the day.

His jaw dropped and he gasped. She was beautiful. A beauty like a storm, skin like snow clouds, eyes like lightning, lips like roses, dark hair like clouds on the horizon. She was tiny. She pulled the hood of her cloak back to swipe hair out of her eyes and… were her ears pointed?

Padraig made the sign of the cross. "Mother Mary, and Joseph!"

"You know of Joseph?" she demanded, suddenly lunging toward him again.

Padraig scuttled to his feet and discovered that he had the reach on her. Grabbing her by the elbow, he turned toward the house, dragging her behind him. "We've got to get you out of the weather and let your mama know where to find you!"

The small woman dug in her heels and batted at him with her free hand. "Are you in the pay of the Queen?" Her voice rose to a shriek, desperate, angry, tearful, "Let me go! Let me go!"

Padraig did not.

Inside, as he turned on the lights, the girl started. "Those are not torches," she said, eyeing the bulbs suspiciously. She turned back accusingly to him. "Have you captured Pixies to do your bidding?"

She seemed to rise in height but as she'd no more than four feet to start with, it was not enough to deter him.

"Where do you live, then?" Padraig said, moving to bar the door and pulling off his soaked jacket. "I'll give your mam a call. In the meantime, I'll get you some tea." He nodded toward her cloak. "You should get out of that or you'll catch your death."

"My death?" the little girl laughed bitterly. "My death is tied to the rose."

"What?" Padraig said, turning back to her. "What are you on about, girl?"

"The rose," the girl said, reaching into her cloak and pulling it out, "when it withers, I die. My brother, the prince, made it so." Her haughty expression faded and she seemed to collapse on herself. "I must find him, he was the only one that ever loved me."

"Who?"

"Gran," the little one said. She saw the confused look on his face and added, "In your world he would have been Joseph."

"Joseph Murray?"

Her eyes lit and her face beamed. "You know him? Oh, take me to him, I beg you!"

"Who are you?"

Her eyes narrowed. "If you hope to ensnare me by my true name, it will win you little."

"I just want to get you home," Padraig said, now certain the girl was touched.

"I will not go home, nor can I," the girl replied. She looked up at him, drew a breath, and became a thing of indescribable beauty, of regal bearing, something unreal, unearthly, and beyond mortal ken. "I am Eilin, princess of the most royal house in the Elvenworld, and I have pledged my blood on this quest."

Perhaps, Padraig thought hopelessly, she was one of those — what did they call them? LARP people? — the city yahoos who played all sorts of games dressed in costume and pretending to be elves and what-not.

"Joseph Murray was born over a hundred years ago," Padraig said.

"Aye, and he was pucked away to Faerie not long after to become my Gran," Eilin said. "He had the raising of me from a baby and I knew him as his ginger hair turned to white." She faltered then, like a candle in a stiff breeze. When she continued, her eyes were pained and tears dripped down them. "This is what it is like to be mortal?" she said, her hand going to her heart. "The beats, they skip and start."

And then she collapsed. Padraig was on her in an instant, scooping her up and racing up the stairs with her in his arms. She weighed nothing. As he elbowed on the bedroom light, he caught sight of one of her ears. It was pointed. And it wasn't makeup or, if it was, it was better than any he'd ever seen.

He placed her on the bed and leaned over her, listening for breath. There was none. He'd been trained, he was a farmer, he knew that doctors were distant, so he quickly put her on the floor and began breathing for her in a desperate kiss that was more air than passion.

Four breaths, pause, listen, check for pulse. None. He gave her a quick chest compression, worried that he'd crush her tininess, then back to her lips for another breath.

He was near the end of his endurance when she gasped and her eyes fluttered open.

"Think you to take liberties!" she hissed.

"Your heart had stopped, you weren't breathing," he told her. "I gave you the kiss of life."

Her fingers went to her lips and her eyes were wide with amazement. "You kissed me and I did not feel it?"

Padraig's expression must have been answer enough.

"Kiss me again," she demanded.

"I'm sorry," Padraig said, "but you're just a little girl."

"Kiss me," she responded in a voice that could not be denied.

He leaned down and pecked her lips, thinking to humor her.

When he tried to draw back, she hissed at him, "I am no child, kiss me proper."

And from that moment on, Padraig was in thrall. Oh, as a young man he had had his share of kisses — and more — but there had never been a lasting spark, a love strong enough to marry a farmer tied to a doomed land. This girl — this elf — this was his life.

"Oh, I am so sorry," Eilin said when they finally broke for air. "I am so, so sorry. I never knew."

"Knew what?"

"I never knew how beautiful it would be to take a mortal's kiss, how much you would lose in it," she told him. She pursed her lips inwards for a moment, then said, "But please, oh please, kiss me again!"

"I will kiss you forever," Padraig promised when again they finally broke.

"No," Eilin said, "we have only until the rose withers."

#

The rose withered in ten days. Eilin smiled at him on the dawn of that last day, and they kissed again — a kiss that seemed to last forever but, at the end of it, Padraig realized that she would kiss him no more.

And so now, the last of the dirt.

There. It was done. She was with her Gran again. The man who'd raised her from infancy, in whose lap she'd slept so peacefully, never realizing the depth of their love.

Above the earth there was only Padraig and the rain.

But not for long. He'd bought rhubarb and beets — she'd told him all about them — and he'd made a promise in the deep quiet parts of his heart. He would never love a mortal again.

He would chase the rainbows. Rhubarb and beets would bring him to the land of his love.

Acknowledgements

These stories span over thirty years of writing, from 1984 to the present. I owe a debt of gratitude to my late mother, Anne McCaffrey for her constant support.

I am very grateful to Bill Fawcett for cajoling me into writing my first story (and my second, and my third, and...).

In these stories you'll find the remnants of my broad education, as I was reared both in the United States and in Ireland. So, occasionally, you'll get *colour* instead of color, and *realise* instead of realize. I am firmly of the opinion that English is subservient to my prose, and plan on changing it, modifying it, and – occasionally – mangling it for my enjoyment.

Any mistakes, naturally, are my own.

About the Author

TODD J. MCCAFFREY IS A U.S. ARMY VETERAN, A CROSS-CONTINENT pilot, a computer geek, and a *New York Times* bestselling author.

He feeds his weirdness with books, large bowls of popcorn, and frequent forays to science fiction conventions. He is the middle son of the late Anne McCaffrey and is proud to list among his credits eight books written on Pern—including five collaborations.

His website is: http://www.toddmccaffrey.org

Printed in Great Britain
by Amazon